Seducing

the

Dragon

(Stonefire Dragons #2)

Jessie Donovan

This book is a work of fiction. Names, characters, places, and incidents are either the product of the writer's imagination or are used fictitiously, and any resemblance to actual persons, living or dead, business establishments, events, or locales is entirely coincidental.

Seducing the Dragon
Copyright © 2015 Laura Hoak-Kagey
Mythical Lake Press, LLC
Second Paperback Edition

Cover Art by Clarissa Yeo of Yocla Designs.

ISBN 13: 978-1942211143

To My Readers

All of your support, word of mouth, and enthusiasm inspires me to keep writing. Thank you!

Other Books by Jessie Donovan

CHAPTER ONE

Evie Marshall pulled her car into the parking area next to Clan Stonefire's main gate and willed her stomach to settle. Sure, she was nervous, but it wasn't because of the dragon-shifters flying overhead or the glares she knew she'd face once she stepped onto their land. She'd worked the last seven years with the Department of Dragon Affairs down in London, and visiting a dragon clan's land wasn't anything new.

Yeah, right. Who was she kidding? Today was different from her other visits. She was here to seduce a dragon-shifter, and not just any dragon-shifter, but Stonefire's clan leader, Bram Moore-Llewellyn.

That was her goal, anyway. Whether she'd succeed or not was yet to be seen.

Her heart skipped a beat at the thought of failure. If she couldn't convince Bram to allow her to stay with the dragon-shifters then the dragon hunters would kidnap her, and maybe even kill her. Their warning last week had been clear: stop working for the Department of Dragon Affairs and join them or be hunted down as if she were a dragon herself.

Inhaling in and out repeatedly, she tried to pull herself together and push aside her fear. The British government had brushed off the threat and wouldn't help her, so she'd do whatever it took to seduce Bram and earn a place in his clan.

Rumors said he was civil with humans, and if she could make him care about her, the alpha dragonman would protect her.

Focus, Evie. Right. Glancing at the clock on the console, she realized she needed to get a move on. From her past experiences down south with Clan Skyhunter, she was aware that while dragon-shifter clan leaders liked to keep her waiting, she had damn well better be on time or face a scolding.

After giving her hair one last smooth and plumping up her slightly too small breasts, Evie grabbed her duffel bag and exited the car. As she closed the distance between her car and the front entrance, it took everything she had not to stumble or twist her ankle on the uneven gravel. She'd worn heels maybe ten times in her life, and despite the hours of practice she'd done over the last week, she wobbled more than strutted with each step.

Shit. Things weren't off to the greatest of starts.

Careful to walk slowly and not fall on her arse, she headed toward the stone structure about twenty feet away, which served as the clan's security checkpoint. Since employees from the Department of Dragon Affairs, or DDA, weren't allowed to drive onto Stonefire's land, Evie went to the smaller entrance and called out, "Hello?"

Soon, a tall man with light blond hair and the ever-impressive thick, twining dragon-shifter tattoo on his muscled arm approached. She might've worked with the dragon-shifters for years, but her heart rate always kicked up when she saw one. They must have some kind of special gene which made them all gorgeous. This man was no different. The way his low-slung jeans clung to his fit body made her a little wet.

If she were lucky, Bram would be a little less attractive. The last thing she needed was to go instantly wet in his presence and start thinking with her lady parts instead of her brain.

Seducing the Dragon

The blond-haired dragonman's voice interrupted her thoughts. "Ms. Evie Marshall with the Department of Dragon Affairs?"

Careful to keep her face calm and collected, despite the butterflies banging around in her stomach, she nodded and handed over her identification papers. "Yes. I'm here to do my post-birth interview with Melanie Hall and to further investigate the death of Caitriona Belmont. My office should've made all of the arrangements for my three-day visit."

The dragon-shifter gave her an unreadable glance before he thumbed through her documents. No doubt, he could hear her heart banging in her chest, or even worse, smell the fact she found him attractive. While he was probably used to the latter, she hoped the former wouldn't raise any suspicions about her reasons for being here.

Only when he nodded and held out the papers for her to take back did she let out a mental sigh of relief. He must believe she was merely here for an inspection.

She retrieved her papers, and then he turned and motioned to another guard a few feet away. "Dacian over there is your assigned guard for the duration of your visit and he'll take you to see Bram."

At Bram, the clan leader's name, her heart gave a few extra hard thumps inside her chest. In less than half an hour, she would finally meet the man who would determine her future.

"Thank you," she said and smiled over at the dark-skinned man named Dacian.

And damn, the defined muscles peeking out from his shirt combined with the striking planes of his face only confirmed her theory of the secret dragon-shifter hotness gene. Her chances of

Bram being less attractive so she could focus were looking slimmer by the minute.

Despite her best smile, his face was guarded as he motioned with his head for them to start walking. Without so much as a word, he turned around and headed down the worn dirt path.

Hmph. Stonefire's reputation about being friendlier with humans than Skyhunter wasn't looking good so far. She bloody well hoped Bram was nicer than Skyhunter's leader, Marcus, or she would most definitely have her work cut out for her.

Since Dacian was already several feet ahead of her, Evie tried her best to both walk quickly and sway her hips in what she hoped was a seductive manner. Her two-inch heels were less than ideal for a lengthy walk to the main living area, but first impressions were important. She would gladly risk sore feet if it meant Stonefire's leader would take notice of her.

Of course, her feet were the least of her problems. Evie had sacrificed a social life, hobbies, and even love to earn a place with the DDA, but those sacrifices now paled in comparison to the task that lay before her. In order to stay alive, she would have to give up not only her body, but also her freedom and her future.

~~~

Bram Moore-Llewellyn attempted to sign his name on the last bit of paperwork for the DDA inspection when he heard a "whoosh" followed by a little baby hand slapping against his desk. With a sigh, he tossed his pen aside and turned wee baby Murray around in his lap before raising him to eye level. "What did we say about knocking papers off the desk?"

Murray looked at him with wide eyes and drooled.

Bram chuckled. "Right, I know you're bored, but the inspector should be here any time now and she needs to see you're doing well."

The baby waved his hands around and started to squirm, clearly not caring about any DDA inspection. Bram lifted the boy above his head and said, "Just another half hour or so, lad, and I'll drop you off at my brother's house where you can play with my niece. You like Ava, remember?"

Murray made some incomprehensible baby noises and Bram took that as a yes. He lowered Murray down and cuddled him against his chest. His inner dragon pushed to the front of his mind and said, *We should keep this young. He is ours.*

He wanted to agree with his dragon, especially since Bram's chances of having children were less than one percent because of infertility issues, but it wasn't what was best for the lad. *He deserves someone with time to take care of him. We are too busy.*

His dragon huffed and Bram resisted a sigh. He'd been having this inner argument for months now. Taking care of a clan with nearly three hundred dragon-shifters was enough of a challenge, but it became infinitely harder to manage his people when his dragon became grumpy and uncooperative.

So much for Bram being bloody good at controlling his beast.

There was a knock on the door and Bram looked down at Murray. "All right, lad, I bet that's the inspector. Be on your best behavior, okay?"

While all the boy did was blink as he gnawed on his fist, Bram hoped the undertone of dominance in his voice would do the baby some good. Like most young, Murray had good days and bad.

Bram hoped today was one of the good ones or no doubt the inspector would make his life hell. Hate was too tame a word for what Bram felt about being beholden to the British government for his clan's survival.

He reached the door and opened it to find one of his guards, Dacian, filling his front stoop. Bram nodded to signal all was well, and Dacian stepped aside. His actions revealed a red-haired human female wearing a light blue blouse that hugged her small breasts, and her wide hips were encased in a black form-fitting skirt. Her dark blue eyes reminded him of the Irish Sea.

As she glanced between him and the baby, surprise flickered and Bram fought a smile. According to his contacts, this woman had been dealing with Marcus, Skyhunter's bastard leader, for years and would never expect a clan leader to answer a door with a baby in his arms.

However, the surprise in her eyes was gone in an instant, replaced with a smile and a look of heat that took both the man and the dragon by surprise. Even his cock twitched at the fiery look.

The redheaded female gave him a slow once over and he came back to his senses. Sure, she was pretty and plump with striking dark blue eyes, but he didn't need this right now. Between selecting a male from his clan to breed with the next human female sacrifice and doubling his clan's efforts against the recent spate of dragon hunter attacks, he didn't have time to bat off a female's attentions. When Bram wanted sex, he found it. He didn't need a mate.

His inner beast growled. *Liar.*

Ignoring his dragon, Bram shuttered his face, hugged Murray closer to his chest, and motioned with his head. His voice was full of dominance when he said, "I have the necessary paperwork inside. Follow me."

He turned without another word. The sooner he finished this interview, the sooner the DDA inspector could leave and become some other male's problem.

~~~

As Stonefire's leader turned his yummy broad back and walked away, Evie felt her temper creeping up. The man hadn't even so much as said hello, let alone asked for her name.

If that wasn't bad enough, he was pulling his dragon-shifter dominance shit on her.

She clenched a fist at her side and tried counting down from ten. If she couldn't calm herself the hell down, she would have zero chance of getting into this dragon-shifter's bed, let alone convincing him to allow her to live with Clan Stonefire.

Taking a deep breath, she followed Bram inside his cottage to the desk at the far side of the room. He picked up a manila folder and held it out just as the baby in his other arm started slapping the dragonman's chest. He jostled the boy as he said, "You'll find everything inside is in order."

Even with a baby in his arms, the man was all business. She wondered if her earlier once-over had affected him at all.

Bram was going to be a tough bastard to crack.

Evie forced a smile and was careful to sway her hips as she crossed the few steps between them. She felt a little silly as she never walked this way normally, but as the dragonman's eyes flickered down to her hips and back to her face, she resisted a triumphant smile. Maybe he wasn't as indifferent as he'd made himself out to be.

The small win cooled her temper. When she reached out to take the folder, she was careful to brush her hand against Bram's. She knew full well this was all an act, but his hand was rough and warm to the touch and she wondered what his strong hands could do to a woman when she was naked and beneath him.

Wait, where the hell had that come from? She'd never had such thoughts around Skyhunter's clan leader, and they'd even shaken hands a few times. Evie would just need to be careful. She wasn't here to fancy the man. She was here to ensure her future and her safety.

Careful to keep her seductress mask in place, she purred, "Thank you."

The dragonman's jaw tightened and he moved away from her to sit behind his desk.

Okay, despite all the online articles saying men loved that kind of husky, low voice, Bram clearly didn't. *I'll just mark it off my list of things to try, no worries. I have loads of other tips.*

As he turned the baby in his lap, he motioned for her to take a seat. Once she sat down, she opened the folder and did a quick sweep, but everything looked filled out correctly. Closing the folder, she eyed the baby bouncing on Bram's leg for a second before she asked in a more usual voice, "Is that Caitriona Belmont's son?"

"Yes, this is wee Murray."

The way the dragon-shifter leader looked down at the little baby boy, full of love and even hope, warmed her heart. Somehow, some way, she needed to find a way to get him to relax like that with her. Only then would she have a chance of seducing him.

Realizing she'd been staring for a few seconds, Evie crossed her legs and leaned forward. While her attire wasn't tart-worthy, she'd unbuttoned a few buttons of her blouse to allow a small glimpse of skin and a tease of what cleavage she had. Bram's eyes did dip down for a second, but then his expression turned back into the hard one from his greeting at the door.

The dragonman in front of her was more resistant to her act than she liked. From his glances to various parts of her body, she had a feeling he was attracted to her, but her current techniques weren't working.

Since Bram responded better to her business tone, she continued in it. "Your latest report to the DDA says the boy is still being fostered between several clan members. When will you have a permanent home for him?"

The dragonman's eyes turned hard. "As you can see, the boy is happy. When I find the right family for him, then he'll have a permanent home, not before."

She didn't like his dominant tone, but she was experienced enough to keep her voice level. "The contracts signed between you and the late Caitriona Belmont clearly stipulates that in the event of her death, you have six months to place the baby in a permanent home or we will assign him one. It's been five months already, so time is running out."

Bram hugged the baby close and Murray stopped moving to stare up at Stonefire's leader. Bram's voice was as dominant as ever when he replied, "Maybe you should remember we're living beings with feelings too. Would you want your child fostered to a random person or placed with someone who will love him or her?"

Evie resisted a frown. "Of course you have feelings. I never claimed otherwise. Now who's being judgmental?"

As soon as the words left her mouth, Evie regretted them. Somewhere between the door and this moment, she'd fallen on her DDA training instead of her supposed seductress persona.

Shit. She might've just bollixed this up.

Bram silently stared at her until little Murray started crying. He broke her gaze to look at the boy as he said in a gentle tone, "Sssh, lad. Nothing is amiss." The boy's cry increased in volume and Bram looked back to her, his expression once again neutral. "I need to see to Murray's care. We'll continue this discussion tonight over dinner. Dacian will escort you back here around seven p.m. and you can report to me what you find today."

A snippy reply was on the tip of her tongue, but she managed to hold back. Things had devolved quickly and some time apart would not only allow her to cool down and regroup, but to also find out a little more about Stonefire's leader from the human sacrifice she was here to visit, Melanie Hall.

"Fine, I'll come round about seven p.m." She stood up and held the manila folder against her chest. She wanted to walk out without a word, but after working with Marcus, Skyhunter's leader, she decided to fall back on the other clan's protocol to avoid angering Bram further. "May I be dismissed?"

Something she might call amusement flashed in his eyes. She clenched her jaw and wondered why following protocol would be funny.

Then, despite her slowly simmering temper, she forgot about everything else as Bram stood up, filling her vision with a broad chest and strong, muscled arms cradling a crying baby.

She finally forced her gaze up to meet the tall dragon-shifter's light blue eyes, but his expression was back to that bloody unreadable one. He nodded. "You may go, Evie Marshall."

18

She blinked. He did know her name after all, and she sort of like how it sounded in his Scottish accent with a hint of Northern English. Maybe one of his parents was Scottish and the other English. That would explain it.

Get it together, Evie. She wasn't here to get to know the man; at least, not until she'd secured her safety.

Evie nodded. "Right, till tonight then."

She turned before Bram could say anything else and decided what the hell; she should make an impression. She carefully swayed her hips as she made her way across the floor. It was ridiculous, but she swore she could feel his eyes on her quite sizable arse.

Maybe, despite the rough start, she had a chance after all.

CHAPTER TWO

If Evie's newfound hope at maybe succeeding with Bram wasn't enough, she didn't stumble or trip over her heels the entire way to Melanie Hall's house.

Even if she had, it wasn't like her assigned guard would have noticed. After asking to see Melanie, the dragonman had just kept walking, expecting her to follow. But he looked young, maybe twenty, and all dragon-shifter males were broody and irritable at that age. After all, according to her textbooks, that was when their inner dragons started demanding sex on a more regular basis.

Dacian stopped in front of a two-story stone cottage with what she assumed were bushes in front of it. Having spent a good chunk of her life in London, Evie was no gardener, but the vegetation was definitely wild.

Since her brain always did that, fluttered about from one topic to the next, she merely brushed it aside and knocked on the door. A few seconds later, it opened to reveal yet another tall, muscled dragonman holding a baby.

Really, did all of the dragon-shifter males around Stonefire go around carrying babies?

As he glared down at her, the male patted the small baby's back, as if he were burping the little one, and growled before saying, "I don't know who you are and I don't like it."

Seducing the Dragon

The dragonman's accent was purely from the North, unlike Bram's. "I'm Evie Marshall with the Department of Dragon Affairs. Your clan leader should have notified you of my upcoming visit. Is Melanie around?"

"Melanie is busy. You can wait out here until she's done."

If she thought Bram had stoked her temper, this man had done it with a handful of sentences. Luckily, she didn't need to try to seduce him, so she put on her take-no-shit attitude and said, "Look, I get that you might not like me. Most dragon-shifters don't like the DDA, but it's my job to make sure Melanie Hall is well and I'm not leaving until I see her. Now, where is she?"

Before the dragonman could reply, a female voice drifted down the stairs behind him. "Tristan, who's there? Is it the DDA?"

So, he'd known full well who she was. Well, if he was going to play games, so would she. She shouted loud enough that the woman would be able to hear her. "Yes, I'm Evie Marshall. Can you tell your dragonman to let me in?"

There was a snort from Dacian's general direction, but when she glanced over, he had the same expressionless face as before.

Tristan said, "Shut it, Dacian, or I'll tell all of the young females you have herpes. Then you'd only have your hand for relief, and it would get quite tired before long."

Evie blinked and looked back to the dragonman with the baby, but he was still burping the little one with his hardass expression unchanged.

Before Dacian could reply, thuds sounded down the stairs at the same time as the American female voice said, "Tristan, move and let her in."

After one more good glare, Tristan stepped aside to reveal a smiling, short woman wearing loose clothing with another baby in her arms.

Melanie put out her hand and Evie took it to shake. As Melanie dropped her hand, she said, "Sorry about Tristan. The babies are barely a month old, and to say he is protective would be an understatement."

Tristan stepped closer to Melanie. As the other woman leaned against her dragon-shifter, a surge of jealousy shot through Evie; due to the death threats and the dragon hunters, she'd accepted she'd never have that kind of closeness. But sometimes she wished it could be different.

Rather than think of what she couldn't change, Evie focused back on the present. "While Skyhunter never had a human sacrifice stay on after a birth, the male dragon-shifters were always protective of their young." She tilted her head. "May I come in?"

Melanie stared at her a second, assessing her, before she nodded. "Sure, follow me." Melanie looked to Tristan. "Could you make us some tea, love?"

He grunted and nodded. With one last glare in Evie's direction, he disappeared into the house.

As Evie followed Melanie down the hall, she heard the front door close behind her. A quick look told her that Dacian must be waiting outside.

Evie stumbled and turned her head back around. She definitely needed to watch where she was going. Her poor feet didn't need any extra abuse today.

As they entered the living room, Melanie plopped down in an overstuffed armchair and Evie took the couch across from her. Before she could ask a question, Melanie said, "I've never seen a

DDA inspector wear such a tight skirt, let alone unbutton her blouse down to her cleavage."

Evie blinked. "Pardon me?"

Melanie placed a pillow under her arm holding the sleeping infant. "Most inspectors dress overly conservative to avoid any extra notice. Wearing clothes like yours will make the men drool, and as far as I understand it, you'll be dismissed the instant you have sex with a dragon-shifter. So, I'm guessing there's a reason for you dressing that way, am I right?"

Evie had heard the rumors about Melanie Hall being observant and forward, but the woman's accuracy made her uneasy. If she could guess Evie had a second motive from a mere glance, what else could the woman guess after an entire conversation?

Evie would just need to be careful. "I'm not here to discuss my wardrobe or the rules of the DDA. I'm here to see how you're doing and to investigate Caitriona Belmont's death."

At the mention of the dead woman's name, sadness filled Melanie's eyes. "Cait died in childbirth. I'm not sure what there is to investigate."

The genuine sorrow in Melanie's voice eased some of her irritation at the woman's earlier words. "There were some concerns during the autopsy. I just need to make sure we have all the facts before we close the case. While none of her relatives have asked about her, the DDA wants to be ready in case they ever do make a request."

Melanie looked like she wanted to say something, but she looked to her baby instead. As she stroked the little one's cheek, she finally said, "Cait was unhappy. I won't deny it, but I truly believe if she'd lived to see her son, she would've bounced back eventually."

"I think we're in agreement about that. I just came from Bram's office and Murray Belmont was there." Melanie merely nodded, so Evie pushed. "The baby seems well-behaved and cordial. I can't understand why he hasn't been placed with a permanent family yet."

Melanie looked up and gave Evie yet another assessing stare before she said, "Bram is the one who'll have to answer that question. If he won't, then I'm sorry, but no one else here will do it either."

"So it's true then, about you being loyal to Stonefire."

Frowning, Melanie said, "Of course. They're Tristan's clan, which makes them my clan."

The way Melanie said it, as if it was a simple truth, amazed her. In all the years Evie had worked with the DDA, she'd never come face-to-face with a human who had chosen to stay with a dragon-shifter out of love. If that wasn't fascinating enough, Stonefire had two humans who'd done so; the other was a woman named Samira.

Since all of her seduction research would mean nothing if she couldn't understand the dragon-shifter males better, she needed to nudge the conversation in that direction. It might make Melanie suspicious, but Evie would have to chance it; there were only a few hours between now and the dinner with Bram. "How did you do it, then? Convince a dragon-shifter to fancy you?"

Melanie blinked. "Only women who can't conceive dragon-shifter children are promoted to DDA inspector, which means you couldn't put yourself up as a sacrifice even if you wanted to. So why would you ask me that question?"

Her estimation of Melanie Hall's knowledge of the DDA just went up a few notches. Few people knew that little requirement.

Not missing a beat, Evie said, "When I worked with Clan Skyhunter, women always asked me how they could do more than merely breed with the dragonmen. I'd like to have an actual answer for them next time, because it always broke my heart to tell them 'I don't know'."

It was true. Usually desperate women offered themselves up as human sacrifices to the dragon-shifter clans to either earn some money or to obtain a vial of dragon's blood to cure a loved one's sickness.

While few were ever physically harmed due to the contract both the dragon-shifters and human women signed, too many had been shunned or verbally abused. Maybe things were different with Stonefire, but Skyhunter had been bloody unkind to their sacrifices. She hoped she never had to work with them again.

The other woman adjusted the blanket around her baby as she murmured, "Be strong, be honest, and be open-minded. That's what it takes to soften a dragonman's heart."

~ ~ ~

Once Bram had dropped off wee Murray at his brother's house, he'd wanted nothing more than to shift and take a short flight to clear his mind of Evie Marshall's enticing arse. However, before he'd had the chance, Melanie had called him with her concerns about the DDA inspector and he'd had to use his small amount of free time to think of a strategy for this evening.

The human female could be a threat to his clan. He needed to find out the truth.

His inner dragon growled. *We will find the truth. If she's in trouble, maybe we could help her.*

Right. Leave it to his dragon to presume the woman was in trouble rather than thoughts of betrayal. *Stop thinking with your cock, you ruddy beast. What if she works with the dragon hunters? After all, they're getting bolder by the day.*

Before his dragon could reply, a knock sounded on his front door. As he always did with strangers, he put on his stern, brick-wall expression before he opened the door.

He'd expected Dacian, but instead, he was greeted with the sight of Evie in a tight yellow dress, her straight red hair billowing over her shoulders. His inner dragon growled in appreciation at the way the stretchy dress hugged the female's body. From her small chest, to her round stomach, to her wide hips, the dress left little to the imagination. Then his eyes fell to her short hem, which highlighted the smooth, creamy skin of her legs.

Find out the truth. Help her. Maybe she'll reward us and let us fuck her.

Only because of years of experience did Bram keep his expression neutral at his dragon's words. *Shut it.*

The beast fell silent and went to the back of his mind. Not even his dragon was going to challenge his dominance right now.

Finding his voice, Bram said, "Ms. Marshall." He then eyed Dacian behind her. "Dacian, you're dismissed. I will take over Ms. Marshall's guard duty for the rest of the evening."

His young guard nodded and walked away, leaving him alone with the inspector. He stepped aside and gestured for her to enter. In return, she gave a sexy smile that shot straight to his cock.

His dragon hovered at the edge of his mind, but Bram decided he needed to get Evie talking before the beast started with his sex fantasies. Once Bram had dealt with Evie, he would find a female to ease his dragon's lust before their next meeting.

"Come in. I don't know what Skyhunter ever made you do, but we're informal here. I usually eat in jeans and a t-shirt."

Her eyes roamed his chest before settling on his crotch. It took every bit of restraint he had to keep his cock from going rock hard.

Looking back up, Evie shrugged. "I never dressed like this for Marcus, only for you."

His dragon was pleased at the way she said it so matter-of-factly, but his human-half grew suspicious.

He decided to put an end to the female's silly antics. He wanted to pass the inspection, end of story. "You're a DDA inspector. Stop flirting and do your job."

Fire flashed in her eyes, but it was gone before he could blink. Much like before, he guessed she was trying to tame her temper.

Her tone was surprisingly even when she replied, "I am doing my job, thank you very much. Have you ever thought that maybe I'm just trying to test you? The other inspectors have talked about you, and I'm trying to find out the truth."

He crossed his arms over his chest. "Right, go on, then. Tell me what they said about me so I can call bollocks."

From the corner of his eye, he saw her hand clench and felt a small rush of satisfaction. Getting an opponent angry usually led to them saying more than they normally would.

Evie studied him a second before she walked past him to the couch on the far side of the room. Once she sat down, she crossed a leg over her knee and said, "No."

His expression faltered. "What?"

She placed her hands on her knee and straightened her shoulders. "No. You ordered me to come here for dinner and to ask me about what I found today, so that's what I'll do. There is absolutely no reason I have to tell you anything else."

Shutting the front door, he strode across the room to stand a few feet in front of her. He gave her his best piercing stare as he said, "You're on Stonefire's lands, lass, and I'm the law here. You'd best remember that."

She raised an eyebrow in nonchalance. "Empty threat and you know it. My report determines the future of your clan, so you might want to start being nice to me."

"Are you really going to challenge a clan leader? One word of you hopping into a dragon-shifter's bed will get you sacked."

"Is that what you do, then? You toss the human females to the beasts and let them go at it?"

Bram knew her words were meant to provoke, but she'd touched on his honor and he wasn't having it. He spat out, "If that's what you think, then you'd best leave right now and send another inspector. I want a fair chance, and I won't get it with your prejudices."

"My prejudices? You're the one who inferred you would lie about me having sex with a dragon-shifter to get me fired. Maybe I should remind you that one mention of you threatening me, and that's it, no more sacrifices."

"Yet you can insinuate that I allow my dragonmen to force themselves on the human females, and think that's okay? I don't know what Marcus does down south, but up north, we have pride and respect for those who are helping our clan to repopulate."

She opened her mouth just as his mobile phone rang. *Thank fuck.* He needed time to cool his head or he might say something that could really hurt his clan.

Without a word, he turned his back on the infuriating female, and took the phone out of his pocket. Glancing at the screen, he pressed receive. "What's up, Kai?"

Kai, one of the clan's Protectors, answered, "There's been another breach on our border. The dragon hunters attempted an ambush on the east side."

Walking to the far side of the room, he switched to Mersae, the dragon-shifter language and said, "Was anyone injured?"

Kai answered in the same language. "One of the newer Protectors-in-training has a nasty gash, but she'll survive."

Satisfied his clan members were alive, he barked, "Then tell me the rest."

"We only managed to capture one, a mid-rank dragon hunter with a Carlisle branch tattoo. He's not saying much, but what he's said so far worries me."

He didn't like the sound of that. "Spit it out, Kai."

"Well, he says he knows Evie Marshall."

CHAPTER THREE

When Stonefire's leader started talking on his mobile phone in the dragon language, Evie took the opportunity to count to twenty and back down again. Trying to follow Melanie's advice of being strong without letting her temper loose was harder than she'd imagined. She'd have to work on that, especially since Evie couldn't be completely honest with the dragonman. At least, not yet.

His eyes on her body at the door had boosted her confidence. Despite their argument and her temper slipping loose, there might still be a chance.

Or, so she thought until the dragonman turned around with a fierceness in his eyes that made her heart skip a beat.

The dragons didn't teach humans their language, so she had no idea what he was barking into the phone, but his tense body and the tone of his voice told her it wasn't good.

When Bram shut off his phone, she steeled herself for what was to come. Most humans would cower under the dragonman's current stare, but she'd worked with dragon-shifters for seven years now. She could take any dominance bullshit they threw her way.

Still, as the seconds ticked by in silence, she started to get a bad feeling in the pit of her stomach. Rather than wait for Bram to speak, she blurted out, "Why are you glaring at me like that? If it's about my so-called prejudices, you never gave me a chance to respond. If you would just listen—"

"Enough."

Despite her resolve, Evie fell silent at his tone.

He motioned for her to stand up and then crossed his arms over his chest. At first, she merely raised her chin in defiance. But as one minute ticked by, and then another, she finally gave in and stood up.

Bram moved closer, until he was less than a foot away from her. Ignoring the heat radiating off his body, she looked up into his eyes and raised an eyebrow. "Well? How long are we going to stand here in silence? I'm hungry."

Searching her eyes, he moved a hand to grab her chin. The feel of his rough, warm skin against hers sent a rush of heat through her body, and it took every ounce of resolve she had not to draw in a breath. Yes, she needed to get him naked and over her, but not until she knew why he was staring at her with such contempt.

She tried to break free of his grip, but his fingers tightened as he said, "Tell me now, Evie Marshall, why are you here?"

Shit. She needed to be careful here. "I told you already. I'm here to check in with Melanie and investigate Caitriona's death."

"And what else?"

"What makes you think there is anything else?"

He leaned down until she could feel his hot breath against her cheek. "We both know there is something else. If you cooperate, it will make things a whole hell of a lot easier for you."

Evie's heart thumped inside her chest. Did Bram truly know her other motive for being here or was he merely bluffing?

She was starting to think her plan to seduce Bram Moore-Llewellyn was a bad idea.

Thankfully, due to her years of drama in school, she was able to not show any outward sign of her doubts as she said, "Innocent until proven guilty, Mr. Moore-Llewellyn. Tell me why you think I have an ulterior motive."

"Three words: Carlisle dragon hunters."

Evie's stomach dropped. How the hell did he know about them?

Raising an eyebrow, Bram said, "I thought so. You're pretty good at hiding your true thoughts, but right now, I can see the fear in your eyes. Tell me why."

Out of nowhere, Melanie's words from earlier sprung into her mind, *"Be strong, be honest, and be open-minded. That's what it takes to soften a dragonman's heart."*

Would the truth really work, even with the fierce man currently glaring down at her? Or would it push him away, dismissing her problem as none of his concern?

Considering she was trapped on the dragon-shifter's land with no allies, it wasn't like she had a choice. If she didn't tell him, he would probably kick her off Stonefire's land and right into the hands of the dragon hunters. The British government hadn't taken her seriously before about the death threats, and most certainly wouldn't now. She wouldn't have anyone to protect her.

Yet if she told Bram, then maybe, just maybe, he would help her; at least, if she were honest.

She had only one choice, really, and taking a deep breath, she tried to figure out what to say that would convince the dragonman not to instantly hand her over to the dragon hunters.

SEDUCING THE DRAGON

~~~

Bram could smell Evie's fear but he wasn't sure if it was for him or for the dragon hunters. From what he'd seen of the human so far, he'd guess the second. Yet she'd been lying to him since she'd stepped foot on his land, so who knew; she could be more afraid of him.

His dragon pushed forth in his mind. *She is afraid. Not of us. Help her.*

He wanted to ask how the bloody hell his dragon knew she was in trouble, but while he trusted his dragon with his life, his beast didn't like giving details.

Still, even if she were afraid of the dragon hunters, she needed to tell him the truth or he'd boot her off his land and ask for another inspector.

His dragon growled. *Don't do that.*

Before he could tell his other half to shut up yet again, Evie took a deep breath and he focused on her words as she said, "I requested to be transferred here from London so I could ask for your help."

He raised an eyebrow. "Why would you do that instead of asking your human government for help?"

"I already tried, but they won't help me without more proof. Rather than risk getting myself killed while I did that, seducing you seemed like the better option."

Bram frowned. "Seduce me? Lass, you'd better start at the beginning and get to the point. I have a dragon hunter to question."

Her eyes widened. "One of them is here?"

He grabbed her arms and instantly regretted it as her soft, smooth skin sent a thrill through his body. This close, Evie's scent was a mixture of woman and something wild, and he'd been trying to ignore it for the last five minutes. But with the combination of her skin under his hands, his cock was very much standing at attention.

If that wasn't bad enough, Evie continued to stare into his eyes as the scent of her arousal reached his nose.

His inner beast went crazy, and said, *See. She is not afraid of us. She wants us. Help her and then fuck her.*

Bloody hell, what was wrong with him? He hadn't been this randy since he'd been a lad of twenty. She was just a woman, for fuck's sake, and he could have his pick.

Growling again, his inner beast hissed out, *Don't push her away. She is different.*

Okay, he had no fucking idea what that was supposed to mean.

He pushed both his dragon and his lust aside to focus back on protecting his clan. "Start talking, Evie. Now."

"Let me go first."

Rather than argue and waste more time, he released her and crossed his arms over his chest again. "Now talk."

A defiant glint flashed in her eyes, but thankfully, the female had some sense and she started talking, "Over the last few months, the dragon hunters have been targeting DDA employees. And anyone who doesn't listen to their 'warning', which is more a death threat and being shot at, ends up dead."

This was the first he'd heard of this. From here on out, he would have his people monitor the human news channels more closely. "Wait, why? The dragon hunters want us and our blood; humans have nothing to offer them." She raised an eyebrow, as if to call him out on his claim, but he didn't back down. "Your blood can't heal diseases and be sold on the black market."

"You're supposed to be clever, Bram. We have value, more than you think. What do you think would happen if more DDA inspectors were killed and people stopped volunteering for the job?"

It was the first time she'd said his name, and the way her London accent rolled over his name pleased him.

Focus, oh, great leader, focus. He could just demand the answer from her, but for some odd reason, he wanted her to see he had a brain.

Then it hit him why the inspectors could be targets. "Without you and your coworkers, the human sacrifice system would cease to be. Without human females, our numbers would dwindle again."

She nodded in approval. "Right, which means with fewer dragons, the hunters can ask higher prices on the black market whenever they harvest a captured dragon."

"You say 'harvest' and I say 'torture'."

Shaking her head, she said, "Don't turn this into me not caring about your kind. I've pretty much given up my life to help the dragon-shifters, and what did I get in return? An endless parade of humiliation and irritation. Sometimes I wonder why any of us stay with the department."

His inner beast growled at the thought of anyone humiliating this strong woman. Bram agreed with his dragon.

His curiosity piqued, he said, "I'm not Marcus. You'll face no humiliation here as long as you tell me the truth." She looked unconvinced, so he continued, "You spoke with Melanie earlier today. Was she afraid of me? Did she have an endless line of complaints about me? Or anything else that contradicts my claim?"

She paused a second, before answering, "No. She's extremely loyal to you."

"Exactly. I treated her fairly from the moment she set foot on this land, just like I do with all the sacrifices. Hell, I was even helping Cait with her fear of dragon-shifters up until she died."

Both man and dragon took a second of silence to remember the woman who'd suffered so much and had tried to come back, only to die in childbirth. To this day, he blamed himself for assigning Neil as her dragon-shifter. The bastard never should've been allowed a human female. In Bram's opinion, banishing the arsehole had been too easy a sentence, but the only one that had legally been open to him.

Evie touched his arm and he looked back into her eyes as she said, "You truly feel sorry for Caitriona's death, don't you?"

"Yes."

Her eyes searched his for a few more seconds before she nodded. "I believe you. I'll tell you the truth."

Her acceptance made his dragon hum.

For a second, he stared down at the beautiful redhead standing before him and savored the feel of her hand on his arm. The urge to haul her against him and kiss her was overwhelming, but there were a million reasons why he couldn't.

Still, his voice was husky when he said, "So tell me how seducing me was supposed to help you?"

Licking her lips, her grip tightened on his arm before she said, "I was hoping that if you slept with me, I might be able to convince you to let me stay here. Sex was only part of my plan; I was hoping to make you care for me too, especially since one of the former DDA inspectors let slip that you can't have children and thus can't have a sacrifice."

Seducing the Dragon

~~~

As the words left Evie's mouth, she instantly felt equal parts daft and callous. She'd just admitted to using something extremely personal against Bram. Why, oh why, had she told him that part? Preying on his infertility would most assuredly sting his dragon-shifter ego.

Yet rather than shout or go mental like Skyhunter's leader most assuredly would've done, Bram merely stared at her in silence.

Okay, she'd admit that his cool, blue-eyed gaze was prodding her to fidget, but she wouldn't do it. She needed to be strong and plead her case. Evie refused to think of what would happen if she failed.

Bram took a step back, forcing her to release her grip on his arm. Her stomach flipped as her heart rate kicked up. Was the distance a sign that he was going to dismiss her?

When Bram finally spoke, his voice was low. "I don't know how any of you lot found out about that, but it's clearly my business and mine alone. Tricking me into helping you is also not the way to garner my help."

Since he hadn't outright dismissed her yet, she risked a question, "So, does that mean you'll help me?"

"To be honest, I don't know. But to even consider it, you're going to do something for me without putting up any fight."

Uh oh. She didn't like the sound of that. "What, exactly, am I supposed to do?"

Pointing to the couch, he said, "Sit down and wait there."

In normal situations, she would balk at following an order such as that one, but this wasn't just any situation. These next few minutes would determine her future, so she sat down.

Nodding, Bram headed toward his desk and fished something out of one of the drawers. When he stood up, he had a laptop in his hand. He waved it as he said, "While I go question the dragon hunter, you're going to type out everything you can think of related to the Carlisle hunters, the assassination of DDA inspectors, and what else you know about me and my clan."

So far, so good. "Okay, so if I do all of that, you'll let me stay?"

"I never said that. First, you're going to work on giving me a reason to need you. After all, if you stay on my land and aren't a DDA employee or a sacrifice, then I'll be breaking your British human law. You'd better have some bloody good information for me to try and fight that."

Before she could stop herself, Evie blurted out, "But I discovered a loophole for that."

He raised an eyebrow. "Oh? And what would that be?"

"You're not going to like it."

"Lass, I already don't like this. Just tell me what you've found or you'll lose any chance of me helping you."

She absolutely hated that Bram held all the cards. Still, giving in to someone was better than ending up dead.

Taking a deep breath, she said, "While buried deep into one of the bylaws, there is a clause that legally allows a human to mate a dragon-shifter without being a sacrifice first, provided the dragon-shifter in question is a clan leader."

"Since when? Your government does everything it can to dissuade human-dragon-shifter interactions outside the sacrifice system."

"Yes, but all of their ads and talks are very careful not to mention it's illegal for all dragon-shifters. They use intimidating language and propaganda, and of course people assume it's illegal because of those messages. But when the sacrifice system was set up in the late 1980s, the British government was careful to keep the old law concerning marriages between clan leaders and humans intact just in case things devolved. After all, the old law was used in the distant past to help keep peace between human lords and dragon-shifter leaders."

If she'd surprised Bram with her words, he didn't show it.

"And how, exactly, do you know about this?"

She shrugged. "I have a friend obsessed with everything to do with the dragon-shifters. I reckon she knows more than just about any other human in the world. Well, at least those not living with the dragon-shifters."

Evie left out the part about how she'd been just as obsessed as her friend until she'd joined the DDA. Working for the DDA had killed any romantic notions she'd had of a dragonman sweeping her off her feet.

Bram frowned. "Right, and I'm supposed to mate you and feel grateful since I can't have a sacrifice myself? Or because I can't take a dragon-shifter mate without ruining my clan's future of independence?" He shook his head. "I don't know how you humans view marriage, but we dragon-shifters take mating seriously."

Evie felt her future begin to slip from her fingers. If she didn't say or do something, she'd lose her chance. Bram was by far the most understanding dragon-shifter clan leader in the UK.

Standing up, she took a few steps toward Bram to test out the waters, but he didn't retreat. After taking a few more, she looked up into his eyes and said, "I'll admit that when I first came up with my plan, I didn't take your needs or wants into account. I researched how best to seduce a man, and was going to try everything on that list to snare you, but I never expected for there to be this overwhelming attraction between us."

For just a second, his stern façade slipped and Evie pounced. "Before you try to deny it, kiss me. Just once. If you can pull yourself away and claim there's nothing there, then I'll leave and see if I can make it to America to seek out the number two most likely candidate on my list. Sure, the dragon hunters will probably find me first, but I'll do anything it takes to try to live. I'm not about to let the bastards kill me without a fight."

As Bram remained silent, her palms began to sweat. She'd just put all of her cards on the table. If this didn't work, she'd have to attempt to not only evade the dragon hunters probably waiting outside Stonefire's gates for her, but she'd have to find a way to America to try and seduce another clan leader.

Of course, that plan had been easier to accept in the abstract. Now she'd met Bram, she didn't think she'd ever forget him. No man's touch had ever set her body on fire before, and she wasn't daft enough to think the touch of the next dragon-shifter leader on her list would be able to do it too.

Bram was her best chance at safety, yes, but she also wanted to know what it'd feel like to be kissed by the dragonman standing in front of her.

CHAPTER FOUR

After Evie threw down her proposition, Bram's dragon instantly said, *Yes. Kiss her. We need her. She needs us. It is a good match.*

Stop being so bloody opaque. Tell me why.

His beast growled. *No. Kiss her and think later.*

If not for the human female in the room, he would have let loose a string of curses. Since he knew his dragon was too fucking stubborn to ever back down, he could either listen to the beast and kiss the lass, or he could face days or weeks of the dragon arguing with him.

Looking over at the red-haired human, he had to admit he liked the way her skin felt against his. Not only that, despite working with the DDA for seven years, she'd maintained her spirit and her backbone. If not for the dragon hunters trying to attack his land, that combination might've succeeded in seducing him.

Now, however, he needed to make a rational choice without his cock getting in the way.

If the human became his mate, she could divulge all kinds of information about the inner workings of the DDA. Since Melanie Hall-MacLeod was writing a book about his clan to garner human understanding, Evie's detailed knowledge of human and dragon-shifter law could help Stonefire avoid any kind of lawsuit or possible backlash.

In addition, if she had a way of contacting this dragon-shifter obsessed friend of hers, Bram could find out more about the old laws and what he could or couldn't do in the present day.

Yet if he took her as his mate, not only would his chances of having children go from one percent to zero since all DDA inspectors were incompatible, he might never find the partner he so desperately wanted to help with clan matters. As he eyed her body in that tight yellow dress, he knew he'd enjoy fucking her, but he wanted more than just sex. He wanted what Tristan MacLeod had found with Melanie.

His dragon pushed to the forefront of his mind. *Stop thinking and kiss her. It will be good.*

The beast's words prodded him to make a decision. What his heart wanted didn't matter. He was clan leader, and provided the human female gave him information, she could help give his clan an advantage over both the sacrifice system and British politicians in general. That was more important than him finding love.

It was time to kiss the living shit out of her and see if she could handle a dragon-shifter. As much as she could help his clan, he would never be able to tolerate a life of her being afraid of him. He would give it his all and see how she reacted.

Laying down the laptop, he ordered, "Come here."

Without a word, she moved to stand in front of him. Evie's addictive scent wafted up to his nose, causing his dragon to hum. *Kiss her.*

He reached out and pulled her soft body flush against his, her heat making his cock pulse. She let out a little noise of surprise, but she quickly recovered and placed her hands on his chest. Too bad he was wearing a t-shirt so he couldn't feel her soft skin.

Squeezing her soft body tighter, he murmured, "Get ready, human, because your life will never be the same after you've kissed a dragonman."

Her lips parted to say something, but he lowered his head before she could speak. The instant he touched her soft, warm lips with his own, heat flashed through his body. Her soft skin and sweet scent weren't enough; he wanted, no needed, to taste her.

Seaming her lips, she finally opened and he growled as he explored her mouth. She tasted just as sweet as he'd imagined, but he needed more, much more.

As he stroked his tongue against hers, Bram moved his hand to her arse and squeezed, loving how she pressed even closer against him. Then the female moved her hips and it was Bram's turn to moan at the friction against his cock. The bloody seductress knew what she was doing; he'd give her that.

Wanting to take the power back, he slapped her arse and Evie arched her chest against his. His dragon hummed. *More, take more.*

Moving a hand to the back of her head, he tilted her for better access, determined to devour her sweet, hot mouth. A mouth he'd very much like to feel around his cock.

~~~

When Bram's lips touched hers, all of Evie's trouble and nervousness morphed into something much hotter. The simple touch of his strong, warm lips sent wetness rushing between her legs. Then he parted her lips with his tongue before invading her mouth, and she nearly cried out at his taste.

Bram stroked and explored, making clear who was dominating whom. In most circumstances, Evie wouldn't put up with that shit. But as his teeth clashed against hers right before he gripped her arse possessively, she decided that when it came to snogging and sex, she might just like a man taking control.

Unable to resist, she moved her hips against the hard bulge at her stomach, and this time, Bram let out a sound of pleasure.

Despite being pressed up against his chest, it wasn't skin-to-skin contact, and she needed to feel the warmth of his skin. However, before she could move, Bram slapped her arse and the mixture of the sting and heat made her pussy throb.

This dragonman seemed to know how to turn her on.

Desperate for his skin, she moved her hands from his chest to his neck. She then pressed her hard nipples against his chest and was rewarded with a moan. While this dragonman might like to take control, she had her own sort of power over him, and she wanted the chance to use it again.

Don't think of the future. Focus on driving the man crazy in the present.

Then Bram pressed his cock harder against her stomach. If what she felt through his jeans was anything to go on, the rumors about the dragon-shifters and their long, thick cocks were true.

Before she could move her hips against that deliciously big bulge again, he slapped her arse once more before turning them both around and lifting her to sit on his desk. As he moved closer, her legs opened to accommodate his trim hips, her skirt riding high on her thighs in the process.

Yet the man never moved to touch between her legs, not even with his barely restrained cock not more than a few inches from her core. Deciding to take matters into her own hand, she scooted to the edge of the desk, but just before her clit would've made contact, Bram broke the kiss to stare into her eyes.

His eyes were dilated and filled with a hunger that shot straight to her pussy. The dragonman wanted her.

Placing his rough hands on her upper thighs, her core pulsed at the contact. If he'd only move his hands a little further...

Shuttering his expression, he severed contact and stepped back before he said, "You'd be a good fuck. I'd give you that."

Suddenly feeling exposed, Evie closed her legs and tugged down her skirt. She knew she had no right to demand anything, but his words stung a little. There was so much more to her than a pussy to be used for some man's cock.

At least there was a positive to take from his words; Bram might yet take her as his mate and protect her from the dragon hunters.

Determined not to let the dragonman know how his words affected her, she straightened her shoulders and said, "Well?"

"You've earned the right to show me you have something to offer Stonefire in the way of information." Pointing behind her, he continued, "Hand me that laptop."

While he hadn't said outright that he was attracted to her, his cock had betrayed that little fact earlier, so she focused on passing the next test. She picked up the laptop and handed it to him. "What do you want to know? And how long do I have?"

He moved toward the table on the far side of the room, and opened the laptop. "Start with the Carlisle dragon hunters. Then move on to the DDA inspector deaths, and finish with the little known knowledge concerning dragon-shifters that you learned from your friend."

Frowning, she hopped off the desk and barely managed to keep from toppling over her heels. "All of that could fill a book. Tell me, how long do I have?"

After typing in what she assumed was a password, he looked over at her with expressionless eyes. "Until I return from questioning the dragon hunter."

"Wait a second, that's nowhere near enough time for me to do a proper job. On top of that, I didn't bring my glasses with me and the screen will blur after a few minutes."

Bram stood up. "Considering your future and life is at stake, I suggest you find a way to make it work."

She opened her mouth, but Bram beat her to it. "I don't care about your excuses. Type like your life depends on it, because, after all, it does."

Taking a step toward him, she couldn't hold back her temper. "Is this how it will be between us, if I do pass these mysterious tests of yours? Because I assure you, I don't like arseholes and being submissive to your every order is not my style."

Shit. The instant the words left her mouth, she regretted it. *You're supposed to woo him, remember?*

Yet Bram looked unfazed. He moved to the door and motioned toward the laptop. "Provide some information first, and then we'll worry about what might happen in the future."

The dragonman exited the door and she heard the lock click.

Bastard.

With Bram gone, a flood of emotions hit her at once. Hope, that she might be able to live past the week; confusion at how the dragonman went from hunger in his eyes to ordering her about like a soldier; and irritation that she didn't have enough time to do a proper job at her task.

Oh, and not to mention her wet panties were a physical reminder of whatever else she thought of the dragonman, one kiss was all it took to turn her on like no man had done before.

His earlier words echoed inside her head, *"Get ready, human, because your life will never be the same after you've kissed a dragonman."*

Damn the man. There was no way she could let on that he'd been right. She doubted any man, dragon or human, could ever possess her mouth in the same sexy way.

Forget about the kiss and focus on your task. One thing was certain, she'd never have another kiss with Bram if she couldn't prove she had information he could use. And she wouldn't lie to herself; she very much wanted the dragonman to kiss her again. Just thinking about all that raw, sexual heat and power focused entirely on her made Evie shiver.

She inhaled and exhaled a few times, stretched her arms over her head, and moved toward the laptop. Thinking about Bram and his hot kisses would have to wait.

Typos be damned, Evie opened a word processing document and went to work, typing as fast as she could without really being able to see what she was doing.

~~~

Once out of his cottage, Bram took a deep inhalation of the cool evening air in an effort to clear his head of Evie's scent of woman and sex.

Stepping back from her spread legs and switching back into 'clan leader mode' had been one of the hardest things he'd done in a while. She'd been wet and willing for him, and with a few more kisses and caresses, she probably would've let him fuck her.

His inner dragon growled. *Why did you stop? You ache. She aches. You both want it.*

It's not that simple.

Why not? Sex makes everyone feel good. It is simple.

At least his dragon's words weren't desperate and filled with an intense need, meaning Evie Marshall hadn't initiated the mate-claim frenzy.

He should have felt relieved, but a small part of him was sad at that thought. Her being his true mate would've made the future so much easier and more certain.

His inner beast chimed in. *It can be certain. Choose her. She is soft with fire. She is a good fit.*

The dragon was too bloody perceptive. Few people ever stood up to him, let alone a mere human, and once Evie let her temper truly shine, it would be fun to provoke her.

Nearly missing a step, Bram brushed that thought aside. There was maybe a five-minute walk between his cottage and where the Protectors of his clan kept any prisoners and Bram needed to think of what he would ask during his interrogation. The dragon hunters were a growing pain in his arse, to the point that Bram had become more involved with the prisoners instead of merely letting Kai and his team handle them.

From right after Tristan had been shot down by the Carlisle hunters nearly eight months earlier, the Carlisle dragon hunters had grown bolder with each attempt at either capturing one of his people or sneaking onto his land. If he didn't know his people as well as he did, he might think he had a spy in his midst. There had to be another way they were getting information.

SEDUCING THE DRAGON

Remembering Evie's words about the hunters killing DDA inspectors, he wondered if the two were connected. He'd have to look into it and find out.

Reaching the two-story brick building with walls of reinforced steel, Bram put on his take-no-shit expression and walked through the door.

The young injured Protector-in-training, Nikola, sat in a chair just inside the place. Bram glanced to her bandaged arm and shoulder and then back to her dark brown eyes. "Still trying to prove yourself worthy of your fame?"

The young dragonwoman shrugged and then hissed at the pain as she clutched her arm. She finally managed, "People will always treat me special, so I figure I need to do something to earn that regard."

Nikola—or, rather, Nikki to most of the clan—was the child of the first human sacrifice sent to Stonefire twenty-five years ago. Despite her best efforts to discourage it, many of the older dragon-shifters showered her in affection and extra attention; to them, she was their first hope of one day repopulating their numbers to what they had once been.

Frustrated with the unwanted praise, Nikki had decided on becoming a Protector. So far, it hadn't changed how the older dragon-shifters treated her.

Bram, on the other hand, treated her like any other young dragon-shifter. "Well, you can't earn anything if you're dead. Next time, don't be daft."

"How do you know I was daft?"

He raised an eyebrow and the female dragon-shifter sighed. "Right. You're a bloody mind reader, that's why."

"It's my secret power. Now that's settled, give me the update. Has Kai found out anything?"

Waving a hand to the closed door down the hall, she said, "He's been in there with the hunter ever since he rung you. Kai did say that he'd prefer you do the special knock to announce your presence rather than just barging in."

The request was reasonable. "But before I go, you're going to tell me how you were injured."

While no one liked to share their failures, most especially a Protector-in-training, Nikki knew better than to try to withhold information from him. After standing up, she met his eyes and said, "While tackling our current prisoner to the ground, one of the other hunters shot me."

"With a regular gun?"

She nodded. "Yes. No one has yet seen the laser-type gun the hunters used on Tristan all those months ago."

No doubt, the hunters were saving it for a special occasion. "Since you'll be out of commission for a while because of your injury, I may have a job for you."

Usually Bram wasn't the one to give her assignments, but if Nikki was confused, she didn't show it. "As long as you clear it with Kai first, sure, I'll do whatever you need."

"Good." He looked toward the door. "Keep the same rules in place while I'm in there with the hunter. Only those with high-level clearance are allowed to disturb me. In addition," he turned back toward Nikki and said, "I need you to call Arabella MacLeod and give her my order to go to my cottage and watch my guest."

The dragonwoman frowned. "What guest?"

"Evie Marshall, the DDA inspector."

Nikki looked confused, but she merely bobbed her head.

With that, Bram headed toward the door at the far end of the hall. Arabella would seem a strange choice to most of his clan since the dragonwoman still hated all humans except for her sister-in-law Melanie, but Bram didn't trust another male to be in the same room with Evie. If she pulled out her seductress charms, she could probably find out all sorts of information he didn't want made public.

No, Arabella not only preferred men and would be resistant to those charms, she would be skeptical and he needed that to give him the peace of mind to focus.

Of course, he tried not to think about how quickly he didn't want other males in the same room with the DDA inspector. The human female was going to be nothing but trouble if he did take her on as his mate.

But a good kind of trouble. It will be fun.

Ignoring his dragon, Bram increased his pace. The sooner he finished interrogating the dragon hunter bastard, the sooner he would see if he would have a female of his own to fuck. Yes, to fuck. He wasn't about to hope for more, especially when he had no bloody idea whether he could trust the lass or not.

CHAPTER FIVE

Evie squinted at the words on the computer screen, but it didn't help make the letters any clearer. If not being able to see properly wasn't bad enough, her blurred vision was giving her a bloody big headache. Astigmatism, combined with slight farsightedness, was definitely not her friend tonight.

She'd typed nearly three thousand words of information, but that was just the tip of the iceberg. Hell, she'd barely finished the introduction about the Carlisle dragon hunters. Still, she'd rather be thorough than gloss over the information. The more concrete detail she provided, the higher the chance Bram would take her as his mate.

His mate. All of that sculpted, glaring, stubborn dragonman could be hers soon. Not that she'd have any claim on his heart. Evie was clever enough to know the mating would be a transaction of sorts: her safety in exchange for information. Still, she couldn't help but wonder what it'd be like to have Bram Moore-Llewellyn naked and unrestrained above her.

Stop that, Evie Marie Marshall. She wiggled in her chair. Sex fantasies would bring back wet panties, and she didn't want Bram scenting it when he returned. The last thing she needed was the dragonman's ego to inflate at how a simple touch or thought about him set her body on fire.

SEDUCING THE DRAGON

Leaning back in her chair, she closed her eyes to clear her mind of Bram when there was a knock on the door. Evie opened her eyes and debated whether she should answer it or not when a muffled female voice sounded from the other side of the door, "Open up, human. Bram sent me to babysit you."

Great. Bram didn't even trust her to stay in a cottage and type without causing trouble. She hoped the rest of her life wouldn't be this way, with a guard watching over her nearly every second of every day.

With a sigh, Evie stood up and moved to the door. Not a complete idiot, she opened the door a crack in case she needed to close it quickly and was greeted by the sight of a pair of woman's breasts encased in a t-shirt. Looking up, it took everything she had not to gasp at the woman's disfigured face.

The scar running down from the woman's right temple, across the bridge of her nose, to her left ear as well as the healed burns on her neck, told Evie the woman's identity; or rather, the dragonwoman's identity. She said, "You're Arabella MacLeod."

The dragonwoman raised an eyebrow. "Great to see I have a reputation. Now open the fucking door before I kick it open."

Evie had to somewhat put up with Bram's bullshit for a chance to stay safe, but she didn't have to put up with Arabella MacLeod's attitude. "If you're going to try to intimidate me, you have a long way to go before you even start coming close to Marcus King's level. How about we cut the tough act and converse on a level footing?"

Arabella crossed her arms over her chest. "So, the DDA inspector has a backbone." While waiting to see what the dragonwoman would do, Arabella kicked the door hard enough to send Evie flying backward on her arse.

Not even her squishy bum could save her tail bone from crashing against the floor. She glared up at the dragonwoman. It was on the tip of Evie's tongue to quote DDA regulations about accosting an inspector, but Evie kept quiet since those laws wouldn't protect her from the dragon hunters if Bram cast her out on her own.

Evie slowly stood up, ignoring the pain in her backside as she said, "Feel better now?"

The dragonwoman blinked. "What?"

"Your capture and resulting torture just over ten years ago is well-known inside the DDA. It's also well-known that you hate humans, so if knocking me on my arse helps to calm you down, then go for it. But if all you're going to do is use me as a punching bag for your hatred, then you can glare at me from across the room. I have shit to do."

Arabella studied her a second and then said, "You're not like the other DDA inspectors."

"Is that a compliment?"

"No."

Evie rolled her eyes. "Glad to see the dragonwomen can be as monosyllabic as the dragonmen. Now, excuse me, I'm going to work on the aforementioned shit I have to do."

Just as she moved to walk, Arabella grabbed her arm and asked, "Why are you here?"

Had Bram already spread her story to all the dragon-shifters? She'd thought better of him than that.

Looking over her shoulder, she answered, "Look, I don't know what Bram told you, but if I don't type out as much as I can before he returns, I might end up in the hands of the dragon hunters. You know what that's like, and no matter how much you might hate my being human, I'm guessing you hate the dragon hunters more, to the point that you wouldn't want them to get what they want."

"And they want you."

Okay, maybe Bram hadn't told her anything. However, it was too late to take it back, so Evie nodded. "Yes. I'm trying to put together some information for Bram, information about the Carlisle hunters. You holding me up and wasting my time is hurting your clan, so let me go so I can finish my task."

Evie never broke her gaze, and after what seemed like minutes, Arabella surprised the hell out of her by releasing her arm and nodding. It seemed her time working with Skyhunter had prepared her well for dealing with Stonefire's overabundance of alpha personalities.

Before the dragonwoman could change her mind, Evie rushed to the laptop, sat down, and started typing again. She was so engrossed in her work that it took her a second to realize that Arabella MacLeod was standing right behind her. Not wanting to waste any more time, she ignored her.

Since Evie could only guess how much Arabella hated the dragon hunters for what they'd done to her all those years ago, she hoped the dragonwoman wasn't going to use the information Evie was typing about the Carlisle hunters for some kind of half-arsed revenge. Especially since, if Evie's memory served her, it had been the Carlisle hunters who'd killed Arabella's mother.

~~~

Bram's ire at the dragon hunter remaining silent for the entire interrogation vanished as soon as he approached his cottage. Despite the darkness of the night, his vision was keen and he could see one of the hinges of his door was hanging on to the doorjamb by one screw. Someone had broken in.

Fuck. Had the captured dragon hunter been a decoy?

His dragon snarled. *Check on the human female. The hunters want to hurt her. We must protect her.*

Bram was on the same page, but instead of wasting time talking to his dragon, he sent a quick text message to Kai before he crept up to his cottage and took a closer look.

The light still glowed from the two front windows, neither of which was broken. Taking a deep inhalation, he didn't scent blood in the air, which was also good. Since his cottage was soundproofed to keep delicate clan matters away from supersensitive dragon-shifter ears, he couldn't hear anything. He needed to check the inside.

Dragon-shifters rarely used guns, and Bram was no exception. His dragon's reflexes had never failed him before, and he would trust them now.

Gripping the doorknob, he twisted it bit by bit until the latch clicked softly. On the count of three, Bram inched open the door and was greeted by the sound of Evie's voice. "The rivalry between the Carlisle and Edinburgh hunters is something to keep an eye on. Pitting them against each other might help loosen their defenses enough to attack."

Some of Bram's tension eased at the lass's voice, and he pushed the door wide open. Evie was standing behind Arabella, who was sitting and typing on the laptop before her. Without thinking, he demanded, "What's going on here?"

Both females turned to look at him. Neither one looked surprised to see him. If anything, they looked irritated.

Evie was the first to speak up. "Doing what you asked me to do—typing up information for you."

SEDUCING THE DRAGON

Bram decided to take the easier route and looked to Arabella. "Explain."

The dragonwoman shrugged one shoulder. "I was tired of trying to decipher her typos, so I offered to type for her."

"Yes, but why, exactly, would you do that, Arabella? Humans and kindness don't usually go together for you."

Evie spoke up, "Leave her alone. You sent her here, so my guess is that you trust her. I see no reason for you to be upset at her typing for me. If you'd allowed me time to fetch my glasses, we wouldn't be having this conversation right now."

Losing his cool in front of Arabella was not on his list of things to do, so he focused on his clan member and said, "Arabella, you can go now."

"But we're not done. All of this information about the Carlisle dragon hunters is fascinating."

Oh, fuck. Arabella didn't need inside information about the Carlisle hunters. She'd made great strides in her PTSD recovery over the last eight months, and he wouldn't put it past her to try to attack the hunters alone. After all, they were the ones responsible for both her mother's death and her scars.

Forcing every bit of dominance he could into his voice, Bram said, "Go home, Arabella. We'll talk tomorrow."

Ara looked about ready to argue, but then clenched her jaw and nodded. She'd never been tempted to outright disobey him before. He blamed the human's influence.

He waited until Arabella stood up and walked out the door before he pinned his best stare on Evie Marshall. "How in the world did you get Arabella MacLeod to not only work with you, but to almost appear to be on your side? And in just under two hours, no less?"

The human female straightened her shoulders. "I know a trick or two when it comes to working with dragon-shifters. Pretty much all of Clan Skyhunter detests humans. My first year was hell until I learned to use their other hatreds to my advantage. I did the same with Arabella. She hates the dragon hunters, and so do I. That hatred was stronger than what dislike she held for me."

Shaking his head, Bram moved to stand next to Evie and instantly regretted it as her womanly scent filled his nose. Just one whiff made his dragon growl. *Kiss her again. She cooperated. Arabella does not hate her. She is good.*

He sent a mental scowl to his dragon. *You are too trusting.*

His inner beast hissed, but Bram ignored him and spoke to the human, "Your cleverness is going to be a pain in my arse."

Hope lit her eyes. "So you're letting me stay?"

The way Evie looked at him, as if he were the only one who could save her life, went straight to his heart. He still couldn't fathom why anyone would want to kill the lass.

It was time to find that out. "Not yet." Her hope died, and he resisted putting a hand on her shoulder to comfort her as he continued, "First, I need to take a look at your information and see if it really is worth the hunters killing you over."

Her expression returned to one of part irritation and part impatience as she gestured toward the laptop. "Be my guest."

Just as he moved in front of the laptop, he heard the human's stomach rumble and his dragon jumped to the forefront of his mind. *Feed her.*

Even Bram felt a little guilty at her hunger. "While I do this, there are some leftovers in the refrigerator you can eat. I hope you like curry."

Raising an eyebrow, she said, "Are you sure it's not poisoned?"

Despite himself, one corner of Bram's lip twitched. "Aye, I'm sure. Now eat before I tie you to a chair and force feed you."

The human looked like she was about to say something, but then shut her mouth and nodded. He motioned to the doorway off to the side. "The kitchen is in there. Come back as soon as you've heated your food."

She gave a mock salute and walked toward the door. For the first time, he noticed she wasn't wearing any shoes. Not only that, her exaggerated hip sway had been replaced with an efficient stride.

The fake seductress had all but disappeared.

Not that he was sad about it. But rather than think too hard about why he liked the changes, he sat down in front of the computer screen and read the first sentence:

At the presend rime, the Carlide hunters numver avout forty.

Rubbing the late-day whiskers on his face, Bram could see what Arabella had meant about deciphering the typos. Reading Evie's notes was going to take three times as long as normal.

With a sigh, Bram went to work.

~~~

As the smell of curry filled the kitchen, Evie's stomach rumbled and she tapped her spoon against the counter in impatience. By now, Bram had to have noticed the plethora of typos in her document. Would he really make her wait until he finished it all before he told her if he would take her on as his mate or not?

Uncertainty was not her forte. Since Evie had been a little girl, she'd always planned out her life: earn good marks, go to university, and work her way up the Department of Dragon Affairs until she could be the Director.

Now, however, all of that planning was irrelevant. All that mattered was staying alive, and everything else would have to wait.

Living in such uncertainty simultaneously scared and irritated her.

Get over it, Evie. She'd dealt with plenty of uncertainty in her job as a DDA inspector; she would just have to use those experiences toward her personal life as well.

The microwave beeped. The sound was a welcome interruption of her thoughts.

For now, she'd focus on eating. Who knew, maybe by the time she'd finished, Bram might have answers for her. Then she could figure out what to do next.

She removed the leftover korma curry before carrying it to the kitchen doorway. Pausing a moment, she took advantage of the situation and simply watched Bram at the computer.

Without his glare or dominance crap, he looked like just a man. Sure, a fit man with broad shoulders, defined muscled arms, and a very lickable-looking tattoo on one of his biceps. Yet with his slightly too long hair brushing against his ears as he leaned over the laptop screen, all she wanted to do was walk over and tuck his hair back behind his ears. She had a feeling no one ever looked after him; being clan leader was a demanding and lonely job.

According to DDA records, Bram worked the hardest out of the five dragon-shifter clans in the UK to pass all of their inspections. Stonefire had by far the least amount of sacrifice-related complaints. Yet despite all of his hard work, Bram's infertility assured that he would never have a female sacrifice of his own. Hell, he might not ever have a mate. Everything he did screamed how he wanted his clan's numbers to rebuild and his infertility would hinder his goal.

Of course, Evie would never be able to give him a child anyway since her DNA wasn't compatible with dragon-shifter sperm. When she'd been nineteen and obsessed with everything dragon-shifter, she'd been tested.

She hoped that would work to her advantage since Bram wouldn't have to feel guilty about taking a likely mother-to-be away from his clan.

At one time, she'd wanted children of her own, but she was far more concerned about living than reproducing.

She probably would've continued staring if Bram's voice hadn't interrupted her thoughts. "You're not eating."

Standing back up, she then moved to stand next to him. As soon as his eyes met hers, she raised the spoon to her lips and took a bite.

Bram's eyes darted to her lips, and that odd heat and awareness shot through her body.

Bloody hell. Since when was eating curry a turn on?

After swallowing the spoonful, she asked, "So? Do you have a verdict yet?"

The heat vanished from his eyes and was replaced by a wry look. "Where did you learn to type, lass? Even if I were blinded right this instant, I could do better."

She narrowed her eyes. "I type fast and make mistakes. It happens. Now, stop trying to change the subject and just tell me straight what you plan to do."

He looked pointedly at her curry and she let out a sigh before taking another bite. Only once she swallowed did he stand up and look down at her. Without her heels on, he towered even more over her. The man was huge.

Crossing his arms over his chest, Bram said, "While I've only read about a third of what you wrote, it's enough for a decision."

The dragonman fell silent and she wanted to kick him and scream for him to just tell her already. When he said nothing, she asked, "And?"

"I want you to pack your things."

Evie nearly dropped her bowl of curry. He was sending her away.

Her heart squeezed and it took everything she had not to start crying. *Pull yourself together, Evie. Fight for it.*

She'd come this far. She wasn't about to give in so easily. Straightening her shoulders, she said, "If you give me a little more time, I'll provide more information. Seven years has allowed me access to quite a bit about the DDA, the dragon hunters, and the other dragon-shifter clans. With my glasses and another chance, I can prove to you I'm worth keeping."

Bram frowned. "What are you talking about? Of course you're going to help me. I'm not about to mate you just so I can fuck you, although I look forward to that."

She blinked. "Fuck me? What? You just told me to pack my things."

"Aye, you're moving in with me tonight."

CHAPTER SIX

Evie blinked and tried to comprehend Bram's words. Rather than say something intelligent, all she could do was echo, "Move in with you tonight?"

The dragonman took two steps toward her before he said, "Aye. Unless you're now having second thoughts?" He gave her a slow once-over before meeting her eyes again. "I was rather looking forward to fucking you."

The bluntness of his words cut through her shock and ignited her temper. "I'm not just going to jump into bed with you without setting things straight between us. If you're being serious about taking me as your mate, then I want to know how it will work, what my role here will be, and how you plan to chase away the dragon hunters. Not to mention, exactly how you plan to fight the British government about my staying here."

"No."

She narrowed her eyes. "What do you mean 'no'?"

He crossed his arms over his chest. "What was it that some redhead said to me earlier today? Oh, that's right, that she was only going to share what needed to be shared. Right now, you're in the 'maybe I'll mate you' stage. We have three days before you're supposed to leave here. In that time, you need to convince me to trust you. Until then, I'll share what you need to know, but not one word extra."

It seemed that her display of strength earlier had come back to bite her in the arse. "If you're trying to intimidate me into doing whatever you say, it won't work. Yes, I need your protection, but I'd rather take my chances with the dragon hunters than turn into a 'yes, dear' complacent idiot."

Bram uncrossed his arms and took the remaining steps between them. "Strong words from a woman all but begging for my help."

As she stared up into his light blue eyes, she could hear the dragonman's breathing and she realized how close he was standing to her. He was being an arsehole, but his heat and scent surrounded her and she remembered what it'd been like to be kissed by this man. Before she could stop herself, her eyes darted to his firm lips.

Then the corner of Bram's lips twitched and she knew she'd been caught. Focusing on her temper, she met his eyes again. "Laugh at me, I don't care. We already know how one kiss from me affects you."

He raised an eyebrow. "I rather thought it was the other way around."

They stared at one another, neither of them speaking. His head inched toward hers, and for a second, she thought he was going to kiss her again, but instead, he placed a finger under her chin. It took everything she had not to shiver as his mostly Northern tones rolled over her. "If all goes well and you have nothing to hide, you'll be in my bed soon enough. Until then, don't lie to me, Evie Marshall, or you will make an enemy out of me."

SEDUCING THE DRAGON

~~~

Bram resisted the urge to stroke the soft skin under Evie's chin. Hell, he was only inches away from her lips, and his inner dragon kept pushing him to kiss her. Even now, his dragon chimed in. *She tastes good. Her scent tells us she wants it too. Kiss her.*

Again, you're thinking with your cock.

She will not betray us.

He tried asking his beast how he could be so certain, but as his dragon had done all day, he remained silent whenever Bram tried to find out specifics about why he trusted Evie.

Rather than think about that, Bram studied the human female's eyes. They were steady, like a calm sea. Despite being in a stressful situation and her life on the line, the woman remained cool.

Sure, she had a temper, but it only seemed to affect her mouth and not her brain. He rather liked that about her. Glancing down at her plump lips, his dragon whispered, *Kiss her.*

No. Instead, Bram looked back into those cool eyes with a hint of fire and forced himself to focus. "Well, are you planning my downfall or should we go fetch your things and bring them here? I think I've growled and glared enough as a warning for you to not fuck with me. I have an early meeting, and whatever you may think, you'll be safer under my roof."

Her eyes widened. "Why? Did the dragon hunter say something during your interrogation?"

Okay, her remembering his errand impressed him a little. "Nothing he said was important. As long as you don't try to stab me in the back and you stay out of trouble, I will let you know if there's an increased threat to your life."

She stared at him and Bram resisted a sigh. He hadn't lied about the early meeting. He was about to say he'd fetch her things himself and lock her in the bedroom when Evie said, "Promise me you'll show me around your land tomorrow for a few hours and I'll stop fighting you for the rest of the night."

Out of nowhere, he couldn't resist saying, "Even if I toss you into my bed?"

Her cheeks flushed and he tried his hardest not to laugh, but failed. The instant he did, Evie straightened her shoulders and tilted her head. "Somehow, I think you like a little fighting in your bed. Compliance is boring."

She turned around and her words created an image of him and Evie naked, rolling around in a meadow, each fighting to be on top. He'd win, of course, and she'd be breathless, flushed, and beautiful as he thrust his cock into her tight, wet heat.

His dragon hummed. *It will be fun. Maybe tomorrow.*

Careful not to reach down to adjust his now semi-hard cock, Bram looked up to see Evie standing at the door staring at him. She cocked an eyebrow. "Well? Say the word and promise me that tour, and I'll go without a fight to collect my things. I might even throw in me only asking a handful of questions instead of everything on my mind during our walk."

All of a sudden, he wondered exactly what was going on inside that mind. This human female's sass was different from any of the females he'd met before.

If he were honest, he might even be enjoying himself right now. "I could just lock you in a room and go myself. Then I wouldn't have to deal with any of your questions tonight."

"Ah, yes, but how do you know I can't pick the lock?"

"It's a deadbolt."

She gave a mischievous smile that sent blood straight to his cock. "I could find a way. I'm quite resourceful."

The picture of Evie standing near the door, her head tilted so her red hair cascaded over her shoulders as she smiled with confidence made his dragon hum. *You like her too. Play some more and sleep later.*

He knew exactly what kind of "play" his beast was hoping for.

Enough. He didn't have time to argue with his dragon. For the sake of his clan, his meeting tomorrow with the Scottish dragon-shifter leader, Finlay Stewart, was too important to attend without any sleep. It'd taken him months of convincing Finn to meet him in person for alliance talks against the dragon hunters. He wasn't about to fuck that up over a female, no matter how enticing she might be.

He walked toward the door, but noticed Evie only had a light coat. He plucked an extra one from the coat hooks near the door, tossed it at her, and said, "Come or stay, it doesn't matter. I'm getting your things now. If you try to run away, just know that my people are watching you and you won't get far."

Without another glance, he walked out the door.

~~~

For a moment, Evie had been enjoying herself. Teasing the dragonman had been a lot more fun than she'd ever imagined.

Then Bram had shuttered his expression, tossing aside the amusement in his eyes. With it gone, she realized how much more attractive he became when he didn't wear his hardass dragon leader face.

Well, then, she'd just have to work on getting the teasing version of Bram Moore-Llewellyn back again. That version she wouldn't mind waking up next to for the rest of her life. Or, at least she hoped it would be for the rest of her life. Bram's half-arsed "maybe my mate" stage bullshit was vague. How she was supposed to convince him to trust her in three days was beyond her. Maybe after a night's rest she could figure it out.

Putting on the coat Bram had given her, she followed him into the dark.

And by dark, she meant pitch-black. The dragon-shifters had exceptional eyesight. According to her textbooks, while their night vision wasn't as keen as their sight during the day, they could still make out shapes in the dark. Evie, on the other hand, was all but walking blind with the lack of street lamps. Then the inevitable happened and she tripped.

Before she could mutter, "fuck," strong arms stopped her from falling. As the large, rough hands maneuvered her upright, she knew it was Bram. Her display of weakness pissed her off. She'd been doing so well with him.

She could barely make out his face, but his husky voice filled her ears. "To save time, I'm going to carry you."

He put an arm under her knees and swooped her up as if she weighed nothing. She squeaked as her body made contact with his chest. "I am perfectly capable of walking by myself. Put me down right now, Bram."

Adjusting his grip on her legs and waist, the dragon-shifter held her tighter against his hard, muscled chest. Despite the layers of clothing between them, the contact sent a sizzle through her body, which ended between her legs.

Bram's voice filled her ears. "No. Why human females feel the need to wear uncomfortable, ridiculous shoes, I'll never understand. Our land here isn't designed for those things. Once you change your shoes, you can walk on your own, but not before. You did bring other shoes with you, correct?"

Before she could help herself, she mumbled, "But you're supposed to like women in heels."

Bram squeezed her. "Why? They hide your true gait. In your case, it is full of confidence and efficiency. You should embrace it if you want to seduce a dragon-shifter."

"You're giving me advice on how to seduce you now?"

She felt him give a half-shrug. "As clan leader, I don't have a lot of time. Don't wear the heels and don't do the fake voice. They hide who you are, which doesn't convince me to take you as my mate."

"So no to the sexy heels, and no to the husky voice. Should I wear a trash bag then too, instead of my form-fitting clothes?"

Even in the dark, she could hear the smile in his voice. "A bin bag would be easier to rip off when I wanted you in my bed."

She rolled her eyes. "Leave it to a man to make a bin bag sexy."

For a second, Bram remained silent and she wondered if she'd gone too far. In the dark, she felt comfortable and had nearly forgotten she was being carried in the arms of a dragon-shifter, in the middle of dragon-shifter land. If she'd rolled her eyes at Marcus down south, she never would've heard the end of it.

But then Bram leaned close to her ear and the heat of his breath caressed her skin. "I'm sure that even if I required you to wear one every night as part of the arrangement of our mating, you'd probably find a way to rebel and wear those bloody awful things that squeeze your body into some unnatural shape beneath it."

She laughed. "Corsets are very 19th century. Exactly how old are you?"

His tone became more distant. "Old enough."

Hmph. Dragon-shifters had lifespans similar to humans, so it wasn't as if she was really insulting him. He couldn't be more than thirty-five or so. She must've touched on a sore spot without even trying. She should drop it, but she added it to her lists of things to find out about Bram.

She frowned. Wait a second, since when had she started a list? It wasn't like she was really still doing her DDA inspector job. Any information she sent back now would be promptly dismissed as tainted the instant her mating to Bram happened. Well, she hoped the mating would happen. And the dragon-shifter hadn't even agreed to mate her yet. It would be dangerous if she became too interested in him too soon. She'd just have to be careful.

Bram shifted his hold on her and soon her feet were on the ground. The dragonman opened the door, leaned around her, and flipped on a light. They had arrived at her temporary cottage.

While she might've protested earlier, she already missed the heat and safety she'd felt in Bram's arms. However, she kept her face brave and confident, not wanting to let on that little tidbit or the dragonman might use it against her. She looked up. "I'll change my shoes and fetch my things. Then you can carry them back instead of me."

Judging by Bram's expressionless face, whatever camaraderie they'd shared on the way here had cooled. That bothered her more than she liked.

Rather than focus too long on that fact, she stepped inside the door, kicked off her heels, and went inside the cottage. She had a feeling their walk back would be mostly in silence.

CHAPTER SEVEN

Bram poured his second cup of black coffee and took a sip. He preferred tea to the nasty black brew, but he needed something to help wake him up and make him more alert for his meeting in thirty minutes with Finn Stewart.

It was all Evie Marshall's fault. He should've been able to nab five hours of sleep, but he'd spent the first two of those imagining her soft, warm body next to his. Or, rather, under his.

And even when he'd finally chased away the sexual fantasies created by both him and his dragon, he'd had a restless three hours of sleep. Evie's comment about age had brought back memories best forgotten. He very much wanted to get the surliness out of his system with the human female, but she slept like a log and was still asleep. Not even banging on the door had woken her.

So much for the female being on edge because her life was in danger.

His dragon chimed in. *She feels safe with us. That is a good sign.*

In no mood to argue with his stubborn beast, Bram pushed the dragon to the back of his mind and went out of the kitchen to his desk. Kai had given the green light for him to borrow Nikki, so he dialed the young dragonwoman. When she answered, he said without preamble, "Nikki, your new assignment starts this morning. You're to be Evie Marshall's full-time guard. I need you here in five minutes to get the female up and out of my cottage before Finn Stewart shows up."

He could hear the confusion in her voice. "Can't you wake her up while I make my way there? It would make things easier."

"I tried. Now, hurry up."

Clicking off his phone, he took another sip of coffee. With Nikki's assignment out of the way, he only had about twenty-five more things to take care of in the next twenty-eight minutes. Melanie always badgered him about hiring an assistant, but Bram liked the work. However, dealing with Evie's situation was going to take more time than he'd like and he might just have to find some help.

His dragon decided to poke his head out again. *Show her around. Bond with her. She's brave but still scared.*

Deep down, Bram knew that too. If he took her as his mate, her whole life would turn upside down. He knew nothing of her family or friends, and getting them onto his land was a problem. He'd been trying for months to get the okay for Melanie's parents and brother to visit, but the British government was being cranky and bureaucratic about the law. Humans weren't supposed to visit, end of story.

Maybe Evie could help us find a way.

His dragon had a point. To placate the beast, he said, *Okay, I'll ask her later. For now, I need to work. Go back to sleep. You need to be alert when Finlay Stewart is here. I need your intuition.*

In response, his dragon hummed and faded to the back of his mind.

Right. Now, he could put things into play without any interruptions. If the meeting went well with Finn, he should start having regular teleconference meetings with the other leader within the next month or two to strategize against the dragon hunters. And if so, he needed Arabella to be ready to talk with the other leader about secure communication channels before Finn returned to Scotland.

He'd just finished sending an email to Arabella when there was a knock on the door that had to be Nikki. Not wasting time, he strode to the door and opened it. "She's upstairs. There's a pitcher in the kitchen you can fill with water and dump on her to wake her up. Get to it."

Trained solder that she was, Nikki nodded and went about her task. It was only when he heard a shriek a few minutes later that he knew she'd succeeded.

And he couldn't help but laugh. What would Evie look like all wet and angry in the morning?

Focus, Bram, focus. Right. Pushing aside his distracting thoughts about a wet, angry Evie, Bram went to work on his list of things to do. His clan came first, no matter how much he wanted to see what Evie looked like right this second.

~~~

Evie had been warm and enjoying a dream about flying on a dragon's back when a blast of ice hit her face. She shrieked and jumped out of bed. Looking around, she saw a female with a dragon-shifter tattoo peeking out of the sleeve of her shirt. She was short for a dragon-shifter and she had black hair, dark almond eyes, and skin with a yellow undertone. She also had her arm in a sling.

She had no idea who this person was.

Evie growled. "Who the fuck are you and why the bloody hell did you feel the need to dump ice water on a sleeping woman?"

73

The dragonwoman arched an eyebrow. "My orders are to get you out of bed and out of the house in the next twenty minutes. It's your own fault you sleep too soundly."

She frowned. "Orders? Who..." Then it hit her. "Oh no, he bloody well didn't."

She moved to pass the dragonwoman, but she moved into Evie's way. "Yelling at Bram won't accomplish anything. Lochguard's clan leader is on his way here and he has a lot on his plate. Don't bother him."

"Lochguard? As in the Scottish dragon-shifter clan?"

For a second, the dragonwoman's brows drew together, and in that instant, she looked pale. "He didn't tell you?"

Somehow, she had a feeling that telling her clan secrets was a big no-no. Evie would use that to her advantage later. "No. What's your name?"

"Nikola. I'm your new guard."

So, she still had a guard. She resisted a sigh as she wiped the water off her face with her sleeve. "Right, Nikola, here's what we're going to do. I need to learn the lay of the land here. Did Bram place restrictions on where I could go?" The dragonwoman shook her head and opened her mouth, but Evie cut her off. "You take me where I ask, and I won't mention your slip-up. Does that sound like a deal?"

Nikola's face turned fierce. "My orders come from Bram, not you. I always tell him the truth. Blackmailing me won't work."

Of course she'd be assigned a loyal guard. Still, she could be of some use. "I admire your spirit, so let's try another approach. How about you ask Bram if I can go out today to explore since he refused to show me around? Promise me you'll ask that, and really push for the decision, and I'll jump into the shower without any more fuss."

SEDUCING THE DRAGON

The dragonwoman hesitated, but finally nodded. "Fine. You have ten minutes to shower, so hurry up."

Nikola left and Evie smiled. Her request might be simple, but she had an ulterior motive. As she moved toward the bathroom, she nabbed her clothes and starting humming. What had begun as a bloody awful way to wake up had turned into a way for her to not only search out the dragon-shifter doctor who could give her the answers she needed to maybe gain Bram's trust, but she could also get under the bloody dragonman's skin.

Yes, the dragonman was in for a surprise.

~~~

Bram glanced at the time. If Clan Lochguard's leader was punctual, Evie had five minutes before the dragonman would arrive.

It was bad enough he'd agreed to Nikki's request to allow her to show the bloody female around in his stead. Now he ran the risk of Evie and Finn crossing paths, and Bram very much didn't want that to happen.

Evie probably didn't know much about Lochguard's new leader. Finlay Stewart had taken over the Scottish dragon-shifter clan six months ago. Few inside the DDA knew much about him since Lochguard had remained isolated throughout the transition and had postponed any inspections or female sacrifice requests. If Evie had heard the same rumors Bram had heard recently about the new leader having more open-minded views on humans and dragon-human interactions, she might've gone to Finn for help instead of Bram.

Yesterday morning, he would've sent the female packing while giving her his best wishes. Yet after kissing the female and holding her soft, warm body against his last night, both man and dragon didn't want Finn anywhere near her. He still didn't know the lass's whole truth, but provided she didn't betray him, he planned to keep her.

His dragon emerged from the back of his mind. *Good. Embrace the truth. She is fire, and you like her.*

Bram grunted, but before he could converse any more with his inner beast, steps echoed down the stairs and he moved from behind his desk to stand at the bottom. Looking up, his heart skipped a beat.

Evie wore a short jean skirt, brown flat-level boots that went to just below her knees, and a blue sweater the same deep blue of her eyes. The top hugged her figure and dipped low enough to show her small cleavage. Even from here, he could make out the lace shapes of her bra through the material. With the added cold, every male in his clan would be able to see her nipples.

His dragon snarled. Her nipples were not for anyone else to see.

He growled. "You are not going outside dressed like that without me."

The human arched one dark red eyebrow. "Since I'm auditioning to be your mate and am, in effect, no longer a DDA inspector, I can wear whatever I want. I'm wearing this."

He ignored the look Nikki was giving him at the news of Evie auditioning to be his mate and moved up the stairs until he was one step below her. Even with the extra step, he was still taller than her. "As a *former* DDA inspector, then you very well know dragon-shifter populations are heavily male. In Stonefire's case, only about thirty-five percent of our clan is female. Dressing like that will attract nearly every unmated dragonman in Stonefire."

"The competition might be good for you."

He resisted a snarl. In normal circumstances, he knew there were a lot of good, single dragonmen in his clan who would make fine mates. Right now, however, they were all enemies.

Gesturing behind him, he said, "You'll wear one of my big coats and not that tiny thing on your arm. My jacket will also cover up your tempting curves."

Evie shook her head. "It's early April, not December. I have a scarf and a jacket. I'll be warm enough since my legs never really get cold."

At the mention of her legs, Bram glanced down at the plump, creamy skin on display. He remembered touching that soft skin yesterday right after he'd kissed the human, and he itched to do it again.

With the sight of her skin, combined with her sweet, womanly scent, his cock was coming to life. He was about to reach out and touch her thigh when Evie broke the spell by clearing her throat and saying, "Eyes up here, dragonman."

Careful to keep his expression guarded, Bram looked up and said, "Your skin and scent are too enticing. Wear the big, heavy jacket or I'll have you locked away for the day."

Evie narrowed her eyes. "No. Until you accept me as your mate, you have zero say in what I do. And even then, it's not guaranteed."

He leaned until he was an inch from the human's face. "If you want my help, you should at least try to listen to me. Fighting me at every step of the way is not helping your case."

"You know what? Fuck you, Bram. You act like you have a claim on me, yet you foist me off on a guard at the first opportunity rather than talk with me. I understand you're busy, but no one wants to mate a stranger. I won't ever try to interfere with your work if it's important, but if you want to fuck me, then you'd better start paying me some attention. Bloody hell, beyond your DDA reputation and your sexy kisses, I know nothing. Do you have family? A former mate? Let alone what plans you have for the clan. Try opening up to me, Bram Moore-Llewellyn, or I'll chance the dragon hunters and find another clan leader to help me."

Fire danced in her eyes. Bastard that he was, the fighting had made his cock hard as stone.

Bram grabbed her upper arm, but before he could continue their argument, a Scottish-accented voice interrupted, "If you're looking for another clan leader, lass, you have one right here and I'll tell you anything you like for a kiss."

Turning around, Bram did his best to hide Evie from Finlay Stewart's gaze. He barked, "You're early."

The leader raised one blond eyebrow. "I know I said to act informal as I can't stand the protocols, but you're close to crossing the line, Mr. Double-Barreled last name."

His inner dragon was snarling. *Get Evie away. She is ours.*

The human half of him, however, realized the enormity of this situation. He was very close to fucking up everything over a female.

As he worked to control his possessiveness, Evie's voice sounded from behind. "Hello, Scottish dragonman. I would introduce myself, but as you can see, I have more than two hundred pounds of dragon-shifter muscle in the way."

Finn chuckled and Bram's dragon snarled louder. He sent calming thoughts to his beast and said, *Behave. I will send her to safety.*

From decades of earned trust, his dragon listened. Bram said to Finn, "Give us a minute and we can start over."

The Scottish leader answered, "Is she your new mate?"

What the other leader didn't say was that it was bad form to flirt with a newly mated dragonman's female; more than one fight to the death had erupted in the not so distant past over such a misstep. Their inner dragons were finicky beasts when it came to mates.

Bram wanted to lie, but knew his ties to Clan Lochguard were tentative at best, so he told the truth. "Not yet, but soon." He turned toward Evie and Nikki. His comments were directed at his young clan member. "Nikki, take her wherever she wants, but bring her back here for lunch. Evie and I need some time to talk." He moved his gaze to Evie. "You'll get some time, lass. Just take the other coat is all I ask."

She searched his eyes a second before nodding. "Asking is all I want." She paused, her voice soft when she added, "Don't order me around, Bram. I don't like it."

Except when she is naked. She will like it then.

Since Finn was in the same room, Bram didn't bother wasting time with his dragon. Instead, he said to Evie, "We'll discuss it at lunch, in private."

The human stood on her tiptoes to glance over his shoulder, acknowledging their audience, and then back to him before nodding. "I hope it's going to be a long lunch."

Rather than comment, Bram headed back down the stairs and stopped in front of Finn. He gestured for Evie to come forward. Ignoring his dragon's snarling, Bram said, "Evie Marshall, this is Finlay Stewart, the leader of Clan Lochguard."

The other dragonman put out a hand. As Evie shook the man's hand, Bram put a hand on her waist and squeezed. She shot him a quizzical glance before she turned her attention back to Finn. "While it's nice meeting you, I expected Dougal Munro."

Finn winked. "Prefer the older men, do you?"

Before the Scottish shifter could flirt any more with his female, Bram guided Evie away as he explained, "Dougal retired six months ago. I can tell you all about it later." He plucked a coat off the peg on the wall. "Try not to get into too much trouble, lass."

Evie gave a mischievous smile and his heart skipped a beat. "That's the fun part."

He nearly groaned, but Nikki came to his rescue and ushered the human out the door before she could taunt him with any more glances or smiles.

He turned toward Finn. The Scottish leader grinned. "We can talk about the alliance later. First, you need to tell me where you found such a fiery female. I could use one myself."

"Lay one hand on her, and I don't care if you're a clan leader, I'll challenge you to a dragon fight myself."

All Finn did was grin wider and Bram knew this was going to be one long meeting.

CHAPTER EIGHT

Evie smiled as she left Bram's cottage. She'd stirred his jealousy, just as she'd intended. The new, youngish and attractive Scottish clan leader had made it even easier to do, but all that mattered was that she had a lunch date with Bram.

Of course, lunch was hours away, and even though the DDA would toss aside any report she submitted, Evie felt the need to investigate Caitriona Belmont's death. With the facts under her belt, she could hopefully direct the new DDA inspector sent to replace her to the truth. If Stonefire was to be her new home, she would need to protect them from the bureaucratic loopholes that could weaken the clan.

Finding out the truth might also help her earn Bram's trust enough for him to accept her as his mate.

Nikola, or as Bram called her, Nikki, stopped and turned around, garnering Evie's attention. Nikki narrowed her eyes as she said, "I will take you where you wish to go, but not until I say that if you hurt Bram, I will make your life miserable whilst you're here."

The fact so many of his clan seemed to love him eased her apprehensions bit by bit. "I have no intentions of hurting him as long as he doesn't hurt me." Nikki nodded and Evie decided to give the dragonwoman a bit more of an explanation. "He's protecting me from the dragon hunters."

Nikki waved the arm not in a sling. "I don't care about the reason. Bram is my leader and I respect his decisions. Just don't hurt him and we'll get along fine."

Since Evie would be spending the next few hours with Nikki, she decided to merely bob her head and push on. "Sounds good. With that out of the way, I need to visit Dr. Cassidy Jackson's surgery and ask her a few questions."

"What for?"

She could simply tell the dragonwoman to mind her own business, but she wasn't a DDA inspector anymore. She needed to try fitting in with the clan members or her future could be extremely lonely here. "There are some questions about Caitriona Belmont's death. I was originally sent here to find out the truth. While the DDA will soon no longer trust me if I'm Bram's mate, I want to find out the truth before the replacement inspector arrives. I want to make sure they don't overlook anything."

"The DDA thinks we killed her?"

Evie eyed the woman a second before she replied. "You act like a soldier, so answer this and I'll give you more information. Are you one of Stonefire's Protectors?"

The other woman raised her chin. "In training, but I'm nearly done."

Each dragon clan in the UK had a group of special ops-like soldiers called Protectors. They each served with the British armed forces for two years before being trained by their respective clans. The fact this dragonwoman was nearly done spoke volumes about her abilities as well as her loyalty. "Right, then I'll tell you this in confidence: The high levels of dragon-shifter hormones in her blood might have caused her death in childbirth."

Nikki frowned. "I'm not a doctor, but I think it's normal for a human who carries a dragon-shifter child to have those hormones."

"You're right, but the levels were exceedingly high, as if someone were giving her extra amounts on the side."

"That's not good."

"No. So the sooner you take me to see Dr. Jackson, the better."

"The clan calls her Dr. Sid, but never in a million years would she try to kill someone." Nikki turned and motioned with her head. "Still, she might have an idea of who could. Follow me."

As they turned down a path on the left, they moved away from the main living community with cottages cheek and jowl and headed toward the wide-open space ringed with rugged hills that was the landing and takeoff area. Or, at least, that was her guess since a large, dark purple dragon jumped up and beat its wings before flying into the distance.

Most dragon-shifter doctors placed their surgeries near the landing area to make it easier to access their most critical patients. While accidents and injuries happened every day, the worst ones were caused by the dragon hunters, especially if the rumors about their recent weaponry upgrades were true.

Within ten minutes, Nikki stopped in front of a three-story house with a large covered, yet open-aired, space on the side used to treat dragon-shifters who were too weak to shift back into their human forms. The dragonwoman said, "Dr. Sid might be with a patient, but she should be here. She can, hopefully, answer your questions. Although I hope you're wrong about someone tinkering with Cait's hormone levels."

Evie nodded. "Believe me, I hope so too."

They entered the house-slash-surgery. Inside was obviously a waiting area with some chairs and a desk staffed by a young dragon-shifter male who couldn't be more than twenty. He smiled at Nikki, but his smile faded when he eyed Evie. "Why did you bring a human here, Nikki? We aren't due for another female sacrifice for a few months."

Rather than let Nikki answer for her, Evie butted in, "I'm Evie Marshall and I'm investigating something for Bram. I'm here to talk with Dr. Cassidy Jackson."

The male dragon-shifter eyed her with suspicion. "If Bram had a human investigating something for him, he would've alerted the clan and he hasn't. Who are you?"

Nikki stepped in front of her. "Leo, she's with me and I'll vouch that she's here to do as she says."

While the action was small, Nikki's defense meant the world to her.

Leo stared at Nikki and finally sighed. "The last time I stood up to you, I ended up with a black eye and a broken nose. Take a seat and I'll let the doctor know you're here."

Nikki nodded and Evie couldn't help but smile. The dragonwoman was a bit like her in that she didn't take shit from anyone.

The pair of them moved toward the nearest chairs and sat down to wait.

~~~

After nearly two hours of back and forth, Bram waited for Finn's answer.

And not just any answer, but the answer that would determine the future of his clan.

SEDUCING THE DRAGON

The tall, blond Scot studied him with his amber-colored eyes. The teasing and flirting from earlier in the morning was gone, replaced with a dragonman with an unreadable expression on his face. The version of Finlay Stewart sitting across from him right now was the version who had won the right to be clan leader.

Finn's voice finally filled the room. "I have one last condition."

He resisted a growl. "I've stated my terms and what I'm willing to compromise on. There's not much room for negotiation."

"This falls within your parameters."

Bram waved a hand. "Well, stop being melodramatic and spit it out already."

"For my people to truly believe you want to work with us, I think we should foster like in the old days."

He frowned. "That hasn't been done for centuries."

Finn shrugged. "I think each of us hosting a clan member or three from the other clan will A) help to show that we're more alike than we give credit and B) allow us to each have a spy." Bram opened his mouth, but Finn beat him to it. "You seem to like the truth, and spy is closer to the truth than a prolonged guest."

"So much for trust."

"Hey, trust will come in time. Nothing happens overnight."

Despite his irritation at all the negotiating, Bram liked the Scottish leader more as time went on. Finn was far more open-minded and forward-looking than sixty-year-old Dougal Munro had been. "Say I agree to the fostering, then what about the details? How long? How many? What role should they play in the clan? I won't send one of my clan members to sit and twiddle their thumbs for months on end, nor will I allow them to be shunned and mistreated."

"I can respect that as I feel the same way. You don't have to send someone today. Let's say, in a month or two? That gives us each time to prepare our clans and hash out the finer points." Finn leaned forward. "I can promise you no harm will come to your clan members as long as no harm comes to mine."

Bram nodded. "I can promise that too, but with one caveat—if any of your fostered clan members try to undermine the well-being of Stonefire, they will be dealt with accordingly."

Finn leaned back in his chair. "I could threaten back the same thing, but I think you're clever enough to expect the same out of me."

"Right, then that's the last of the negotiations for today." Bram stood up. "I'll see you tonight for dinner at the great hall."

The Scottish leader stood and amusement glinted in his eye. "Are we going to see your spirited, delectable female tonight too?"

"She will be sitting as far away from you as possible."

Finn laughed. "No worries, Bram, I'm not about to fight you and throw away these past few hours of boring, tedious negotiations. Life's too short to live through that twice."

Bram wondered if Finn had two personalities. One minute he was stern and calculating, and the next he was jolly and teasing. Bram was definitely going to keep him far away from Evie. He could see the two of them flirting back and forth, which made his inner dragon growl.

Shushing his beast, he pushed on. "You can meet my technology security expert tonight at dinner and discuss your requirements then."

"Why don't I meet with this individual now?"

SEDUCING THE DRAGON

He wasn't about to detail Arabella's past to Finn and tell him how she still had trouble with one-on-one private meetings with strangers, especially with a stranger who could overpower her. The dragonman was barely an ally. "The dragonwoman is busy until tonight."

"A female, eh? Well, then that makes everything better."

Bram was about to warn the other leader to leave Arabella alone when there was a knock on the door. Since the cottage was soundproofed, he moved to the door and opened it. Nikki and Evie stood in front of him.

Before he could say anything, Evie blurted out, "Bram, I really need to talk to you."

"It's not quite lunch time, lass."

The female glanced to Nikki and then back to Bram. "It's important."

Given her tone and expression, he believed her.

Bram looked over his shoulder. "Finn, is there anything else that absolutely must be discussed before dinner?"

"No, take care of your clan." Finn moved to stand next to him and put out a hand. Once Bram shook and dropped it, the Scottish leader looked to Evie and Nikki. "And I look forward to talking with you bonny lasses tonight."

Both females smiled at the other clan leader and Bram growled. Finn laughed at the sound before saying, "Right, I'm going." He gave each of the females a smile and was gone.

Since Bram had various clan members keeping an eye on Finn—much as Finn said earlier, trust still needed to be earned—he stepped aside to allow Evie and Nikki into his cottage. Once he shut and locked the door, he said, "So what's the emergency, Evie?"

The human female unzipped his huge coat surrounding her and then bit her bottom lip. It took everything he had to focus on her words and not her mouth when she released her lip and said, "I think Caitriona Belmont was murdered."

He looked back up into her eyes. "Come again? Caitriona died in childbirth."

Nikki took a step forward. "Listen to her, Bram. I think she's on to something."

Glancing back at Evie, he said, "Okay, then, explain how you reached that conclusion."

Standing this close to the lass, he could hear her heartbeat thumping hard inside her chest. Yet level-headed human she was, she took a deep breath and carried on. "Well, part of the reason I was sent here by the DDA was to investigate Caitriona's death since her autopsy was off."

He nodded. "Melanie mentioned that to me. Go on."

"This morning, I decided to pay Dr. Sid a visit." Bram opened his mouth but she beat him to it. "I know the DDA won't accept any report I write about Stonefire, but I wanted to find out the truth. Not only for me, but for you as well."

His dragon decided to speak up. *She cares for the clan.*

Rather than think about that, he asked, "And what did you find out?"

"I brought a copy of Caitriona's autopsy results with me and showed them to Dr. Sid. I knew high levels of dragon-shifter hormones in a human's blood was bad, but I'm not a doctor."

"Get to the point, lass."

"Dr. Sid explained how the numbers were far too high. In order for any human to have that level of dragon-shifter hormone in her body, she'd have to be given shots or take medication. I guess much like humans have medications for things like thyroid hormone replacements, the dragon-shifters have something similar for the hormone that controls their ability to shift into a dragon."

She looked to Nikki. "You fill him in on the rest."

The young dragonwoman didn't hesitate. "After Sid looked through the lists of dragon-shifters who needed the hormone, one name stuck out—Neil Westhaven."

Neil had been the dragon-shifter assigned to the sacrifice, Caitriona. He'd made the poor lass's life hell, primarily through verbal abuse, until Cait had turned into a depressed recluse. Only because Neil had hidden the female so well from others did Bram miss the human's suffering.

Bram clenched a fist. "But that bastard was banished long before Cait gave birth."

Evie stepped in. "That's true, but Nikki and I did some talking, and we think we came up with an explanation."

Bloody fantastic. The two of them working together would most definitely cause trouble for him in the future. "And that would be?"

"He must have someone here, still on the clan's lands, working with him. Nikki thinks it could explain the increase of dragon hunter attacks too."

Chapter Nine

Evie held her breath while she waited for Bram's response. He had no reason to trust her, but she hoped Nikki's support would convince him to take the possibility seriously.

The tall, muscled dragonman looked from her to Nikki and back again before he said, "Do you have any proof to back up these claims?"

Nikki moved to talk, but Evie put out a hand to stop the dragonwoman. "No, but my gut says it's the right thing. Just think about it. How else would the dragon hunters know each and every weak point on your perimeter?"

Bram looked to Nikki and the dragonwoman squared her shoulders. "I didn't tell her anything that wasn't clan-wide knowledge. Since she's going to be your mate, I reckoned it was okay to tell her that sort of information."

"Fine, okay. Putting that aside, Cait pretty much always stayed in her cottage, and when she wasn't confined there, she came to me, Melanie, or Sid. None of us would ever have harmed the lass."

Nikki piped in. "But whenat about her food? Cait didn't cook and most of her meals were brought to her."

Bram shook his head. "Old Mrs. Duncan is seventy-five years old and doesn't have a traitorous bone in her body. She was loyal to my mother and she's loyal to me too."

Seducing the Dragon

She racked her brain trying to come up with something else when Nikki added, "Let me talk to Kai about this and see what we can find. He's loyal to you as well and would never betray you."

Evie barely resisted hugging her new friend. Nikki may be quite a bit younger than her, but the dragonwoman was worthy of her Protector-in-training status. She would have made a fine DDA inspector.

"Right," Bram said, "talk to Kai and no one else. We're also going to keep a close eye on Cait's son, Murray. While unlikely given that the lad's already five months old and Neil never tried to take him, the bastard might yet come to retrieve his son. Since the male of the current couple watching him is a Protector, Murray should be safe for now. As for the rest, once Kai has a plan, tell him to come here and discuss it with me."

"Yes, sir." Nikki looked to Evie. "I'll see you at the great hall tonight."

Evie had no idea what was happening tonight at the great hall, but she nodded. "Thanks for your help, Nikki."

The woman grinned and was gone, leaving Evie alone with Bram.

She didn't think she'd overstepped her boundaries, but given the dragonman's assessing look, she wondered if she were in for another row.

He took a step toward her, and Evie was suddenly aware of the big, bulky coat she was wearing. In preparation for their possible heated argument, she shucked the jacket. Now she was ready to take the dragonman head on.

Bram nodded at her. "You've done well today, Evie."

She blinked. "Um, thank you?"

A smile tugged at Bram's lips and she melted a little. "You can handle Skyhunter's bastard leader down south, you can sway Arabella MacLeod to your side, and even stand up to me, but you don't know how to handle a compliment. I find that intriguing."

She frowned. "You try working with temperamental dragon-shifters for years and see how often you get a compliment. Half the time, I was lucky to just do my business without someone yelling how humans were weak, disgusting, or the enemy. Add in the humans who view my job as a waste of the government's money, and yeah, I'm not well liked."

Anger flashed in Bram's eyes and they went to slits before going back again. That signaled his dragon was close to breaking free.

Hoping to prevent that from happening, Evie put a hand on his arm. The instant her fingers touched his warm skin and the hairs of his arm tickled her palm, a flash of heat shot through her body. She'd been right to ditch the jacket.

Stroking his skin with her thumb, his eyes were human again when she said, "But you're busy and I don't want to waste time talking about Clan Skyhunter or any of the other rude people I've dealt with over the years. What needs to be done to sort out the dragon hunter problem? Is there anything I can do to help?"

Bram tucked a strand of her hair behind her ear. His fingers lingered on her lobe and she was very aware of the roughness of his fingers against her skin. It took everything she had to focus on his words, especially since his voice was low and extra sexy as he said, "Kai and Nikki will investigate and report to me as soon as they find something. Kai's the best clan member I have when it comes to rooting out secrets. I would trust him with my life, so I trust him in this too."

SEDUCING THE DRAGON

Evie was glad Bram had someone to help him. Of course, a small part of her wanted to be part of his trusted list too. Maybe with time she'd earn a place. Her telling him about Cait's possible murder was hopefully a step in the right direction.

Bram caressed her earlobe again, and thoughts of her future and place in Stonefire fled her mind. A tall, muscled dragonman was looking at her like he wanted to eat her up. Or, if she were lucky, lick her up.

She shivered. The thought of Bram's tongue lapping between her legs made her clit pulse and her heart rate kick up. Glancing to Bram's firm lips, she wanted him to kiss her.

Stop it, Evie. His clan is on the verge of attack with a possible traitor. Right now is not the time to think of the wicked strokes of his tongue against yours.

With incredible effort, she removed her hand from Bram's arm, but the dragonman grabbed her hand and pressed it back against his skin. She looked up and saw the dragon slits flashing in his eyes again.

The dragonman stroked the skin at her wrist with his thumb as he said, "It's lunchtime, lass. Trust Kai and Nikki to do their jobs; there's nothing else that can be done until they've finished their investigation, especially if we don't want to alert the whole clan to a possible traitor. After what you've just uncovered, you've earned an hour of my time. Now, what would you like to do?"

~~~

As Bram stroked Evie's wrist, her heart rate kicked higher with each pass. He could smell her arousal, and he very much wanted to kiss the living shit out of her.

Before meeting this human, Bram would've dove right into his work to see if there was something he'd missed from when Neil had still been part of the clan. He hadn't lied to Evie; he would trust Kai with his life. But without a mate or a family of his own, work was what had made him happy.

Now, however, all he could think about was Evie's touch and his dragon's growling and screaming inside his head. *Let the others investigate. Before tonight, claim her. Do not let the Scottish leader steal her away. Make her want only us.*

He agreed with his beast, and without thinking, Bram pulled the human flush up against his body. She let out a sound of surprise. "Bram?"

He was clan leader. He should push the female away and put the clan first as he had for the last eight years.

But the combination of his dragon's need and her soft belly against his cock was too much. For the first time in nearly a decade, he wanted to take something for himself.

Lowering his head, he kissed her.

Her lips were soft and warm, but nowhere near enough to appease either man or beast. Pushing his tongue against her lips, she opened, and he groaned as her taste surrounded his tongue.

His inner dragon hummed. *More, take more. Feel her skin. Now.*

As Evie met his tongue stroke for stroke, he placed a hand on her upper thigh. The heat of her soft, plump skin seeped through his palm and sent a fresh rush of blood to his cock. Unlike last night, he didn't stop. Instead, he moved until he reached between her legs.

He barely registered the plain cotton underwear. No, all he noticed was how wet and swollen she was for him.

SEDUCING THE DRAGON

Testing the waters, he rubbed her clit through the material and Evie moaned into his mouth. Wanting to see the desire in her eyes, he broke the kiss, and yes, the heat in her deep blue eyes made both man and dragon hum.

He rubbed her clit again and murmured, "I know you wanted to talk, but it's taking everything I have right now not to rip off your underwear and plunge into you. Tell me to stop, and I'll stop."

Silently, he begged her to please allow him to keep going.

Evie laid a hand on his chest and stared into his eyes. One second passed, and then another before she replied in a husky voice, "Promise me you'll talk after, and I'll let you fuck me. Just once."

He dragon snarled. "Just once? Why? Do you want to go after the Scottish leader?"

She narrowed her eyes. "Tame the jealousy, dragonman. There's too much to do for your clan, as well as the fact I refuse to mate a stranger. I want to know something about you, Bram Moore-Llewellyn, because I'm starting to like you."

Her words placated his dragon. *Good human. She likes us. The sex will be good. Hurry. Fuck her. Claim her.*

Bram was a hairbreadth from losing control to his dragon. It was almost as if Evie were his true mate. *Impossible.* Mate-claim frenzies happened with the first kiss and only ended with pregnancy. Since he couldn't impregnate Evie, the pulsing desires running through his body must be something else.

Pushing aside all of his confusion, Bram gave another swirl around Evie's clit with his finger and whispered, "I promise to talk later. Now, will you let me fuck you?"

He pressed against her hard little nub and Evie leaned into his chest. She whispered, "Yes, please. My legs are about to give out."

Bram ripped her underwear and plunged two fingers in her hot, wet pussy. Evie clutched his arm and he whispered, "So wet and hot." He retreated and thrust his fingers again. "Since I only have the one time, I'm going to make you come hard."

Evie opened her mouth, but he wasn't looking for her wit or charm right now. He pressed harder against her clit with his thumb, and she closed her eyes.

Neither man nor beast liked her eyes shut. "Evie, if you want to come, then open your eyes and spread your legs for me."

His dragon growled, impatient to fuck the human, but as soon as her beautiful, dark blue eyes met his, the beast's impatience eased a fraction. When she spread her legs wider, Bram removed his fingers and gave one last order. "Remove your shirt for me, lass. I need to see more of your beautiful skin."

~ ~ ~

How Evie was still standing upright, she didn't know. Bram's thick, rough fingers inside her pussy had been wonderful, his attention to her clit even better. Her former human lovers had all seemed oblivious to the little bud's existence.

But now his fingers were gone, leaving her empty and aching. Part of her wanted to rebel at his order, but she said fuck it. The sooner she could ease the pulse between her legs, the more time she would have to talk with Bram.

And she had plenty to talk with him about.

She reached for the hem of her sweater and slowly tugged it up over her body. Watching Bram's eyes the entire time, she loved how his eyes flashed between slits and round pupils. The sight only reminded her of how she was finally going to be taken by a dragonman.

But unlike her teenage fantasies with an unnamed dragon-shifter fucking her senseless, this time she already knew what Bram tasted like, and how his wild dragon scent drove her crazy.

As soon as she tugged her sweater over her head and tossed it aside, Bram's hands were on her ribcage. The slow, deliberate up and down motion of his hands only made her wetter.

She was close to begging, but she resisted. Giving in would make Bram a little too cocky.

Then his hands covered her small breasts and squeezed, and her brain forgot about everything but his strong, possessive touch.

All too soon, Bram moved his hands behind her and unhooked her bra. As he removed the last shred of material between her breasts and his eyes, his voice was like a whisper against her skin. "So pretty."

She was about to tell him to cut the crap when he leaned down and took her nipple into his mouth. He swirled, nibbled, and sucked her deep. She threaded her fingers through his hair, pulling him closer. "Harder," she whispered.

He growled and the vibrations against her sensitive skin shot straight to her pussy. At this rate, she'd soon be dripping down her legs.

As if sensing her thoughts, Bram reached between her legs and rubbed between her folds. Then he let her nipple free with a pop and she let out a sound of protest. "What? Why? If you're doing this to make me beg, it's not going to work."

Bram chuckled. "Oh, you'll beg eventually. But I think you'll like this."

He removed his fingers from her folds and rubbed her wetness on her other nipple. The sight of it on her breast was oddly arousing.

Then Bram leaned down and lapped at her juices on her skin. *Bloody hell.* The man was lapping as if he'd die if he didn't catch every last drop.

Holy crap, she was close to coming from his tongue...on her breast.

After one last nibble, Bram stood up and said, "My dragon is about to break free, lass, and I need to remain in control for tonight's dinner at the great hall. I need to fuck you. Now."

As much as she wanted to see his dragon break free, she had meant what she'd said earlier about never trying to take time away from anything important. She laid a hand on his chest. "Well, in that case"—she took his hand and tugged—"follow me."

She half expected him to growl and tell her no. But surprisingly, Bram let her lead him to his desk. She hopped up and spread her legs. "Since this is where we first kissed, I think we should also make it the place of our first fuck." Widening her legs, she massaged her breasts as she said, "What do you say?"

~~~

Bram's dragon was raging inside his head. *Brand her hard. She must stay with us. Convince her. Hurry.*

With a growl, he didn't fight his dragon's urges. Instead, he unbuttoned his jeans and unzipped them as he made his way to Evie perched on his desk.

Fuck, her arousal was strong. He'd had the merest taste of her sweet honey earlier. But as much as he wanted to lap between her legs, his cock was hard and pulsing. Combined with his dragon's pounding need, he didn't have the strength to show patience. He'd make his female come, but with his cock and not his tongue.

He quickly shucked his jeans and stood naked from the waist down. As Evie's eyes went to his cock curling up against his belly, a drop of precum seeped out.

"Eyes up here, human female."

Evie smiled as she met his eyes again. "Maybe next time I'll let you stare at my boobs if it means I can stare at your cock."

His inner beast roared. *Fuck her now, talk later.*

If he resisted much longer, he would lose control of his beast for the first time in nearly fifteen years. Still, he couldn't help but say, "We can experiment with that later." He moved between her legs, rubbing up and down her plump thighs. "For now, it's my job to make you forget how to speak."

As she opened her mouth, he positioned his cock and thrust inside her pussy. His dragon hummed at the combined heat and tightness. Spreading his female's legs wider, he pulled out slowly and pistoned back inside her. "I think I'm succeeding."

On the tail end of a moan, Evie whispered, "Just shut it and fuck me, Bram. We can take turns debating who can control whom later."

He smiled. "I'll win."

Evie opened her mouth, but he started moving slowly and deeply. She grabbed onto his biceps in response. When she spoke, it was, "Is that all you got?"

His dragon hummed. *I approve of her. Comply.*

Moving his hands from her thighs to her hips, he pounded harder. From the way Evie's nails dug into his arms to the tightness of her pussy around his dick, he loved every bit of it. Never had a female felt so perfect.

She is ours.

As Evie's moans grew louder, sweat formed on his back. His own orgasm was close, but his female needed to come first. Adjusting his grip, he touched her clit and pushed hard. Evie's nails dug deeper into his skin right before she screamed. As her pussy clenched and released his cock, Bram eased his restraint and increased his pace.

Brand her. Now.

Not sure if it had been him or his dragon to say those words in his head, Bram gave a few more strokes and stilled as he filled Evie with his seed.

When the last spasm left him, Bram leaned his forehead against Evie's. His voice was thick to his own ears. "Did that sate you, human?"

She made a noise in her throat. "It was nice."

He pulled back. "Nice?"

Evie's eyes danced with amusement. "Is nice such a bad word? Shall I say spectacular? Or, how about earth-shattering? Will that ease your ego?"

Pulling her close, until her hard nipples brushed his chest, he murmured, "One day, you'll think 'earth-shattering' is too tame a word for what I will do to you with my cock."

Evie smiled. "I look forward to that day."

While his dragon was half-asleep from their orgasm, he piped in. *She thinks of us in the future. She wants only us. She will stay.*

Bram wasn't as optimistic as his dragon. After all, Finlay Stewart could be a charming bastard when he tried. Still, he'd made a good start. It was time to make even more progress because he wanted to keep this female. She was his.

He squeezed her waist. "As much as I'd like to stand here with your tight, wet pussy around my cock, you'll get cold once you start coming down from your post-orgasm high. Let's get cleaned up and you can ask me what you like."

The mischief returned to her eyes. "Anything?"

"That would be a dangerous promise, given your tendency to surprise me, lass. How about we say most things?"

"I suppose that'll do for now. Although, give me a little time, and I may find a way to revoke your veto."

He shook his head. "I don't doubt it, Evie Marshall." With great effort, he pulled out of her and tugged her off the desk. She stumbled into his chest, and on instinct, he hugged her tight. The way her soft body fit against his sent blood to his cock again.

Bram had a feeling that if he wasn't careful, he could become addicted to this female's body. As it was, he was already addicted to her sass. He only hoped she didn't betray him. His dragon was confident she would stay true, but the bastard still refused to say why and that made him uneasy.

CHAPTER TEN

As Evie finished cleaning up, she tried to concentrate, but the wonderful soreness between her legs was making it hard for her to think about anything but the way Bram had fucked her downstairs on the desk. She'd had her fair share of sexual fantasies, some of which had included a dragonman or two, but none had compared to the real thing.

Not that she would let Bram know that for a while. Teasing him and poking his ego was fun.

Yet she still knew so little about him. While her gut said to trust the dragonman, her head wanted more information.

Opening the door, she paused as she was met with a very naked and aroused Bram lying on his bed. He'd suggested they use his room and bathroom to clean up. She was starting to think he had ulterior motives behind it.

Determined not to let his long, hard cock distract her, Evie leaned against the door jamb and focused on Bram's face. "Expecting something, dragonman?"

He glanced over and smiled. The sight made her heart thump an extra beat.

Bram said, "You straddling me would be nice, but you're the one who wants to talk."

SEDUCING THE DRAGON

Images of her riding the dragonman popped into her head and it took everything she had to push them away. *Focus, Evie. Sex can fade. Find out more about the man and what he does.*

She arched an eyebrow. "Well, you can start by telling me about this Neil Westhaven. You seemed angry, and since he was assigned to the human sacrifice, I'm guessing you're angry at both Neil as well as yourself."

His expression turned unreadable. "Bloody former inspector. Your perception is not going to make things easy for me."

"Of course not. Just like I can tell you're trying to change the subject. Get to the point, dragonman."

A smile tugged at his lips and Evie nearly let out a sigh of relief. For a second, she'd thought Bram would close himself off to her. Promise or not, he was clan leader and was used to doing things his way.

Bram said, "You'll definitely keep me on my toes, lass." Evie opened her mouth to steer him back on track, but he beat her to it. "As for Neil, you're right. I fucked up with that one. Everything looked good on paper, and while I know all of my clan members, some I know better than others. Neil was so determined to get a human sacrifice, mostly because he interpreted it to mean he'd obtain a slave, he even had his references and coworkers lie about him."

"Why would they do that? Surely they knew you'd find out the truth eventually."

"Yes, but from what I can gather, Neil figured I would never toss him out of the clan. He was wrong about that. What he did to that poor human female...you should've seen her, Evie. Cait could barely hold a conversation with anyone until Melanie Hall showed up."

While she knew Melanie was happily mated, a slight flare of jealousy flashed through her body at the other human's name.

Evie glanced to Bram's cock and reminded herself that he was hard and ready for her, not Melanie, and she was able to rein in her temper. Glancing back at Bram's face, she said, "We all make mistakes, Bram." Taking a deep breath, she pushed forward. "I have cost two women their lives in the end."

Bram patted the bed. "Sit and tell me, lass, because I have a feeling it wasn't intentional."

"I've come to terms with that, but you need to do the same."

He patted again. "We'll discuss me later. Tell me what happened. What was it you said? That you didn't want to mate a stranger? I think sharing how we both caused people to die might just be the first step in getting to know each other."

Despite herself, Evie smiled. "That's a hell of a way to do it."

He put out a hand and Evie took it. The warmth of his hand was enticing, and rather than sit on the bed, she snuggled up against him. "No funny business. I'm a little cold and you're warm."

Hugging her tight, he murmured, "I'll promise, for now."

She looked up at his face. "Just like that? No arguing or bargaining?"

"Oh, that will come later. Right now, having you laying on me helps to calm my dragon."

Studying his face, she didn't see his eyes flashing to dragon slits. Part of her had wondered earlier what his dragon had been doing since Evie knew she couldn't be Bram's mate; their first kiss hadn't brought on a frenzy. Yet his earlier behavior contradicted the rumors and reports she'd read about his ironclad control.

Seducing the Dragon

She'd ask him about that later. For now, she didn't want to break the little bubble of truth-telling and sharing. Given all the shit going on with the dragon hunters and Cait's death, Evie didn't know when she'd next get the chance to just talk with the dragon leader. Even if the topic was difficult, he was right. Sharing was the first step in gaining his trust.

Taking a deep breath, the words rushed from her mouth, "They were both sacrifices. The first woman, Jenny, was my very first solo case as a DDA inspector. I was to check on her and make sure she wasn't being abused. The woman was quiet to begin with, but it was only when they found her in the bathroom with her wrists slit and a note nearby that I understood the enormity of her silence. She'd been unhappy, but I hadn't been able to see it."

Bram stroked his hand up and down her arm. "Some people are good at hiding their true selves."

She wondered if his words had a hidden meaning. "I understood that later, after doing more thorough interviews with her family. But for the first few days after I heard the news, I locked myself in my flat and nearly quit the DDA."

"But you didn't."

"No. Interviewing her family helped, as did learning she'd lied about her bouts of depression. Still, it was a blow to my confidence. It took me nearly a year to regain it."

"You have it in spades now."

She smiled against his chest. "With you, it just happens. I had my lapses of confidence with Marcus King down south."

Bram's growl rumbled in his chest. "If that bastard laid a hand on you, I will take care of him myself."

Looking up, she propped her chin on Bram's muscled chest. "Really? You'd throw away everything you've done for your clan for some half-arsed vengeance?"

"Anyone who hurts my female will feel my ire."

Evie frowned. "Your female? You haven't even agreed to let me be your mate yet. Have you changed your mind?"

He grunted. "Tell me about the other female first and I'll answer your question."

Searching his eyes, she knew the dragonman wasn't bluffing. From what she'd learned so far, her stubbornness was only second to his. "Fine. The other woman was Imogen. At twenty-one, she was one of the youngest sacrifices I ever had to monitor. She survived her term and the birth, but a few weeks after she returned to the human world, she left a desperate voice mail saying she wanted to meet me. I tried to convince my superior to let me go, but due to departmental meetings and commitments, I had to postpone our meeting by three days. By the time I was free to check in on her, it was already too late. She'd taken a bottle of pills and overdosed."

Imogen's death had hit her harder than Jenny's simply because she'd tried to help but had been overruled by her boss, who believed bureaucracy must be followed to the letter, no exceptions. That man was now the Assistant Director of the entire Department of Dragon Affairs. If Jonathan Christie ever became Director, the dragon-shifter clans would suffer.

Bram poked her stomach and said, "Tell me what's on your mind, human. I don't like being kept in the dark."

Seducing the Dragon

~~~

Evie's distant look morphed into a glare, and both man and dragon were glad. His female talking about the two women's deaths wasn't easy, but she'd been keeping her spirit up until the very end. Despite their new, fragile bond formed through sharing secrets, he wasn't about to let her stew on her own. If they were to be mates, he wanted to know all of her troubles.

His dragon grunted. *We will always look after her.*

I don't know if she'll agree to that.

I don't care. We will do it anyway.

He barely resisted a smile at his inner beast's certainty. Instead, he poked Evie again. "Well?"

Her brow pinched further. "I know you're used to getting what you want as clan leader, but would it kill you to ask me instead of demand?"

"Oh, wonderful human female beyond compare, would you honor me with your enlightened thoughts?"

The human's glare slipped and her lips twitched. "So you do have a sense of humor."

"Oh, aye. But stop changing the subject. What has you so lost in your thoughts?"

The laugh faded from her eyes. "The second woman, Imogen, her death was completely preventable. My boss at the time prevented me from helping her and possibly saving her life. If that wasn't bad enough, that man is now second-in-charge of the whole DDA." Her brow furrowed. "If he takes over, it'll be bad news for your clan."

He squeezed his female. "Give a dragon-shifter some credit. I do have a trick or two up my sleeve. The DDA might be powerful now, but with Melanie Hall-MacLeod's help, that might soon change."

"What?"

Bram hadn't planned on telling Evie about Mel's plans, but talking with her was easy, especially as his dragon kept sending thoughts of trust to him. "Melanie is writing a book about dragon-shifters to help sway public opinion. Come to think of it, the female has all kinds of ideas of how to improve our image."

"So Melanie is your PR expert?"

He smiled. "I hadn't thought of it in that light, but aye, I think you're right."

The sadness faded from his female's eyes and was replaced with a hint of determination. "Then I think I should help her. If she's good at marketing, then combining that with my insider knowledge about the DDA and British law, we'll become unstoppable."

He could see the wheels turning in her head. But as much as he loved how Evie had moved on from her sadness, he didn't have much time before Mel and Samira would come and take Evie away to prepare her for tonight's dinner.

Just thinking about Evie leaving their side made his dragon snarl. *Before she leaves, ask her. Stop waiting. She is right for us. The clan must know she is ours.*

Then fucking tell me why you're so certain.

No. You feel it too. Trust that feeling. Ask her.

Only because of the female at his side did Bram resist growling. He did want to keep Evie as his female, but his dragon's sudden secretive nature was driving him mental.

His inner beast growled and Bram decided enough was enough. *Fine. I will ask her. Now, shut it so I can concentrate.*

And just like that, his dragon faded to the back of his mind.

Seducing the Dragon

Bloody beast.

Moving a hand to Evie's cheek, he said, "That's a possibility, but it's completely up to Melanie. The book is her pet project." Evie opened her mouth and he moved his fingers to her lips. "We can discuss it later. Right now, I need to tell you about this evening. Especially since Melanie and the other human mated to a dragon-shifter, Samira, will be here soon to fetch you."

Evie moved her lips against his fingers, reminding him of just how soft they were. "If you're expecting me to speak, then remove your bloody fingers from my mouth."

He was tempted to remove his fingers and shut her up by kissing her, but he hadn't lied before. There wasn't time. Not even his still-hard cock lying against his belly would convince him to fuck up the event this evening. "Just listen first. Tonight is a special dinner honoring Finlay Stewart as our guest. Attire is meant to be formal. While you no doubt know what the traditional clothing looks like, Mel and Samira will help you look your best. Everyone will be watching you tonight."

She frowned and mumbled against his fingers. "Care to tell me why?"

Removing his fingers, he placed a finger under her chin. "Because I want my clan to know that you're mine."

Her breath hitched and a feeling of smugness came over him. His dragon hummed. *See? She wants us too.*

She hasn't said yes yet, you bloody beast.

She will.

Evie pushed half-up and looked down at him. "Is this a firm 'Yes, I'm going to take you on as my mate' or another half-arsed way to string me along?"

Calm her fears. Leave no doubts.

Sometimes, Bram wished he could just let his dragon talk instead of conveying the beast's messages. Still, he agreed with him this time. The thought of her walking away from him and leaving with Finn in a few days caused a surge of jealousy to shoot through his body.

Bram rolled on top of Evie, pinning her body to the bed, and leaned in until he was a hairbreadth away from her lips. "Evie Marshall, I want you as my mate." Remembering her request from this morning, he tacked on, "Will you allow me to walk in to the great hall with you on my arm? I can make the announcement tomorrow, as I don't want to take the focus away from Finn, no matter how much I wish I could just kick the bastard to the side and bring you into the limelight."

Evie's eyes searched his. "Are you being serious? I don't want to get my hopes up only to have them dashed later when we have another row."

He moved one hand between them and gripped her breast possessively. Evie sucked in a breath as he said, "You are mine, Evie Marshall, and one day you'll admit as much."

His dragon hummed. *Yes, yes, she is ours. Always. We need her.*

Needing was the last word he wanted to hear right now since his cock was currently cushioned between him and Evie's round, soft stomach. Every instinct he possessed urged him to thrust into the female and make her scream.

Yes, yes, fuck her. If we do it quickly, we have enough time.

But she said only once.

Then ask.

Gritting his teeth, Bram forced himself to ask a different question. "Will you accompany me and agree to be my mate?"

Seducing the Dragon

The human stared at him silently. With each passing second, his dragon pushed harder to take control. *Don't lose her. Make her say yes.*

Evie's London tones snapped him from his mind. "As long as you plan to protect me, then yes, I'll accompany you and be your mate."

Joy rushed through his body and he lowered his head to kiss her.

The kiss wasn't meant to be gentle, and he immediately thrust his tongue into her mouth. As he licked and explored every inch of her hot, sweet mouth, he pinched her nipple and reveled in the vibrations of her moan both in his mouth and from the contact against her chest.

Now, now, do it now. We must fuck her and brand our scent more. Don't let the leader take her.

Only because of years of practice did Bram resist his dragon's commands. Breaking the kiss, he whispered, "Please, Evie, let me take you from behind quickly or my beast will break free and take you every which way until he's sated. I want that, too, but I can't risk the alliance."

~~~

Evie was having trouble thinking. Between the fit dragonman's muscled body lying on top of her to his recent domination of her mouth, her lady parts were very much screaming for attention. Somewhere in the back of her mind, she was glad he'd asked her to be his mate. But as Bram asked to fuck her to calm his dragon, any rational thoughts vanished. All she could think about was the cock currently pressing against her.

"Then take me, dragonman. Doggy-style—or is it dragon-style?—is one of my favorite positions."

With a roar, Bram rose off her body, flipped her over, and lifted her hips before he thrust his long, hard cock into her. Evie gripped the sheets and raised her arse. As if signaling to start, Bram pounded into her, no holds barred.

The speed, combined with how his hard cock was hitting her at just the right angle, made her moan. The sensation was in that wonderful place on the border of pleasure and pain.

Then her dragonman picked up his pace and she cried out with each thrust. She'd never had a man so completely fill her, let alone fuck her as if this were their last moment on Earth. Sometimes she appreciated special attention to her clit, but at the moment, the sheer power and animalistic nature of Bram's movements was bringing her close to the edge.

Then he roared and stilled. She felt him orgasm inside her, and pleasure instantly coursed through her body as her pussy started to spasm in time with her clit. Each hot jet inside her brought another orgasm, until she lost all rational thought.

Only when she felt Bram lean over her back and kiss her shoulder did she come down from her high. His arms were tenderly wrapped around her, the hair from his arms and chest tickling her skin. His voice was low and husky as he whispered into her ear, "Thank you."

Her brain took a second to make a coherent thought before she said, "Mr. Dragon Leader is thanking me? That's new."

His chuckle vibrated against her back. "Don't get too used to it. I only bring out the 't' word on special occasions."

Evie laughed. Bram rose upward, but took her with him until she was leaning back against his chest. She looked into his very human-looking eyes. "Is your dragon doing better now?"

Hugging her tightly, he nodded. "I don't know what's gotten into him. He hasn't been this out of control since I was barely an adult. It's almost as if..."

I was his true mate.

Evie pushed that thought aside. There was no way she could be. According to her testing as a teenager, she couldn't have dragon-shifter children. True mates always reproduced. Always.

Or, so went every documented case she'd studied over the years.

Bram nuzzled the side of her neck and she focused on the here and now. She didn't need to be his true mate to enjoy the man at her back. She was about to ask when Melanie and Samira were due to arrive when he cursed and said, "They're knocking on the door. You need to go."

Snuggling against his hard chest, she murmured, "I don't want to."

Her dragonman chuckled. "So have my sex skills graduated from 'nice' to something much more now? So much so that you can't bear to leave my side?"

She tried to frown, but failed. "Remind me not to compliment you too often or you will become unbearable."

He grinned. "You haven't seen anything yet, lass."

As she smiled widely, a mobile phone rang. Bram sighed. "That would be Melanie. We can talk later, lass. Once I find out information from Kai, I'll let you know if you're in any danger. That'll have to be at the dinner in the great hall, provided we can find a secure place to talk."

He moved away and pulled out from her. She turned around and he cupped her face with his warm hands. "I can't wait to see you kitted out in dragon-shifter attire, Evie. It might just drive my dragon crazy again."

She smiled as he placed a gentle kiss on her lips. Then he pulled away and reached for his jeans. "Hurry, lass. Once Melanie has a task, she's determined to see it through. She'll drag you half-naked through the community if that's what it takes."

Standing on the floor, she looked at Bram's light blue eyes. "Just one question: is being your mate-to-be a secret?"

"Melanie and Samira are fine, but don't go spreading it around yet. If there's a traitor in the clan, I don't want them to hurt you to get at me."

After nodding, Evie took one last look at her future mate and headed for the bathroom, unsure of what the next few hours would bring.

CHAPTER ELEVEN

Bram Moore-Llewellyn sat at his desk. For the last half hour, he'd discussed with Kai, his head Protector, about Evie's theory concerning Neil Westhaven slowly killing Caitriona Belmont with dragon-shifter hormones. With the facts laid out and them both in agreement, he asked, "A theory is great, but we need proof. Has anyone formerly related to Neil done anything out of the ordinary?"

Kai tapped the fingers of his right hand against his leg for a few seconds and stopped. "Yes. I hadn't thought anything of it at the time, but it could be relevant now. Olivia Harris left early this morning, carrying a large suitcase to the landing and take-off area before shifting and gripping the item in her talons. She had a pass to visit the clan in Wales, so the Protector on duty thought nothing of it. In retrospect, she's visited the Welsh clan a few times over the last few months. She might be meeting with Neil."

Olivia had once upon a time been Neil Westhaven's female, but they separated six months before Bram had chosen a male for their next human sacrifice. He had thought assigning Neil to Caitriona would be a good way for his clan member to purge Olivia out of his system. "Find out where she went. It should be easy enough to determine if she went south to Wales or elsewhere, especially since red dragons are the rarest kind. Reach out to our contacts within the human communities to help discover her flight path."

"Nikki has been in charge of reaching out to our human contacts. I'll ask her to do it as soon as we're done here."

Bram nodded. "Good. However, I hope she's done by this evening for the special dinner. I need someone to watch Evie if I'm called away."

"I'll watch the human if that happens. As much as I don't want to go to the dinner and want to focus solely on rooting out more information, Finlay Stewart might take offense at the absence of Stonefire's head Protector."

At the mention of Finn's name, his dragon growled inside his head. *When will he be gone? He prevents too many things from happening. First, declaring our mate to the clan. Second, finding the threats to our future mate.*

We need his alliance. He will leave tomorrow. Be patient. Will you allow Kai to watch Evie?

Yes. He knows the identity of his mate. Why he ignores her, I don't understand.

Leave it be. It's his choice.

With a grunt, his dragon faded to the back of his mind, allowing Bram to focus on Kai. "Thanks for offering. You're one of the few males both me and my dragon will allow near Evie." Kai nodded. With Evie's safety taken care of, he moved to the next item on his list. "Right then, before I dismiss you to do your magic, there's one more thing I want to put into motion."

"What?"

"I want someone focused on questioning the dragon hunter we have in custody. If Olivia and Neil are leaking information, and who the hell knows what else, he may be able to confirm it.

Seducing the Dragon

You and I have a lot on our plates already. Is there anyone amongst the Protectors you trust to handle the prisoner?"

"Zain would be a good fit. He's a newer Protector, but his performance is nearly as good as mine."

The corner of Bram's lips ticked up. "I didn't think anyone could be as good as you, not even me."

Despite his attempt to lighten the mood, Kai's face remained serious. "If you didn't have all of your clan leader duties, I'm sure you'd have enough time to train and surpass me. Frankly, the amount of paperwork involved with your job makes me break out in a sweat."

Bram full-on smiled. "It's not so bad." He crossed his arms over his chest. "Now, tell me why you'd pick Zain, and convince me to trust him."

"He's dedicated, carries out even the most menial tasks I've assigned him without complaint, and not even my most thorough background check could find anything suspicious. Add that to his experience of working with the human intelligence collection assets division of the armed forces a few years ago, and he's our best chance at not only finding out about the attacks, but why the dragon hunter let slip he knew Evie Marshall."

Yes, find out why. We must protect our female. Bram sent thoughts of silence before he replied, "The dragon hunter mentioning Evie by name worried me before, but knowing Neil may be involved, worries me further. Still, as much as I want to know the connection, why should we trust Zain?"

"I believe in him. He has no family apart from the clan as a whole. He'll do anything to protect us."

His head Protector may only be thirty years old, but he acted far older on most days. Bram's inner beast piped in. *Zain is good. I never get a bad feeling from him. If Kai trusts him, we should too.*

While not the most fact-based endorsement, he treasured his dragon's intuition. "Right, then involve Zain, but slowly. Have him interrogate the dragon hunter and see what he can find. If he's successful, then share a little more until you feel confident sharing everything. I also want him to keep us both updated every hour, even if it's just with a text message saying he's found nothing new."

Kai nodded. "We have two hours before the clan gathers for the dinner in the great hall. It's enough time for me to fill in Zain and have him start his interrogation."

"Good. Once that's set up, make sure to escort Evie, Melanie, and Samira to the great hall. I need to meet with Arabella right before the dinner starts, which means I can't do it myself. I don't want to take any chances with their safety. If anything were to happen to the three human females on my land, the human media would soon rustle up a witch hunt against us."

The other male stood up. "Anything else?"

"Just be careful. Olivia is our main suspect for betrayal, but there could be other traitors in our midst. I'm not the only one with someone to protect."

"I'll do my job as I always do."

Sometimes, Bram wished his head Protector would be a little more open and forthright, but that wasn't Kai's personality. Bram was one of the few people who knew Kai's greatest secret, but it wasn't Bram's place to push on the matter. Well, at least until it caused his Protector to lose focus and put the clan in danger. So far, Kai hadn't shown any of those symptoms.

He stood. "Of course you do, or I wouldn't trust you with the safety of my future mate."

Kai turned to go but then turned back around and said, "Is she your true mate? Is that why you've claimed her so quickly?"

His dragon huffed. *It's none of his business. Evie is ours. That is all that matters.*

Still not telling me your reasons?

Silence was his answer.

Rather than try to make his dragon talk, he said to Kai, "I don't think she is, no. But she has knowledge to help our clan. Just like you do everything in your power to protect the clan, so do I."

Kai looked unconvinced, but rather than argue, the male nodded and left Bram alone in his cottage.

~~~

Evie was waiting for Melanie Hall-MacLeod to bombard her with questions. Ever since she'd whisked Evie from Bram's cottage, the woman had been pointing out houses and businesses and explaining them as if she were a tour guide. Despite her earlier behavior when Evie had still been just a DDA inspector, Mel wasn't being as blunt as before.

However, ten seconds after she, Melanie, and Samira entered Mel's house, she turned toward Evie and said, "Tell me what's going on with Bram. He couldn't keep his eyes off you the entire time we all were saying goodbye. His eyes even flashed to dragon slits once."

As she looked from Mel to Samira and back again, Evie debated her options. These two women knew the ways of dragonmen well, and probably could already guess Bram's attraction to her. Denying it would be a waste of time.

She also needed to convince Melanie to tell her more about this mysterious dragon exposé book of hers. The truth might win the other woman over. "He said I could tell you two and no others. Bram is taking me as his mate."

Mel placed her hands on her hips. "Did you trick him? Or force him? You can't be his true mate, so I'm trying to figure why he'd agree to that."

Evie resisted blinking. That wasn't the response she'd expected. Still, as much as she wanted to fit in with the two human women in the clan, she wasn't about to take their crap.

Evie took a step toward Melanie. "I'm sure people questioned your relationship with Tristan in the beginning. I expected better of you, but you're just as judgmental as the dragon-shifters I've dealt with over the last seven years. Without giving me a chance, you think you've figured it all out."

Mel's hands fell to her sides as she narrowed her eyes. "I don't know how Skyhunter treated you, but my motives are true. Bram is my leader. I only want what is best for him."

Evie clenched her fists at her sides. *Resist the urge to tell her to fuck off and mind her own business. Remember, she wants to help the clan improve their image. Bram needs her help.*

With a deep inhalation, she forced her temper down a notch. "He's your leader, yes, but how well do you know him? I don't need the mate-claim frenzy to entice the man to open up to me. He has more burdens than you can imagine. I can help with that."

Samira stepped between them. "Melanie, you're getting nearly as bad as Tristan when it comes to protectiveness." She turned her deep brown gaze to Evie. "How about we get you ready for the dinner? I'm sure you have questions that need to be answered. You might not be a sacrifice, but not even your experience with the DDA will prepare you for mating a dragon-shifter."

120

Taking another deep breath, Evie forced her tone to be more even. "I spent seven years with the Department of Dragon Affairs and a year before that in an intensive dragon-shifter study course. Seeing as I surprised Bram with some of my knowledge, I wouldn't dismiss me just yet."

Melanie frowned. "You knew something about dragon-shifters that Bram didn't?"

She nodded. "Yes, and if you ever stop interrogating me, I want to propose working with you on the launch of your book. My knowledge concerning British law alone is worth a lot to you."

The two women glanced at each other. Evie knew these two had had months to get to know each other, but she hated being the outsider yet again. Except for her one dragon-shifter obsessed friend, Evie had been pretty much alone for the last seven years.

Most humans didn't like to associate with a known DDA employee. Talk shows and conspiracy blogs had convinced too many people that dragons liked to pick off the DDA employees; associating with one would make you a target as well.

Add all of that to the recent targeting of DDA employees by the dragon hunters, and, yeah, people weren't exactly lining up to be her best friend.

Melanie was the first to speak again. "Let's try this again. I think my mate's behavior is rubbing off on me, and I need to tone that shit down. Just let me say this—if you hurt Bram, I won't forgive you. He sacrifices a lot for the well-being of the clan, and while I think he likes you now, I don't want him to suffer in the long run."

Staring at the other woman, Evie decided her best chance at eventual acceptance was to start over. Even if her connection to Bram was new, she already felt protective of him. Maybe explaining that would ease Mel's worries. "Look, from what I've seen of Bram so far, he's a strong, funny and clever dragonman. As long as he doesn't betray me or break my heart, I won't do the same to him. After all, he's taking on a lot more than just a mate with me."

Mel frowned. "That's a bit cryptic. Care to explain what you mean?"

Honesty, Evie. Keep at it. After all, these people will soon be your clan too. "The dragon hunters want to kill me. Bram is mating me to protect me. In exchange, I'm offering him information. Since even Arabella was interested in my information, I can only imagine your whole clan would like my insider knowledge."

Samira interjected, "Arabella? You met her already?"

Evie nodded. "She was sent to babysit me last night. I only managed to type out the information about the dragon hunters, but she absorbed every word."

Melanie sighed. "Of course she would." She waved a hand in dismissal. "I'll talk with Ara later since she's supposed to attend tonight's dinner. She might very well be planning something daft, such as going after the dragon hunters alone."

Evie frowned. "I might talk with her too. Taking on the dragon hunters by herself is bloody idiotic. We need to make sure that doesn't happen. After all, there are other ways to go after them, ways that will sully the hunters in the eyes of the human public."

Mel nodded. "I agree. She might be my sister-in-law, but Arabella doesn't necessarily listen to me. The more people watching Arabella, the better." Melanie paused a second, then added, "Ara keeps her distance, but persistence pays off in the end. She could use more friends. I hope you give her a chance."

SEDUCING THE DRAGON

In one way, at least, Arabella MacLeod was like her. "She's clever and doesn't beat around the bush. We should get along fine." She looked from Mel to Samira and back. "Right, I think we'd better start with dressing me up. I'm not a smart dresser, so you two are going to have to help me with the hair and such."

Samira smiled and placed a hand on her back. "I live with two males, so I take any excuse I can get to dress up another female."

Evie gave Samira a wary glance. "Just don't go overboard."

Samira pressed against her back, urging her to walk. "Don't worry, dragon-shifter traditional dress is quite simple, really."

Evie resisted a sigh. "Yes, I know, but the dresses are like half an outfit. Is there a way to cover up some of my skin? Bram doesn't need the distraction."

Mel beat Samira to a reply. "Even with some kind of unique leotard underneath, he'd still be distracted. Dragon-shifter males love to see their females in the traditional style. Just wait until you get the mating band with his name engraved on it. That'll really turn him on."

Rather than comment on the far-off look Melanie had in her eye, no doubt she was thinking of her own mate's reactions, she turned toward Samira. "I don't want fifty bobby pins in my hair with enough hairspray to coat an entire room. Do something simple."

Nodding with an evil glint in her eye, Samira replied, "Simple. Yes, Bram will like that."

She sighed. While she'd had a few boyfriends over the years, she'd never taken hours to get ready. Make-up made her face itch, for one, and heels made her trip.

Before she could tell them Bram preferred her natural, Samira and Mel discussed all the ways they could do her hair with less than ten bobby pins. The style names went over her head.

Still, as the two other women talked, a sense of peace came over Evie. She wasn't naive enough to believe these two women were now her best friends, but just spending time with other humans was nice. At the rate she'd been making tentative friendships, Evie would soon have more friends than she'd made during her entire life. Being dragon-obsessed was starting to pay off.

CHAPTER TWELVE

Arabella MacLeod took one last look in the mirror and wished breaking it would erase the image in the reflection. While she'd had ten years to grow accustomed to the scars on her face or the pink, crinkly healed burns along her neck, shoulder, and arm, most of the clan had barely learned to stomach her face.

Yet Bram was making her attend the fucking gathering despite her wishes. Any excuses she'd thought of had been shot down. If she wouldn't meet the Scottish leader in private, then she'd have to do it during the gathering. She was Stonefire's best tech expert, and Bram wanted things to run smoothly, as well as securely, with their fragile new alliance with Lochguard.

Fine. She could meet with the leader at a gathering. A room full of people would help stave off her memories. They might even help keep her episodes at bay. But the gathering was formal attire, which meant wearing half a bloody dress.

As a teenager, she had loved the traditional dresses which fastened over one shoulder, hugged her breasts, and flared out at her hips, but no longer. Her tattooed arm was burn-free, but even with the strip of material over the shoulder of her healed burns, her other upper arm was pink and wrinkly.

In other words, ugly.

She shouldn't care, but this was the first formal gathering she would attend in nearly a decade. At that moment, her heart thumped in her chest as her stomach churned. Unless the Scottish leader decided to dance around the great hall naked, everyone would be staring at her and talking about her. She was "poor Arabella".

She narrowed her eyes. *Well, fuck them.* Putting her shoulder back, Ara turned from the mirror and headed toward her front door. She may still be afraid of her inner dragon and have flashbacks of her time with the dragon hunters, but she could take care of herself. She would prove it at the gathering.

Snagging her cloak and tossing it over her shoulders, Ara exited her house and into the brisk April evening air. Her cottage was quite far from the main living community, but she loved to walk. The silence always brought a sense of peace.

Within ten minutes, she could see the outline of the great hall.

She arrived early, just as Bram had requested, so as she approached the giant brick building, the area was mostly empty. Five or six dragon-shifters raced in and out of the hall with the meal preparations, but they were so preoccupied, they didn't even notice her.

Tugging her cloak tighter around her shoulders, she entered the great hall and looked around the long, rectangular space for Bram. She spotted him in a corner talking with a tall, blond dragonman she didn't recognize. His hair was short, yet his face was covered in a blond scruff, which was an odd contrast to his formal, kilt-like attire. While his dragon-shifter tattoo was on the arm turned away from her, she knew every dragon-shifter in Stonefire by sight and he wasn't one of them. The unfamiliar male had to be from Lochguard.

Her stomach churned even more. As her heart rate kicked up, a small sense of panic crept upon her. Why would Bram ask her to meet alone with the other male? The blond was tall, muscled, and could pin her down without breaking a sweat.

Much like how the dragon hunters had pinned her down as a teenager before torturing her.

Closing her eyes, Ara breathed in through her nose and out her mouth. Bram was in the same room. He would never allow anyone to hurt her. As long as he remained, she could handle meeting the other male.

Her distress brought out her inner dragon. The beast rarely spoke to her, but it sent wary thoughts of calm. A year ago, Ara would have run from the room and tried to banish the beast from her mind. Yet after nearly nine months of counseling and encouragement from her brother and his mate, she had the strength to say, *It will be okay. Go back to sleep.*

Her dragon gave a soft roar before retreating. Maybe one day, Ara would be able to converse and work with her inner beast like every other dragon-shifter, but it was not that day.

"Ara."

As soon as she heard Bram's voice, she opened her eyes. An apologetic expression was written all over her leader's face as he continued, "Finn came early. I told him to wait over there, but if you're up to it, we can talk to him now. I'll be right there beside you, so you won't have anything to worry about."

While a part of her was relieved Bram would protect her, another part was embarrassed. The Scottish leader didn't need to know how broken she was. Deep down, she wanted to experience a fresh start with someone who hadn't coddled her over the past decade. That was part of the reason why she'd agreed to be in charge of tech security with the Scottish clan.

Curious to see how the Lochguard male reacted to her, she glanced over at the blond Scottish dragonman. She steeled herself for pity, but was surprised to see only curiosity.

His look solidified her decision. Looking back to Bram, she said, "You have a lot to do. Introduce us, and as long as we stay in this main hall, I should be able to survive answering his tech questions and requirements."

"Are you sure?"

She nodded. "Setting up the future teleconferences is part of my job for the clan. I'll find a way to make it work." Her clan leader studied her and she resisted the urge to lash out. She wouldn't make Bram appear weak in front of the other leader. "I can handle it."

With a nod, Bram ushered her over to the Scottish leader. Up close, he was taller than she'd thought. She had to look up to see his eyes, which were an interesting mixture of brown with gold flecks. The curiosity from before lingered, and she couldn't make out an ounce of pity, making her uneasy.

Then he grinned and Ara drew in a breath. It took everything she had to focus on his words as he said, "Bram said his tech expert was a female, but he forgot to mention she had beautiful brown eyes, the exact color of dark chocolate."

Bram growled at her side. "Finlay."

Finn grinned wider. "You said honesty was the best policy. I won't lie about her eyes."

Arabella blinked. She couldn't remember the last time a male had praised her. She knew she should scowl and tell him to stop it, but she resisted.

Instead, she said, "My eyes have little to do with my brain. The sooner you ask your questions and tell me your requirements, the sooner you can go flirt with the 'lasses' as you Scots say."

Seducing the Dragon

The Scot winked at her. "I like a lass with bite."

Ara felt a flush coming on. *Fuck, I won't let this flirt affect me. Think of your work.*

Her mind filled with security protocols and encryption sequences, and her mind calmed once more. *Right, now stop acting like a schoolgirl and carry on.*

She arched an eyebrow. "If listing all of your female preferences in one go will help you focus, you have thirty seconds. Go."

Finn laughed. "Direct and to the point, I like it." Crossing her arms over her chest, she raised her other eyebrow. Finally, Finn put his hands up. "Okay, okay, I'll stop." He leaned in a few inches closer. "For now."

Standing so close, she could see even more gold flecks in his eyes. His spicy male scent also surrounded her; woods with a hint of peat.

With any other strange male, she had little doubt she would be in a complete panic. However, one second ticked by and then another, but if anything, she felt a sense of peace.

Bram cleared his throat and pushed Finn away from her. "Talk, Stewart, or be on your way. Our alliance agreement doesn't include you flirting with every female on my land."

The Scot held her eyes for a few more seconds before looking to Bram. "Aye, well, I've always found humor makes everyone feel better. They say it's the best medicine."

Ara raised her chin a fraction. "Right, then. The thirty seconds I offered you have more than passed. Start talking business or I will insist Bram find someone else in your clan to reach out to me."

Amusement flashed in Finn's eyes. "Oh, aye? And here I thought Bram was the clan leader."

Shit. She hadn't meant to overstep her bounds. Because Bram had been friends with her brother since childhood, Bram often let her get away with more than he'd allow other clan members. She needed to fix this situation. "Bram is the leader. He and I discussed the terms earlier. I'm sure with all your flirting, he didn't have a chance to go over the finer points of meeting with me."

She knew Bram's eyes were on her, but she refused to look over at him. For some reason, the Lochguard leader provoked her. No doubt, Bram would have questions. Questions she really didn't want to answer.

After one last look, Finn's eyes became serious. "Right, then, lassie, tell me what sort of encryption you plan to use. The dragon hunters are becoming tech savvy and the more barriers we have in place, the better."

Ara blinked. "Do you understand the different types of encryption or shall I explain it in laymen's terms."

"Before becoming clan leader, I earned a degree in computer science and worked part-time with our own tech expert as a sort of apprentice. Only when the leadership position became open, did I give it up. This is more an interview for your skills than a question and answer meeting for me."

Bram interjected, "Arabella is the finest we have. She can do whatever you ask."

Warmth from Bram's praised filled her, but Ara focused on Finn. "No, it's okay, Bram. Maybe I can teach him a thing or two and knock down his ego a notch."

Finn's smile was back. "I'd like to see that, Arabella MacLeod."

His words were a challenge, a challenge she wanted to tackle. Any uneasiness or worry she'd felt upon first seeing the

Lochguard leader vanished. Instead, she was determined to knock the cocky grin from his face.

Looking to Bram, she said, "I can handle it from here, Bram. I'm sure there's lots to do before the dinner officially begins."

Her leader searched her eyes. They asked if she were sure, and she gave an imperceptible nod. Her leader looked to Finn. "You do anything to upset her, and the alliance be damned, I'll have your bollocks on a platter before the night is done."

Finn raised an eyebrow. "Hurting the lass is the last thing I wish to do. After all, she'll never flirt with me again if I piss her off."

Ara opened her mouth to protest, but then Finn placed his hand on her back. She tensed a second, waiting for the fear to consume her, but it never came. Her dragon peeked her head out inside her mind. *He won't hurt us.*

She blinked. Her dragon hadn't spoken to her in months. She nearly asked what she meant, but the beast was back in the far reaches of her mind before she had the chance.

Finn pushed gently against her back. "Now, tell me your plans for our security, and don't leave anything out."

Rather than focus on all of the oddities of the evening, such as with her dragon speaking to her and Finn's touch not inciting a panic, Arabella concentrated on her work. As she told Finn of her plans, she was just a female talking to a male without any stress or fear. Apart from Bram or her brother Tristan, she'd never experienced this sense of comfort before. It was almost as if her attack ten years ago had never happened.

Almost.

~~~

Bram watched the Scottish leader walk away with his hand on Arabella's back and barely resisted running after him. Only because Ara seemed at ease did he stay put. For the first time since he could remember, Ara wasn't shying away from her true self. The brief flash of dragon slits in her eyes signaled even her inner dragon was speaking to her.

As much as he didn't like to admit it, having an outsider talk and flirt with Arabella might be good for her. Regardless, he'd keep an eye on Finn. The man flirted with everyone and he didn't want Arabella to be hurt later on.

His dragon said, *You worry too much. Arabella is becoming stronger. She is also surrounded by clan. They will protect her.*

Considering how much his dragon had roared earlier to get Finn off their land, he was now defending him.

If Bram were a drinker, he would definitely start drinking

Rather than start an unwinnable argument, Bram checked his mobile phone, but there weren't any updates from Zain yet.

He clenched his free hand. Usually, Bram didn't mind playing politics, but tonight, it was just bloody annoying because it prevented him from protecting both his clan and his soon-to-be mate.

"Bram."

He looked up and saw Samira walking toward him. While her dark hair was swept up and her make-up done for the dinner, she was alone.

He met her halfway and said, "Is anything wrong? Where are Melanie and Evie?"

Samira smiled in the calm, collected way she always did. "They're just outside. Evie mentioned how you wanted to walk in with her on your arm." She paused, and then winked. "I also think you need a minute alone with her."

He grunted. "Alone is probably not a good idea."

Chuckling, Samira placed a hand on his arm. "Mel and I will be a few feet away. We won't let you ravish her in front of the clan."

Rather than react, he merely nodded. "We need to hurry. I want Evie up front with me before most of the clan arrives."

Walking toward the entrance, Samira glanced over at him. "May I ask why?"

Samira was loyal to her mate, Liam, who was loyal to Bram. Still, he would keep the details vague. "There is a constant threat to her life and I'd rather keep her where I can see her. If you and Mel spot anything suspicious, let me know. I have several people watching out for threats, but the more the merrier."

"Sure. She could always stay with one of us if you need to leave."

"Somehow, I don't think Evie would appreciate a babysitter."

Samira smiled. "I think you're right about that. She's more headstrong than Melanie, and I didn't think it was possible."

His dragon chimed in. *We like her strength. It is not a bad thing. And I agree. Someone needs to stand up to you.*

His dragon preened and Bram resisted rolling his eyes.

They reached the entrance and Bram smoothed the dark red fabric of his dragon-shifter attire. His life was about to change forever once he claimed Evie unofficially. Yet, his only regret was someone would steal her from him.

His inner beast growled. *We will protect her.*

He and Samira walked out the door. A few feet away stood Evie and Melanie, both of whom were wearing cloaks against the cold, with Kai at their side. Despite the other two, he couldn't tear his eyes away from Evie. Even with her body hidden by the cloak, her dark red hair was swept up off her face, exposing the pale skin of her neck.

He resisted the urge to go over and nibble said neck. His dragon tried to break free, but Bram kept him firmly locked away. For once, he wanted to be in control. His beast would understand.

Maybe.

Not caring about the three pairs of eyes watching him, he approached Evie and traced a finger down her cheek. "You clean up nice."

She raised an eyebrow. "I thought you didn't like it when I hide my true self."

"You're not. I can see your neck, and it's beautiful."

Even in the darkening sky, he could see her flush. When she didn't come back with a retort, he narrowed his eyes. She was restraining herself in public. He didn't like it.

Before he could open his mouth, she placed a hand on his chest. "Do you have a few minutes to talk with me alone? Or are there clan matters you need to attend to?"

He placed his hand over hers, not wanting her fingers to become chilled in the cool evening air. "I will make time for you." Melanie let out a soft sigh, but he didn't take his gaze from Evie's as he said, "Kai, take the others inside. I can watch Evie for a bit."

As soon as the others had left, he squeezed the hand against his chest. "Now, what did you want to talk to me about?"

Chapter Thirteen

Evie's heart was beating double-time. She was part nervous about her appearance, but she was also very aware of Bram's hand squeezing hers. She liked his warm, rough hands. She would like them even more if both she and Bram were naked and back in his cottage.

Stop it, Evie Marie. Just stop it. Right, she wasn't a teenager. The evening was important for Bram and his clan. She needed to pull herself together.

Still, she couldn't resist taking a step closer to Bram before she answered, "I don't know how to act in front of everyone. I don't want to disrespect your position, but I also don't think I can sit quietly and smile the whole night. What should I do?"

Bram caressed her cheek again and she resisted leaning in to his touch. "Evie Marshall is asking me how she should act? I never thought I'd see the day."

She slapped his chest with her free hand. "Stop it. I'm trying to figure out how a clan leader's mate is supposed to act in front of the clan. Skyhunter's leader never had a mate while I was assigned to them. When we're alone, of course I won't hold back, but I don't want to embarrass you, let alone myself, tonight. Especially with Lochguard's leader in attendance. This alliance is important to Stonefire."

Even in the dim light, she could just make out his eyes flashing to slits and back. Without thinking, she blurted out, "What did your dragon say?"

Bram gave a wry smile. "You sure you want to know?"

She frowned. "Bram Moore-Llewellyn, don't waste time by making me ask twice. I only ask questions I want to know the answer to."

He put up his hands in surrender. "Fine, fine. My dragon said you are worthy of being a clan leader's mate. You think of our needs even if it means toning down your feisty personality. Therefore, we should fuck you later until you scream, as a reward."

She raised an eyebrow. "You sure that's your dragon talking, or is it your cock?"

Bram laughed and it warmed her heart. He pulled her up against his body and lowered his head until it was a hairbreadth away from her lips. His breath was hot against her skin as he said, "My dragon pretty much controls my cock, lass." He brushed his lips gently against hers. "And believe me, you haven't seen anything yet. He's been holding back."

The thought of Bram taking her even rougher and harder than earlier, when he'd fucked her from behind, made her shiver. "Well, then tell me how to act so we can survive the night and return to your cottage." She nuzzled his cheek. "I want your dragon to come out to play with us."

Her dragonman growled before taking her lips in a demanding kiss and pushing his tongue inside her mouth. After what seemed like only a few strokes, he broke the kiss and she whimpered, "Why are you teasing me? That wasn't a real kiss."

Squeezing her tighter against him, he murmured, "I had to stop or I would've taken you out here in the cold."

SEDUCING THE DRAGON

"So I reckon that means we should head inside soon?" He nodded. "Right, then tell me how to act, Bram."

"Be yourself. The only thing I ask of you is to not castigate me or Finlay Stewart in front of the clan. Everyone else needs to learn how to hold their own with you."

"I'm an outsider and human to boot. Not everyone will accept that. If I'm to be myself, I won't take their shit."

"Good. I might not have known you long, but my dragon trusts you, which means I do." He leaned over to her ear and whispered, "With the possible threat to the clan and yourself, I don't want people thinking you're an easy target. The more strength you project, the more time they'll take to plan how to nab or hurt you, which gives us more time to find the threats."

The fact Bram worried about her did strange things to her heart. For so long, she'd had to exude strength to survive her job. She'd never had someone to lean on, yet she knew implicitly Bram would help her. All she had to do was ask.

After only two days, she was already growing fond of the dragonman who would soon be her mate. Maybe one day, if they continued to be honest and open, she might even grow to love him.

But it wasn't the time for sentimentalities and dreams of the future. "Okay, I can do that. At some point, though, I need to see a picture of Neil and anyone else connected to him. The DDA doesn't keep pictures on file, as you know, which means I'm going to have to treat every stranger as a threat. That's going to make getting to know the clan difficult."

Bram nodded. "We'll set that up as soon as possible. For tonight, either Kai or I will watch over you. Don't leave without either one of us at your side."

"What about Nikki?"

"She's working on something for me. And as fond of Melanie and Samira as I am, they won't be able to stop Neil if he goes after you. Liam should be along later to help, but Tristan is home with the twins." He squeezed her. "I know you hate having a babysitter, lass, but it's just for one evening. Can you abide it?"

She smiled. "Since you asked, I think I can manage it. Just make sure to keep me in the loop. If you try to hide information for my safety, I will be pissed. You wanted honesty from me, and I expect the same."

He gave her a gentle kiss. "I will. I'll even give you a full brief later." He released her and put an arm around her waist. "Now, are you ready to take on a dragon clan?"

She straightened her shoulders and raised her chin. "Bring it."

Bram grinned. "There's the spirit I love so much."

He caressed her side with his fingers. Even through the cloak and her dress, his touch was like a brand, sending heat through her body straight to her lady parts.

Before she could think about what he might do later with the aforementioned parts, the dragonman's voice snapped her back to the present. "Right, lass, then let's go."

~~~

As they entered the great hall, Bram resisted the urge to haul Evie tightly against his side and growl at the other males looking their way. It might be early yet for the dinner, but there were already ten or twenty clan members inside.

And too many of them were single dragonmen.

138

Seducing the Dragon

His dragon didn't help matters by roaring inside his head. *We should not be here. We should be home with our female. The others are thinking of ways to steal her.*

Stop being daft. They are just curious.

No. Look at the lust in their eyes.

Bram tried to push his dragon aside, but the beast resisted and roared again. *No. You will not protect her. I must do it.*

Of course I'll protect her. We must be here for a few hours. It's for the future of the clan. Don't you want to protect them?

His dragon fell silent. Protecting the clan and their young was one of the few things that could rival protecting a mate in a dragon's list of priorities.

His inner beast's voice was sullen when he replied, *Don't let the Scottish leader touch her.*

I'll try my best.

His dragon somewhat pacified, he scanned the room until he found Kai on the side with Mel and Samira. Once the Protector gave him a nod that all was well, Bram led Evie up to the front of the room where the dais for him and Finn was located. A quick glance told him Finn was still off to the side talking with Arabella. Or, rather, flirting with Arabella. He couldn't tell if Ara was distressed or not, but before he could act, Evie's voice broke his thoughts.

"It looks like Finn has met his match."

He glanced to Evie, who was smiling. "Arabella looks irritated to me."

"There's a fine line between irritation and enjoyment. Personally, I think they're hitting it off, which is strange given what I've heard about Arabella MacLeod."

He motioned with his head for them to take a seat at the table. Evie unfastened her cloak, slipped it off, and Bram's jaw fell open.

The dark blue material of her dress not only made her skin glow, it hugged her breasts before cascading over her round stomach until it brushed the floor; the tease of curves and skin made him hard.

Since it was only fastened over one shoulder—for easy access for a dragon-shifter to change forms—one of her pale shoulders was bare. In that instant, he wanted to lick every inch of visible skin. The precious time from earlier hadn't been enough to sate his desires. Not even close.

Evie raised one dark red eyebrow. "What? It's a dress. You've seen me with less."

He stepped close and took a deep inhalation of her scent. "Yes, but you're wearing the traditional dress of my kind and it's one of the sexiest things I've ever seen."

His female frowned. "Don't be ridiculous. It's just some blue material. Believe me, you haven't seen sexy yet."

With another step, he whispered against her cheek, "Maybe I should add that as a condition to our mating—you need to dress in your sexiest clothing for our post-mating ceremony night."

He could hear her thundering heartbeat and smell her arousal. Good. She could suffer just as much as he. If Bram wasn't careful, everyone in the room would know he had a hard-on.

Evie brushed a hand against his chest. "We'll see if you earn that as a reward or not."

He smiled. "You are a conquest I'm going to enjoy very, very much, Evie Marshall."

Seducing the Dragon

Before she could reply, he turned them toward the table and gently pushed her toward their chairs. As much as he enjoyed standing close to his mate-to-be and teasing her, he needed to sit down to hide his hard cock. For the next few hours, he would think of his clan and not a naked Evie under him as he pounded into her tight, wet pussy.

Pushing those thoughts aside, he sat down and placed a hand on Evie's thigh under the table. The contact reassured both man and beast of how she was safe. Before he could stop himself, he squeezed her plump flesh.

Mine, his dragon said.

Ignoring him, Bram decided conversation would help drown out his inner beast's demands and he switched back to a safer topic. "Arabella's had a difficult time getting past her trauma from a decade ago, but ever since Melanie forced her way into Arabella's life, she's been doing better. Her biggest struggle is accepting her inner dragon. But, to be honest, she was more at ease with Finlay Stewart earlier than she is with most of the members of our clan."

Evie laid a hand on his arm. "I'd take that as a good sign. Besides, don't worry. If Finn hurts her, he'll have to deal with me."

Bram snorted. "And what if he shifts into his gold dragon form?"

"Really? A gold dragon? As if his ego wasn't big enough. Anyway, yes, I can handle his dragon form. After all, I have a few tricks up my sleeves."

"But, lass, you aren't wearing any sleeves."

She gave him a glare and he grinned.

He leaned over and whispered into her ear, "All right, then, care to give me a few hints about these tricks? That way I can prepare for your attack. I can't have you besting me and trying to take over the clan."

Evie laughed and the sound not only warmed his heart, it made his dragon hum and then say, *She is light. She will make us happy.*

Still not telling me the why yet?

It doesn't matter. She is our best chance.

His dragon's answer only stoked his curiosity further. *We'll discuss this again when I have time.*

Evie's voice quieted his dragon. "I think keeping you on your toes will be good for you."

Squeezing her plump thigh, he whispered, "Aye, I suspect it will. But the sooner you share your knowledge, the sooner I can incorporate it into my grand plans."

She glanced up into Bram's light blue eyes. "Provided you reward me as promised earlier, I'll start tomorrow."

"I don't recall promising anything."

Her hand went to his thigh, sending blood straight to his cock. Never breaking eye contact, she moved her hand a few more inches. The pulse between his legs grew more insistent. If she would only move her hand a little further…

A male cleared his throat and it broke the tension. Bram narrowed his eyes and looked up to see Finn grinning. It took everything he had not to punch the Scottish bastard in the face as the Scot said, "Do you need to go for a quickie in one of the side rooms? I can hold the fort if you do."

His dragon snarled. *He is too close. Send him away.*

I can't. He will help the clan.

Bram focused on the other leader. "Did you finish with Arabella? What's the result?"

"Aye, the lass knows what she's doing; I'll give her that. I'd like for her to come to my lands to work with my IT person to set things up."

"I'm not sure if that's such a good idea, Stewart."

"Well, Arabella said she'd think about it. So you might want to talk with her."

Bram leaned forward. "That's pushing the boundaries, Finn. You should've asked me first."

Finn shrugged. "The lass might've said no if I waited to do that. This way, it's a maybe."

He stared at the other leader, torn between the male's interest and effect on Ara and his disregard for Bram's position. Before he could think of how to reply, Evie touched his arm and said, "People are starting to file in. Finn might want to take a seat."

The politeness of her words brought his anger in check. He missed her blunt nature. He could just imagine her telling them to stop their 'who has the longest dick' contest to sit their arses down. Maybe one day the alliance with Clan Lochguard would be close enough to unleash Evie Marshall on them.

He smiled at that thought.

Finn gave him an assessing look. "I hope that smile wasn't for me. Otherwise, I may have to sit at a table on the far side of the room."

Bram shook his head. "Sit down, already. Your smartass comments can wait."

Finn replied, "Then it was about me." Bram growled. Finn winked and rubbed his hands together. "Okay, it's time to get this dinner started. The sooner your clan knows who I am, the sooner they will all start loving me."

Only because of years of practice dealing with dragon-shifter egos did Bram not roll his eyes.

Evie leaned against him. From the way she turned her face into his side and shook, he could tell she was holding in a laugh. His dragon was not happy about her reaction.

Still, Bram was currently in control and he kept his dragon in check. He motioned to his other side. "Sit next to me. I don't trust you with my female."

As Finn moved to sit next to him, Bram took a deep breath. Between Evie's heat and scent surrounding him and Finn's man-whore behavior, it was going to be a long evening.

CHAPTER FOURTEEN

Evie's stomach hurt from holding back her laughter. Watching Bram and Finn together was better than any TV program. To be honest, the two were already acting more like brothers than two clan leaders with a new alliance.

Of course, that bode well for Stonefire.

Bram squeezed her thigh and whispered, "I need to make an announcement, lass. Keep Finn away whilst I give it or my dragon will cause problems."

Looking up into his eyes, she nodded. "Okay, but you have nothing to worry about. You're the only dragon-shifter I imagine undressing inside my head."

Her dragonman let out a strangled sound. "Lass, you're not helping matters."

She laughed. "You said I shouldn't castigate you in front of the clan. You said nothing about me not teasing you."

"You're clever."

"Of course I am. Now, go do your duties before you become sidetracked again."

Leaning down, Bram placed a gentle kiss on her lips and murmured, "Just remember that I'll have my payback tonight. I think I'll make you beg before I let you come."

Heat coursed through Evie's body as wetness shot between her legs. The end of the dinner couldn't come soon enough. "Hurry up, then."

Her dragonman chuckled, gave a warning glare to Finn, and then moved to the front of the dais. She took a second to admire his broad back. The way his plaid-like outfit cascaded over his arse was quite nice. Earlier, she'd wanted nothing more than to slip her hand underneath the hem of his kilt-like outfit and prove he wore nothing.

Still, Finn's interruption had been a good thing. It seemed that whenever she was alone with Bram, her lady parts took control and they very much didn't care what was happening around them. Somehow, she didn't think giving Stonefire's clan leader a hand job in the middle of dinner would leave a good impression with the clan.

Bram's voice boomed out over the mostly full hall and she listened, "Thank you all for coming. Tonight is the beginning of something which will benefit our clan more than anything else we've done over the last decade. You may have seen him around, but Finlay Stewart, the leader of Clan Lochguard, has agreed to become our ally."

A wave of reactions coursed through the crowd. Everything from dropped jaws to indignant cries. Clearly, the Stonefire dragon-shifters hadn't expected the news.

Bram put up his hands and continued, "I understand some of your concerns, but Finlay Stewart isn't Dougal Munro. His ideas and plans for the future are similar to my own. While the alliance is new, I think it is promising. Especially as his clan can help with the increasing number of attacks by the dragon hunters." There was more murmuring before Bram's voice echoed through the room once more. "Rather than me tell you about Finn, I'm going to step aside and allow Lochguard's leader to say a few words. Listen to him and give him a chance."

Motioning with his hand, Evie watched Finn move from behind the table to stand next to her dragonman. They were of equal height, but Finn was somewhat leaner. Still, she wouldn't take his leanness to mean weakness. Given what she knew of how dragon-shifter clan leaders were chosen, with grueling trials over multiple days, anyone who won the right to the position possessed a great deal of strength and fortitude.

Someday, she wanted to ask Bram how he'd won the right.

But then Finn's Scottish tones filled the hall and she focused on the present. "I understand your concern and your wariness. My clan is the same way. However, combining the forces of Stonefire and Lochguard will increase our reach and ability to control our destinies. Our territories combined cover more than half of the isle of Great Britain. If we can convince the humans of our respective territories to not fear us but rather to become interested in us, we may be able to sway the South of England and Wales, even with the harsh reputations of the leaders there."

He must be talking about Melanie's book. The knowledge only made Evie more determined to help Mel and make the launch a success.

Then the Scottish leader gave a sweeping bow and the murmurs of the audience increased. Once he stood tall again, he continued, "That bow was my invitation to dance with any members of the clan who wish to sneak a peek at me. I prefer females myself, but, hey, I don't want to deny any males who might fancy me a bit."

Evie smiled as laughter echoed through the hall. The Scottish leader did seem to know how to win a crowd.

Then Finn turned toward Bram and put out a hand. Without hesitation, her dragonman took it and leaned to Finn's ear to whisper something.

Once Bram gave the other dragonman's back a clap, he said, "Now, that's enough of the formalities. If Finlay Stewart is to dance with anyone who fancies a chance, we'd better get started."

As the crowd settled to the tables and chairs at the edges of the room, Finn went out to the dance floor and was immediately accosted by five young dragonwomen. No doubt, they were just the start and he would be dancing all evening.

Bram sat down by her side, and without thinking, she leaned against him and said, "That was quite the performance, but it seemed to have worked. Did you plan it earlier?"

"No. The Scottish bastard likes to act in the moment, but I'm going to enjoy watching him dance with whoever wants a chance. I think he underestimates how tenacious the younger, unattached clan members are."

"You did well yourself, mister, but I'm glad you didn't offer the same chance."

Bram's voice was full of amusement. "Oh, aye? Why not?"

She frowned up at him. "Because I would've had to chase them all away and I'd rather spend the time sitting next to you so I can cover you in my scent. I'm pretty sure that's how part of the territory marking goes, right?"

As soon as the words left her mouth, she regretted them. The only time she knew for certain that a person would carry a dragon-shifter's scent was when a female was pregnant.

The thought that Evie would never carry Bram's scent squeezed her heart.

Seducing the Dragon

No. There is more to building a life than having children. Besides, there were always children who needed a home. That thought reminded her of little Murray. Maybe they could take him in and raise him. She might not know what the hell she was doing at first, but Evie's determination would hopefully pay off in the end. Bram seemed to like the little tot. Not only that, she would love to see even more of her dragonman's softer side. Nothing brought out a soft side like a baby.

With Bram and Murray, Evie could finally have a family again. She was an only child and her parents had retired to Spain years ago. She rarely saw them.

As much as she was growing to like the image of her and Bram with Murray, she still barely knew her dragonman. Hell, they hadn't even been officially mated yet.

If that wasn't enough, there were also the dragon hunters to worry about as well as the threat from within the clan.

Since Bram had remained silent, she changed the subject and lightened the mood again. "Before half the clan needs you and while I have you here to myself, tell me something I don't know about you, maybe even something no one else knows."

As he poured their drinks, he said, "I enjoy the human sci-fi show *Doctor Who*."

Evie blinked. "The children's program about a time-traveling alien? Really?"

Bram chuckled. "He's a bit different from everyone else and sometimes feels isolated. As a dragon-shifter clan leader, I can empathize with his situation. Or, I used to." He glanced at Evie. "Now, I have you."

She stopped breathing at the hunger and longing in his eyes.

Her dragonman caressed her arm and she shivered as he said, "Maybe once things settle down and the threats are taken care of, we could watch it together."

She would agree to watch anything if it meant she could curl up against Bram's side. While she'd never really thought about it before, she yearned to do all the small couple things regular people did. Since she wasn't with the DDA anymore, she might just have the time to manage it.

She was about to tease her dragonman about his revelation when he frowned and reached into the sporran settled over his crotch. As he pulled out his mobile phone, she bit back a smile; the phone was on vibrate and must've given his cock a surprise.

Bram answered the phone and his expression went hard. Her amusement faded as she listened to him say, "Slow down, Vivian. Tell me, is Quinn okay? What about Murray?"

Her gut told her that whomever Bram was talking to, it was related to either the dragon hunters or Neil Westhaven.

~~~

Clenching his fist to channel his anger at the news of the attack on his clan, Bram listened to the female clan member's reply. "Oh, Bram, Murray is gone. They took him."

He growled, "Was it Murray's father? Did Neil Westhaven attack your mate?"

"No, it wasn't Neil. The two kidnappers were human. S-she did something to Quinn. He won't wake up."

Hearing the pain of one of his clan members helped to switch to clan-leader-mode. "Vivian, you already told me you called Sid. If there's a way to help him, she'll try it. For now, just keep an eye out for any other intruders. I'm coming over. Call me the instant anything seems suspicious, understand?"

While the worry was still in Vivian's voice, the dominance in his voice kicked in her dragon instincts and helped her to focus. "I can do that. And Bram, I'm sorry about Murray. I know you trusted us to protect him, and we failed."

"No, Vivian, it's my fault. I'll explain later, but there's no way I'll allow you to take responsibility for my fuck-ups. Once you hang up with me, call Kai and catch him up so he can send help while I warn the clan. I'll be there soon."

He clicked off the phone and resisted the urge to smash it into a million pieces.

His dragon snarled. *No time for sadness. We will find them and punish them. We must protect our clan and retrieve the young.*

A hand touched his arm, and he looked over to see worry etched into Evie's face. "Tell me what happened and how I can help."

"I need you to go with Liam, Mel, and Samira to Mel and Tristan's house while I go to investigate another attack."

"I will, but first, tell me very quickly what's going on. If it's related to the dragon hunters, I might be able to help."

His dragon urged him. *Tell her.*

Needing the anchor of her body, he put an arm around her. Some of his anger faded at the touch, which helped to clear his mind.

He leaned into her ear and whispered, "A human female broke into Quinn and Vivian's cottage and stole wee Murray. Vivian assumes the human was a dragon hunter. If that turns out to be the case, do you know of anything that will knock out a dragon-shifter to the point they are in a coma? Most human-made drugs are useless against our metabolism."

"Murray's gone?"

Thinking about the little spirited baby boy in the hands of his enemies only increased his blood pressure and fueled his angry. He should've increased security around the lad earlier. Apparently, one experienced and well-trained Protector wasn't enough anymore.

With herculean effort, he pushed his fury aside. He'd channel it later and use it on the hunter arseholes. "Yes, they took him. I will do whatever it takes to get him back, but for right now, I need you to concentrate, Evie. Do you know of anything I could use to help Quinn? In a minute, I'm going to have to make an announcement to the clan about the attack. If there's any sort of good news or hope I can pass on, I'll use it."

Evie bit her thumbnail for a second and then widened her eyes. "I don't know if it's what you're looking for, but I've heard rumors about some of the latest weapons developed by the dragon hunters. Believe it or not, one rumor talks about using one of the oldest methods to incapacitate a dragon-shifter. The concoction had been lost for centuries, but a historian recently discovered it and made it public."

Fucking fantastic. "Spit it out, lass."

"A delicate mixture of ground periwinkle flower and mandrake root will knock out a dragon-shifter in seconds. Not only that, it prevents them from shifting for days. Something to do with a hormone imbalance. Historians and scientists decided the mixture was probably responsible for so many English knights slaying your kind in the past."

"So, in the twenty-first century, the hunters have fallen back on technology from the Middle Ages?"

Evie poked his chest. "Sometimes relics are useful. Without them, I wouldn't be able to mate you."

"Fair point. Is there an old fashioned cure to go along with it?"

His female shook her head. "Not that I know of. But if it's just a hormone imbalance, I'm sure Dr. Sid can fix it."

He took one last deep breath of Evie's scent to calm both man and beast before releasing his hold on her. "I'll pass on your words to Sid." Standing up, he ran a finger down Evie's soft cheek. "Thank you, Evie."

She nodded. "I'll try to think of anything else that might help you while I'm with Melanie. Just make sure to keep me in the loop." She took one of his hands and squeezed. "Now, go take care of our clan."

Staring down into Evie's dark blue eyes, a sense of rightness settled over him. It was hard to believe it'd only been a few days since he'd met his female. Now, the thought of anyone else being by his side seemed impossible. She was turning out to be exactly what he needed in a mate.

With one last squeeze of her hand, he released it and turned toward the clan. A quick look confirmed Vivian had called Kai and his Protector had left to set things in motion.

His mind a bit more at ease knowing that, he clapped his hands and whistled as loud as he could.

The music died down and he easily spotted Finn in the crowd. As soon as their eyes met, the Scottish leader's demeanor tensed.

But he'd talk with Finn later. His first priority was to warn the clan.

Sweeping his eyes across the crowd, he willed his voice to be strong. "I'm ending tonight's festivities. There's been another attack, and I want everyone to go home and be alert, just in case more invaders are on the way. I already have our Protectors taking care of things."

Murmurs of "What happened?" and "Was anyone hurt?" filled the room. Raising a hand over his head, the noise died down and he continued. "I will give more details as time goes on. For now, if anyone sees a strange human or Neil Westhaven, I want you to contact me immediately. Also, thanks to Evie Marshall, we have information about a new possible threat from the dragon hunters. She is part of the clan and may be the key to our winning the fight against the hunter arseholes. While I look into this newest threat, I can't always be by her side. I want you to treat her as my mate, because she soon will be."

He hadn't intended to make that announcement, but with the oncoming chaos the next few days were sure to bring, his clan needed to know. Especially if he went on a mission and Evie was left on her own.

Judging by the whispers and looks darting to Evie behind him, he needed to end this now or he'd never be able to leave. Mustering every bit of dominance he possessed, he said, "Now, go home and prepare in case of an attack. You'll receive further instructions shortly."

Bram looked back to Finn for a second, hoping the leader would understand the need to come back up to the front, then turned from the crowd to signal he was done. Evie was already on her feet and moved to his side. "You shouldn't have credited anything to me. They're just rumors."

"Most rumors have a grain of truth to them."

Finn ascended the stairs and prevented Evie from replying by saying, "Tell me what's going on, Bram."

Staring at the Scot, Bram knew this was one of those moments which could change the future of his clan forever. If he trusted Finn with the details of the attack, the dragon leader could either use it help him or use it to exploit a weakness.

His dragon chimed in. *Tell him. He is good with Arabella. He will help us.*

Bram didn't like his dragon picking up on Finn's actions toward Ara, but he'd deal with that later. For now, he'd trust his dragon's intuition, especially given his beast's reluctance earlier. "The short version is someone attacked and kidnapped one of our young. Once I make sure Evie is taken care of, you can come with me. I'll discuss the details on the way."

Finn growled, "Why would someone steal one of your young?"

He nearly blinked at the sudden change of attitude. He was starting to see more and more why Finn was the leader of Clan Lochguard. Still, Bram was in charge. "I'll fill you in later."

He turned toward Evie but saw Liam, Samira, Melanie, and Arabella making their way up the stairs. Once they were close enough he could whisper, he said, "Liam, I want you to take the females to Tristan's house. The two of you are to guard them with your life, especially Evie. Someone kidnapped Murray, and Evie could be next."

Liam nodded. Melanie took a step forward and asked, "Do you know who it was?"

"Evie can fill you in and I'll give the rest of the details when I return to collect Evie." He looked at each one of his clan members standing in front of him until his gaze rested on Evie. "And you be careful, lass. I know sitting around and doing nothing isn't your way, but I don't want to have to worry about you."

His female moved in front of him and placed a hand on his chest. "As long as you promise to be careful, too."

He nodded, gave Evie a much too brief kiss, and motioned for them to leave. As he watched his female leave, Finn said, "She'll be safe. She's a clever lass. Not to mention she was a natural with her behavior earlier, when she politely told us to sit the fuck down. She'll be an asset to the clan and make a fine mate." Bram glanced to Finn and the Scot continued, "Now, let's start walking so you can tell me the details. The sooner I know the facts, the sooner I can help your arse out."

With a nod, they walked toward the hall exit.

CHAPTER FIFTEEN

The entire walk to Melanie and Tristan's cottage, Evie tried to recall anything she might know to help Bram. She knew a lot about the dragon hunters. There had to be a pebble of knowledge inside her head that could help her dragonman.

So far, her only real lead was the possible use of a mandrake and periwinkle concoction. Most of the dragon hunter gangs were little more than bullies looking for ways to fund their drug and sex addictions. None of them would have bothered to keep a dragon-shifter alive if given the chance; they'd just drain him or her of blood, sell it on the black market, and spend the profits. Most of the hunter gangs were lucky if they caught one dragon a year.

However, because of strong leadership, certain gangs planned for the long-term and had a far bigger reach than their immediate territories. Those dragon hunter gangs usually took down dragons in other countries with laxer laws and then shipped the blood to developed countries to earn the most profit.

The small group of resourceful, and therefore powerful, hunters possessed the patience to crack the exact amount of each ingredient needed to knock out a dragon-shifter without killing them. Bram had mentioned the Carlisle hunters earlier, and they were one of the more powerful and successful gangs.

Not much was known about Carlisle's leader, Simon Bourne, apart from his ability to rein in and control the Carlisle hunter gang to follow his orders. In the five years he'd been in charge, the Carlisle branch's reported violence had decreased while their profits increased. Rumor said they hunted dragons in the Russian wilderness to fund their operations. The DDA had been trying to obtain proof, but relations between the UK and Russia were less than friendly.

With all of Bourne's success, Evie had no idea why he'd want to kidnap a five-month-old half-dragon-shifter baby. Dragon blood couldn't heal any diseases until a dragon-shifter reached adulthood.

Then it hit her: Bourne had the patience required to develop his own blood farm system. True, dragon-shifter blood was worthless for curing diseases before maturity, yet if the Carlisle gang kept children locked away from infants until adulthood, they could make complacent blood slaves. They'd no longer need to risk their lives illegally hunting dragons.

Since the DDA was currently investigating a corruption scandal amongst the Cumbria Constabulary, who oversaw both Stonefire's lands as well as the city of Carlisle, it was more than possible Simon had bribed the police to look the other way and avoid raiding his properties. A monumental task considering the destruction a rogue, unsocialized dragon could wreak on the public if they ever broke free.

Without thinking, she muttered, "So much for protecting the public."

Liam, being a dragon-shifter, had exceptional hearing. He turned toward her and said, "What do you mean 'so much for protecting the public'? Bram is doing everything he can."

Evie blinked. "I wasn't talking about Bram. I know he would cut off his right arm if it meant protecting the clan."

Mel piped in. "Then tell us what you were thinking, Evie. Sometimes voicing your thoughts helps to connect the dots. It also gives us the chance to help you, if you need it, since you're new to Stonefire."

She glanced around at the quickly darkening sky. "I'd rather not do it outside."

Mel threaded her arms through Evie's and increased her pace. "Then let's hurry up. We're nearly there."

Five minutes later, Mel shooed her mate away from the door and guided them inside. Before Tristan could do more than frown, Melanie said, "All right, now talk. I'm dying to know what you're thinking."

Bram's earlier statements about the extent of what Melanie would do to find out what she wanted was proving true. Not even Mel's frowning mate could sway her from her current task.

Evie looked at every person in the room before she said, "I may have an idea of why someone would want to take Murray. There's always the possibility his father wanted him, but given that Neil hasn't tried to take the boy in five months, my gut says it's something else."

Mel allowed her mate to put an arm around her waist as she said, "Then tell us, already."

"The Carlisle dragon hunters are managed by Simon Bourne. That man has been under investigation for years for various accusations, although nothing has stuck. While I have no proof to back-up my claim, Bourne has the patience, resources, and intellect to implement long term plans."

Tristan grunted, "Get to the point."

She raised an eyebrow but it wasn't the time to challenge the dragonman. "If Bourne started collecting children now, then in ten or twenty years he could have his own supply of dragon blood to sell. The money he earned over time would give him tremendous amounts of power."

Liam interjected, "But given what I know, the dragon hunter we captured yesterday wants you. That makes little sense with your theory. Why mention your name if they're after the children? You might be Bram's mate-to-be now, but you weren't when you first stepped on this land."

It was hard to believe she'd only arrived yesterday. "Bram and I discussed this last night. If the hunters scare away people from applying to work for the DDA, the sacrifice system would crumble. Your numbers would dwindle, which would eventually lead to the loss of any power over the human governments."

Melanie finished her thought. "But if someone like Simon Bourne had a steady supply, he would have the power to ask for what he wanted from either the wealthy and desperate or the government."

"Exactly. Murray's kidnapping could've been in the works for a while. Bourne no doubt has spies everywhere and a parentless dragon-shifter baby would be easy pickings for him."

Arabella, who had been unusually quiet, spoke up, "Tell us what you know of Simon Bourne, Evie. We might be able to find a weakness to pass on to Bram."

"First, someone needs to fetch a laptop so I can access the DDA database and then let's all sit down. If Murray's kidnapping is just the first wave of trouble tonight, then we need to save our energy. Standing around is an unnecessary waste."

A cry sounded from upstairs. Melanie looked up and said, "I need to check on my babies." Looking back at Evie, she continued, "I'm bringing them downstairs, too, just to be safe. Tristan can find the laptop and get you settled in."

Melanie rushed up the stairs. As the group moved to Mel and Tristan's living room, Evie took a deep breath. If Bram hadn't found something during his own investigation on the attack, taking down Simon Bourne might very well fall to her. She only hoped she could still log into the DDA information database. Unless someone had tipped them off, it shouldn't be a problem. If her access had been revoked, however, Bram's clan might very well depend on her memory.

Talk about pressure.

~~~

Thanks to Evie's information about the periwinkle and mandrake root, Sid had been able to revive Quinn after a few different shots to balance out the hormones in his body. Bram was patiently waiting for the dragonman to wake up enough to talk.

Kai and Finn were checking the perimeter for clues. The darkness was no match for dragon-shifter eyesight and they hoped to find something, especially if the attacker had been human. Even if they'd had a flashlight, without ample lighting to guide them, they could easily trip and drop something without realizing it.

While bleary-eyed, Quinn took one last sip of water from his mate and said, "I don't remember much, except that there had been two figures before Vivian rushed in to investigate the door being kicked in."

Bram looked to Vivian. He'd waited to ask some of his questions until he could question them together in case one of their answers spurred the memory of the other. "You had been in the nursery. Do you remember hearing any sounds near the window or the room?"

Vivian brushed her mate's forehead as she shook her head. "No. Murray's room was the most secure place in the cottage. The room only had two small windows that no adult could fit through. Being on the second floor added another layer of protection."

"Quinn, can you remember anything about their appearance? Or even their accents?"

The male shook his head. "Nothing except that the first person had been female. Then something pricked my side, and the world went black."

Vivian added, "That's right. When I came downstairs to find Quinn unconscious, the woman ran just as I heard the loud noise upstairs, the one we later found out was the result of them blowing a hole in the wall farthest away from the baby." She swallowed. "To think, one wrong calculation and they could've killed Murray…"

Quinn gave his mate's hand a weak squeeze just as Sid stepped from the side of the room. "Bram, wrap it up. The injection was a temporary fix. He'll be out again soon. I need him to sleep so I can run some more tests."

He wanted to argue, but Sid crossed her arms over her chest and raised an eyebrow. Bram knew that look—she'd find someone to drag him out of the cottage if need be. As the clan's head doctor, she was one of the few who could do so when his presence or actions risked a patient's life.

"I'm done for now, but keep me updated on Quinn's status." He looked to the couple. "And if you remember anything, let Sid, Kai, or me know, but no one else. I don't want the information to fall into the wrong hands."

Both Quinn and Vivian nodded. Bram stood up, squeezed Sid's shoulder in gratitude, and went outside. He had hoped for more information, but Quinn was exhausted and pumped full of drugs. He would have to question them again later.

SEDUCING THE DRAGON

He found Kai and Finn squatting on the ground near the rear of the cottage. He joined them and said, "Shoe prints. It looks like there were three people total."

Finn nodded as he pointed to the smaller set. "This is the female's." He motioned toward the other two. "And two males."

Bram looked to Kai. "Did you find anything else? While knowing there were three people is a start, I'd like something more concrete."

Kai stood up. "Not yet, but while most of the clan was at the gathering, some stayed home with the old, the sick, and the young. I'll have some of my team question them."

Bram also stood. "No, the Protectors should focus on the perimeter and known weaknesses. I can question the possible witnesses."

Before Kai could reply, Finn said, "If you'll let me contact my clan, I can have some of my Protectors fly south to help you out. Too much work will cause stress, which will hurt you in the long run with daft mistakes."

Bram studied Finn's face in the near-darkness. He wanted to believe he could trust the Scottish leader, but the alliance was new. However, he did trust his inner dragon, so he spoke to his beast. *What do you think? Should we ask for his help?*

There was a long pause before his beast replied. *Yes. I think he wants the chance to see Arabella again. He will help us and not betray us.*

Is there something you're not telling me? Earlier, you couldn't stand him.

Circumstances have changed.

His dragon retreated and Bram knew that was all the answer he'd receive for the time being.

He met Finn's eyes. "I would be honored to accept your offer of help."

One corner of Finn's mouth ticked up. "That's quite formal, Bram, but I'll take it. Let me call my people and they should arrive within the next hour."

"Thanks, Finn. Make sure they come in from the west." Finn nodded, pulled out his mobile phone, and walked away. Bram looked to Kai. "With the extra help, have someone question the witnesses instead of me. Evie might have remembered something we can use, and I'd like to hear her out." After ensuring Finn was outside of hearing distance, he whispered, "Any news from Zain?"

Kai also kept his voice low. "Yes, but I don't know the details. He didn't want to risk telling me over the phone."

"I'll stop by and chat with him first. Reach out to me when you're done."

With a nod, Bram walked toward where Zain would be interrogating the hunter. He would do his job as he always did, but for the first time in his life, a part of Bram wanted the work to be over so he could make sure his mate-to-be was safe. He'd sent her to Melanie and Tristan's house, which included two babies. If the intruders were still on his land, they could be targeting other children too.

With a quick text to Kai, he asked for the dragonman to alert all families with small children. Bram wasn't about to let any other young be stolen. Hopefully, between Zain and Evie, he could figure out what the bloody hell was going on and stop it. The British government wouldn't help him even if he asked. Stonefire would have to take care of its own.

Chapter Sixteen

Evie had just finished downloading as much information as possible from the DDA database when there was a knock on the door. Since Melanie and Arabella were sitting with babies in their arms, Tristan moved to answer it.

When she heard Bram's voice, she let out a sigh of relief. Maybe his presence would help with her ever-growing stress levels. Everyone had been asking her questions left, right, and center. Bram would help ease the burden.

She knew it was selfish given Bram walked every moment with the burden of the clan on his shoulders. Even though she was usually good at adapting to new situations, becoming a dragon-shifter's mate, along with trying to stay alive and find a way to protect an entire clan, was a bit overwhelming. Add that to not enough sleep and worrying about how something could happen to Bram if he went after the dragon hunters himself, and she was close to cracking.

Bram walked into the room and she did a double-take at his grim expression. "What happened now?"

He walked over, took the laptop from her hands to hand over to Liam, and forced her to her feet. Once he had an arm around her waist, he growled and said, "I need to move you somewhere safe. Now."

Placing a hand on his chest, she said, "Why?"

"The hunters are planning to kidnap you."

"We already knew that. There must be more."

Her dragonman looked around the room and then back to her. "The dragon hunter we captured, well, we've finally managed to extract some information from him. He confirmed there is a traitor within the clan. After tonight's dinner, the hunters will know you're to be my mate." He squeezed her close against his chest. "They'll use you against me, lass, in ways I don't even want to imagine. They may already be hiding on our land, waiting to pounce."

Melanie's voice sounded behind Bram. "You can't exactly lock her in a cellar and throw away the key."

Bram looked over his shoulder. "You may have learned a lot since arriving here, Melanie Hall-MacLeod, but you don't know everything. I have somewhere safe to stash Evie. Very few know of the location, and I plan to keep it that way."

Tristan spoke up. "I won't ask for the location since not knowing will keep my family protected, but who will take her? The clan needs you here. Will you be able to control your inner dragon with another person watching her?"

Evie patted Bram's chest. "He's right. As much as I want to keep you close, the clan needs you more."

"I'll see you settled; otherwise, I'll become useless. I'm barely keeping my dragon under control as it is. I need to protect my mate if I want to protect my clan." He glanced to Liam and Tristan. "You two should understand that sentiment."

Her heart warmed at his fierceness. "Then we'll do whatever is necessary to get your dragon under control so you can return as soon as possible."

Keeping one arm around her waist, he turned to face the others in the room. "I'll be in constant contact with Kai, Tristan, and Finlay Stewart, monitoring the situation from my secret location. Thanks to technology, I'll still be available to the clan."

Arabella frowned. "Why include the Scottish leader? You barely know him."

"He's offered to help and I took him up on his offer." Tristan, Liam, and Melanie all spoke at once, but Bram merely put up a hand and they fell silent. He continued, "The reasons are my own. While I'm getting Evie settled, I want all of you to be on alert. Our prisoner also told us how the hunters are targeting children, in addition to Evie."

Evie jumped in. "If that's the case, then I might know what the Carlisle gang is up to." After explaining her theory about Simon Bourne making his own blood farm, she added, "Once I have the chance, I'll reach out to my friend who knows more about dragon-shifters than just about anyone alive. She might have contacts in Carlisle who can help us."

Bram nodded. "I have contacts, too. Since a clever man wouldn't hide dragon-shifters in the city, I reckon they'll keep Murray and any others in the surrounding countryside. We'll find the lad and bring him back once we have a concrete plan. There no bloody way I'll allow them to keep the wee one." He looked to Tristan, then Liam and back again. "All of you should stay together here to protect Annabel, Jack, and Rhys. I know it might be a bit crowded, but the more adults here to watch the children, the smaller the chance they'll be stolen." Once Liam and Tristan nodded, he spoke to Arabella. "I know this is a lot of people for you in one place, but I want you to stay here, too. You can trust everyone in this room. They will look out for you and protect you, if it comes to that. You have nothing to worry about."

The dragonwoman's lips pressed together before she replied, "I understand."

"Right, with all of that settled, I need to take Evie to the safe location. The longer we linger, the greater the chance they'll try to take her."

Bram pressed against her back, but she put out an arm to stop him. "Wait." Looking to Melanie, she asked, "May I take the laptop with me? I'll find a way to share the information with everyone, but if I'm going to be spending a lot of time locked away, I can use that time to dig through the data and look for something useful."

Mel nodded. "Sure. Ara always keeps a back-up one here anyway, so we can use that if we need it."

Taking the laptop back from Liam, she nodded at Bram that she was ready.

As he guided her toward the back door, she felt a tiny bit of reluctance. Staying alive was top priority, but she was growing fond of her new friends. It was going to be hard to be alone once Bram left her to take care of his clan.

Not that she would ever try to stop him from doing that. Still, she wondered where the secret location he'd mentioned was and exactly how they were going to get there. It wasn't as if she could shift into a dragon and fly beside her dragonman.

~~~

The second they were outside the cottage, Bram's dragon finally broke free inside his mind and roared. *Protect her. Hold her. Don't let the hunters find her.*

I'm trying.

Now, do it now or I'll make you do it.

STOP. If you take control, you might hurt her.

Never.

"Bram? Are you okay?"

Evie's voice broke through his thoughts. The split-second distraction allowed him to stash his beast to the back of his mind again. "It's my dragon. I don't know how much longer I can keep him back. His usual restraint and logical brain are gone."

"What can I do to help? Anything?"

He pushed gently against her lower back. "Just keep walking and talking. I'll have to let him out to shift into my dragon form, so I just need to contain him until we reach the takeoff area."

"We're traveling by dragon? How? I somehow doubt you have a saddle or harness I can just strap on and ride you like a giant, flying horse."

Despite everything going on, he smiled. "Even if I did, I don't think I'd trust you with the reins."

She slapped his chest with the back of her hand. "Be serious and tell me."

His dragon was trying to force his way out again. He grit his teeth and said, "While carrying a dragon-shifter in human-form is rare, it does happen. Especially when a dragonman or woman is injured. We have a large basket with handles to carry them. You'll step into the basket and I'll pick you up with my talons once I'm in the air."

"A basket? You mean like the ones used for a hot air balloon?"

Clever lass. "Yes, it's very similar. I hope you're not afraid of heights because this is the fastest way for me to take you to safety."

Even in the faint light of the moon, he could see her wry look. "Just don't play tricks and 'drop me' so you can catch me again. I'm not a fan of roller coasters, and I may be sick all over your dragonhide." She frowned. "What color dragon are you, by the way? I'm supposed to mate you, yet I have no idea."

His inner beast poked out. *Let me take over and show her. Words are not enough. I will protect her.*

With a growl, he forced his dragon back again and squeezed Evie's soft sides. Even through her cloak, he could feel the warmth radiating from her body. The touch helped him to focus. "Blue. I reckon you could call it a cerulean blue, which is the best kind."

Evie's voice was light. "I don't know about that. I always fancied the purple ones myself."

Blue is better. Let me show her.

Stop it. We're nearly to the takeoff area. Let me explain more to our female so she isn't afraid of us.

Quickly. There is danger everywhere while we remain here. You may think you can protect her, but a dragon can do it better. I am stronger. This is a fact.

Shut it. "Evie, under normal circumstances, I love when you tease me. But right now, love, I'm close to losing control. Every time you mention how another dragon is better, it drives mine a bit crazier. Until you're safe, we need to feed his ego. Can you do that?"

She leaned against him and his inner beast's attempts to break free lessened just a tad. "Then make sure he knows that while it's a bit selfish of me, I'm glad you're the one taking me to safety. I know it's odd considering I only met you the other day, but whenever you're near, I feel safe."

The words warmed his heart. "I feel the same way, lass, and once all of this is over, I plan to mate you in front of the entire clan so I never have to let go of you."

"Bram."

Seducing the Dragon

Squeezing her tightly against his side as they walked, he picked up his pace. It was going to be hard enough to leave her in the morning. He'd best treasure what time he had. After all, he would do whatever it took to rescue wee Murray from the dragon hunters, even if it meant leading a team himself on a raid. There was always a possibility he could die.

Not that he'd mention that to Evie, at least until his dragon was under better control. He needed her to not only tame his dragon, but also to pick apart her brain. If he told her about his plans to rescue Murray, she would argue and be unwilling to do what needed to be done so he could focus.

Luckily, she remained silent during the last few minutes of their walk. They approached the takeoff area and headed for the covered space next to Sid's surgery-slash-cottage. Once Sid's staff finished preparing the basket for his female, he'd have to hand over control to his dragon. He only hoped Evie could handle him in dragon form. His beast was in no mood to be polite or restrained.

~~~

Evie watched as the two teenage dragon-shifters finished preparing the large basket for her use. While a bit larger than the type of baskets used for hot air balloons, the rectangular shape was similar. Well, except for the large, metal upright handles attached to the two longest sides of the contraption.

Since Bram hadn't released her since they'd left Mel and Tristan's cottage, she snuggled against him. "Are you sure they'll hold? Your talons are sharp and could rip the basket to pieces with one wrong move."

Much as his voice had been since leaving the cottage, it was tight with restraint. She wondered how much longer he could control his dragon. "I would never hurt you. Barring a high tech laser cutting through the material, it'll hold."

"If you say so." She looked at her dragonman, the moonlight highlighting the planes of his face. "Tell me what will happen if you lose control of your inner dragon on the way to this location. I need to be prepared."

He clenched his jaw. "A dragon protecting his or her mate is unpredictable. He will do whatever he bloody well feels like. I'll see everything happening, yet I have little control over his actions until I manage to take control again. However," he brushed her cheek with his free hand, "he'll never hurt you, love. Never."

It was the second time he'd called her love, but since this was the North of England, she forced herself to not read too much into it. Everyone from bus drivers to shop clerks called a woman "love".

She nodded just as the two young dragon-shifters approached them. The teenage boy with red hair spoke up. "It's all ready, Bram."

"Right, Miles, then off you go. I know you two have a tendency to sneak off, but until this dragon hunter situation is cleared, stay where you belong. I can't waste the resources to go looking for you if you get lost."

"Yes, sir. I understand."

The teenagers walked away and Bram slowly released his arm around her waist. Cupping her cheeks, he kissed her gently and pulled away. "Right, lass, I'm going to shift now. Remember, if the chance arises, feed my dragon's ego or I'll have the devil of a time shifting back once we reach our destination. Even then, if I do shift back, he may try to claim you once before he hands the reins back over to me. I hope you allow it."

Even in the mostly darkness, she could see the worry in his eyes. "Don't worry, Bram, I've worked with dragon-shifters for a long time. It's going to take a lot to scare me away, and I doubt you'll ever do so. I agreed to be your mate, which means accepting both sides of you. If your dragon needs sex to clear his head, then I'll do it."

"Don't be too enthused about it. You tired of me already, lass?"

She smiled. "I want to say something, but I can't. This feeding your dragon's ego thing is one of the hardest things I've ever had to do."

Bram chuckled. She loved the deep, throaty sound. "It won't be for much longer, and then you can do your worst." He kissed her nose. "And I look forward to it."

Resisting the urge to hug him and never let go, she gave a light push against his chest. "Before something bad happens, let's get this party started. I want to watch you shift, then I'll crawl into the basket."

With a nod, Bram released his hold and walked ten feet away. She could barely make out his outline in the faint moonlight. Would she even be able to watch him shift? She'd only seen a dragon shift a handful of times, one of which had happened during her training. Disappointment flooded her at the thought she couldn't give Bram's dragon the proper attention he deserved. *Later. I'll fawn and swoon over his dragon form later.*

As her dragonman unfastened the strap over his shoulder, she decided the darkness might be a good thing after all. Then she wouldn't be distracted by his naked, toned, and lickable body.

The sound of his clothes falling to the ground filled the air right before his body gave off a soft blue glow. Admittedly, she'd never seen a dragonman shift at night. She had no idea their bodies glowed in the process; daylight masked that little secret.

Two seconds later, the glow intensified as Bram's arms and legs grew into appendages with sharp-tipped talons, a tail and wings extended from his back, and his head morphed into the long, narrow snout of a dragon. The twenty-foot-tall dragon glowed for a few seconds before the light faded. Even with the brief glance, she itched to touch the bright blue of Bram's dragonhide.

The dragon huffed and motioned his head toward the basket. "Right," Evie said before rushing over to the contraption. Gawking would have to wait.

As soon as she crawled over the four-foot-high wall of the basket, Bram jumped into the air and beat his wings to hover in place. He slowly maneuvered to where she waited and delicately gripped the metal rings. The twenty-thousand pound plus dragon above her head had far more grace than she'd believe possible.

With precise movements, the bottom of the basket gave way to her weight as they rose into the air. Since peeping over the side of the basket would be useless in the dark, she tugged her cloak tight around her body and closed her eyes to enjoy the sound of dragon wings beating above her as the wind rushed through her hair.

CHAPTER SEVENTEEN

The steady rhythm of his wings helped Bram to rein in his inner beast, just barely. He had a feeling once they arrived at the safe spot, his dragon would want to claim Evie to cover her in their scent before he had to leave again.

Under normal circumstances, he would love nothing more than to pull Evie close and devour every inch of her body. But his clan needed him. If his beast lost complete control, he would let them down. His actions might even kill them.

Maybe if he knew the reasons behind his dragon's protectiveness of Evie, he could think of how to rein his beast back under his control later. Then he would be able to help his clan.

While he had a chance, Bram decided it was time to wrangle some answers out of his beast. *Tell me why you are so possessive of Evie.*

She is ours. That is all.

There is more you're not telling me. I don't understand why, either. You've always been open with me. We are one, and keeping secrets from one another is counterproductive.

To be happy, you must want her for her.

Bloody beast, I already do. What aren't you telling me?

I will tell you when you're ready. For now, I will protect her.

At the finality of his dragon's tone, he growled inside his head. Deep down, he might know what his dragon was withholding, but it was dangerous to hope. True mate or not, he was keeping Evie Marshall.

His secret hideaway wasn't too far from Stonefire's land by dragonwing, and within ten minutes, he circled around the jagged peaks below a few times to ascertain if any humans were around. The land below him was part of the Lake District National Park, which technically belonged to the humans. However, the nearest village was miles away, and there were very few roads. Since it was only April, not many ramblers hiked the area either.

Bram had chosen this spot within months of taking over the clan. Every leader liked to have a safe haven. While no one wanted anything awful to happen, it was always good to prepare for the worst.

He was certain Evie would be safe here.

His inner dragon growled. *I don't want to leave her alone. We must protect our mate.*

Trust me.

Maybe. I will make sure no one will doubt she is ours. She must carry our scent.

Bram had been afraid of this. *We don't have time for sex. We need to question Evie for answers.*

No. We must make sure everyone knows she is ours. I will fight you to make it happen.

The urge to fuck his mate coursed through his body. His dragon roared inside their head. *We are here. I will gain control before we land. We will fuck her and scent mark her. No male must come near her.*

As his dragon pushed to take control, Bram pushed back. He might be strong, but he was aware of how this was a losing battle. Images of him and Evie from earlier, when he'd fucked her from behind, flashed inside his brain. The dragon-half wanted Evie. If Bram was decoding the dragon's feelings correctly, he wanted to protect the mother of their children.

Impossible. Evie couldn't be pregnant, nor would she ever be. She was incompatible.

Wrong, wrong, you are wrong. She will be mother to our young. I will brand our scent strongly. No males will dare approach her.

His dragon's words piqued his curiosity. *Tell me what you mean about her being mother to our young. Tell me, and we can fuck her once.*

I will fuck her anyway. I don't need to bargain.

Since his dragon was stubbornness incarnate, Bram knew this was a losing battle. It was best to agree for now and pounce when his inner beast least expected it. Post-orgasm, he should be able to regain command of his mind.

Still, it was best to allow his beast to think he won for the time being. *Fine, if we fuck her, will you allow me to talk to her again?*

Yes, after.

Okay, we fuck her. But be careful. She is in the basket. We must lower her gently. Don't take her until she's inside our secret place.

Of course. I would never hurt her.

Beating his wings in long, slow motions, he carefully maneuvered his dragon's form down through the jagged rocks. With great care, he laid the basket on the ground, released the metal rings, and moved to the side where an open area would allow him to land.

The second his legs touched the ground, images of kissing Evie, touching the soft skin of her breast, and finally fucking her flooded his mind. As wrong as it was given all the shit going on, his dragon's need was spilling over into his human-half.

As his dragon repeated *Fuck her* over and over inside their head, he imagined his talons becoming hands, his snout shrinking to a chin and nose, and his wings merging into his back.

Usually when he shifted back into his human-form, his dragon would quietly retreat and either sleep or observe what Bram did. However, that wasn't the case. His beast was shouting inside his head.

Fuck her. Now. We need her. Hand over control to me or I will lock you inside our mind and fuck her until I'm sated.

Alarm filled his mind at his dragon fucking Evie for as long as he liked. *Just give me a few more minutes. We can fuck her soon.*

Determined to keep his human half in charge long enough to guide them inside, he ran over to Evie's basket. She was already standing and staring at him. However, the constant pounding of his dragon's need prevented him from noticing much about her face, let alone her feelings. Until he thrust his cock into her, he wouldn't be able to do anything.

"Come. We need to hurry. My dragon needs to fuck you."

Grabbing her hand, he pulled her along to the secret entrance.

~~~

Less than a minute after standing back on solid ground, Evie was being pulled along by a very naked Bram to some secret location so he could fuck her.

Her legs wobbled a bit as she tried to match her dragonman's pace. The urgency in his voice had been real; she only hoped there was something other than rock at his secret hideaway. Her arse really didn't want to sit or lay on cold stone or damp grass.

Soon, they were walking underneath the cover of trees and she had to rely on Bram's guidance. It was pitch black and she couldn't see a bloody thing.

Bram finally whispered, "We're nearly to the entrance. I will carry you."

Before she could so much as say his name, he plucked the laptop from her hand and her stomach bounced against Bram's bare shoulder. The heat of his skin seeped through her cloak and dress. Combined with his earthy male scent filling her nose, a tingle raced through her body.

Considering all of the shit going on, it was wrong, but the bouncing motioning as he moved made her a little wet. His dragon was about to take control. She wanted to see it.

It will help him, remember. It's not just you being horny and irresponsible. Sure, she'd go with that.

The air became damp and cool, telling her they were inside one of the rock formations she'd just made out in the moonlight earlier. Just as she wished, there were lights; brightness flashed and she closed her eyes. Opening them slowly, her eyes adjusted to see a room furnished with a bed, a sofa, a small kitchen, and even overhead lights. "How do you power the lights?"

Bram grunted. The next thing she knew, he tossed her onto a soft mattress. *Well, at least it's not stone.*

He towered over her and his eyes were flashing rapidly between slits and round pupils. The strain in his voice was pronounced, to the point he enunciated each word when he said, "No questions. Just strip or I'll rip them."

Normally, she'd ask him to rip her clothes off as that had always been a fantasy of hers. However, she didn't want to destroy the beautiful traditional dragon-shifter dress Samira had given her, so she needed to get naked.

Sitting up, she undid her cloak and tossed it aside. As she fumbled with the tie over her shoulder, she glanced to Bram. Her eyes were drawn to the motion of his arm; he was stroking his cock in long, slow movements.

"Hurry, Evie. My dragon's so close."

"Right."

The tie finally came undone, and she wiggled out of the dress. No sooner did she toss it to the floor than Bram was on top of her. He murmured, "Mine," before he kissed her. His tongue pushed into her mouth at the same time he thrust his cock into her wet pussy. Evie cried out in surprise and Bram moved his hips, his cock pounding in and out of her in deep strokes.

The movements of both his tongue and his hips increased, until she couldn't resist digging her nails into his back. She could think of nothing but the dragonman currently owning her mouth with his tongue as he pounded relentlessly into her pussy.

He only broke the kiss to shout as he stilled inside her. As he came, pleasure exploded through her body in orgasm.

She'd barely stopped spasming when Bram took her breast in his hand and squeezed. His eyes were purely slits now. His dragon was in complete control.

She wanted to ask him if his human-half was coming back when he growled. "Mine. Again."

Pinching her nipple, he once again moved inside her. With each thrust, he pinched a little harder. Even without touching her clit, she felt the pressure building.

Bram's hand went under her arse and lifted, changing the angle of his thrusts. Holy hell, her dragonman's dick was hard as stone, which made his movements that much more delicious.

With one last twist of her nipple, she screamed as Bram roared. Her orgasm intensified with each jet of semen inside her.

Seducing the Dragon

Lights were still dancing before her eyes when Bram pulled out of her. *Good. Maybe his human-half has returned. There's so much we need to do.*

Forcing her gaze to Bram, she saw the dragon slits and started to worry. "Bram?"

Growling, Bram flipped her over and entered her pussy from behind. She cried out in a mixture of pain and pleasure. She didn't understand what was happening. Bram had said after fucking her once, he should be able to wrestle control of his inner dragon. Yet he was already on the third go, his dragon fully in charge.

She could barely concentrate as her dragonman played with her clit. His touch was addictive and made it difficult to concentrate.

Yet a small part of her brain knew the clan would need him. What would she do if his human-half never regained control? *No.* Whatever it took, she needed to find a way to bring Bram's human-half back.

Then Bram pinched her clit, banishing all thoughts but the feel of his strong, warm fingers. Another pinch and her pussy clenched and released his cock in orgasm as he continued to move, his motions almost desperate.

Somehow, some way, she would have to find a way to bring the clan leader version of Bram Moore-Llewellyn back to the forefront. How she was going to do that, however, she had no idea. Especially since Bram chose that moment to come inside her, and his semen sent her into another orgasm, scattering her thoughts.

CHAPTER EIGHTEEN

Evie feigned sleep. It was the only way Bram and his dragon would stop fucking her and leave her alone. If it weren't for all the shit going on with the dragon hunters, Murray, and threat of another attack, she would love getting to know Bram's dragon half in bed.

But the rough, slightly kinky sex with a dragonman would have to wait. She needed to think of a way to help Bram's human-half regain control or the clan could be in danger. No doubt, Kai could hold Stonefire together for a short while, but without a clan leader, Stonefire would be vulnerable and the Carlisle dragon hunters would take advantage.

Yet despite how important it was to bring Bram's human-half back, none of her training at the Department of Dragon Affairs had prepared her for a dragon going into a sex frenzy. According to her textbooks, a male dragon-shifter went into a frenzy when he discovered his true mate and wouldn't stop until he could scent she was pregnant with his child. Which, in Evie's case, was impossible.

Although, given Bram's need to claim her, she wondered if maybe her test as a teenager had been wrong. There was also the possibility that humans didn't know as much about dragon-shifters and their biology as they claimed.

SEDUCING THE DRAGON

There's no time to wish or hope to be Bram's true mate despite the test results saying you can't conceive a dragon-shifter's child, Evie Marie. His clan needs him, so think of a way to bring the human-half back to the forefront. No one else can do it.

Talk about pressure.

Focus, Evie. Running through the what she knew, the only thing she could think of which might work was to use Bram's earlier comment about feeding his dragon's ego. She didn't want to sooth the dragon; however in this case, poking the dragon's ego might work. Anger tended to blind a person and make them lose control. If the dragon lost control, there was a small possibility Bram would pounce upon the opening and take over.

Of course, she could be completely wrong and make things even worse. A sex-crazed dragon was bad enough; what would a pissed off dragon look like? Even though she trusted Bram never to hurt her, she had no idea about his inner beast. Clan Skyhunter hadn't allowed her to roam their lands and study how any of the couples interacted. Was it even possible for a dragon-shifter to harm his or her mate?

Bloody hell. She hated not knowing. As soon as everything was righted with Murray and the clan, she was going to take Melanie and Samira up on their offer to learn more about being a dragon's mate.

First, however, she needed to deal with Bram. She refused to believe he was a lost cause. Mostly because of the strength of Bram's will, but also because Evie wasn't about to let anyone else die on her watch. To prevent that from happening, she needed to keep Stonefire cohesive.

Then you'll just have to succeed and bring Bram back. No worries, right? Evie resisted a wry smile. The situation with Bram was the farthest thing from a "no worries" scenario.

Pushing aside the inkling of doubt, Evie focused back on her task. She would bring Bram back, but she wasn't stupid. If she was going to stand up to a sex-crazed dragonman and try to make him angry, she needed to prepare for the worst-case scenario. Evie needed a weapon.

Keeping her eyes closed, she recalled every detail she could about the room. Granted, she'd only seen it in snippets at a time, but she was trained to notice details. A human sacrifice's life often depended on it.

There was the bed under her side, which was next to an end table with a lamp. Since the lamp was small and currently the only light source in the room, she couldn't use that. The tiny kitchen was on the opposite side of the room from the bed. Bram was currently rustling around over there. Since she didn't possess super-human strength, she couldn't lift the sofa and toss it at Bram's head to distract him and find a knife.

No, her only option was to find something inside the small bathroom. Dragon-possessed Bram had allowed her to use the toilet in private once before. It was time to see if he would allow her again.

Taking a deep breath, Evie slowly sat up, trying not to wince at the soreness between her legs. Before she could even think about the last time she'd been this sore from sex, Bram was standing in front of her. His pupils were slits, meaning his dragon was still there.

His voice was low and growly when he said, "I must scent you more. Again."

Evie put up a hand. "Please, let me use the toilet first."

"Then again?" She nodded and Bram moved aside. "Hurry."

SEDUCING THE DRAGON

When faced with a possibly irate and soon-to-be out of control dragonman, Evie pushed aside her soreness and rushed into the toilet. Once she locked the door, she turned toward the sink. Despite the bathroom being inside a cave, the sink and toilet were simple yet modern with nondescript white porcelain. Bram had spent some time constructing the cave hidey-hole.

Squatting down, she opened the door to the cabinet under the sink and peeked inside. There was toilet paper, soap, shampoo, and a plunger.

A quick glance around the bathroom told her there was nothing else apart from the shower stall, a few towels on a rack, and the toilet itself. Reaching inside the cabinet, she took the plunger and stood up. No doubt, the wooden handle would break if she had to swing it at Bram's muscled body, but at least then, she could use the jagged edges, if it came to that.

Catching her reflection in the mirror, Evie tried not to smile. A naked woman holding a plunger like a cricket bat was not something you saw every day.

Pull it together, Evie. This plunger might end up being your ticket to freedom if things go south.

With one last deep breath, Evie tightened her grip on the plunger and opened the door. It was time to provoke a sex-crazed dragonman.

~~~

Inside the partition of his mind, where Bram's dragon had put him, Bram paced. Right before Evie had gone into the toilet, he had noticed a determined glint in her eye. What in the bloody hell was she up to?

His inner beast might be too preoccupied with sex, but Bram wasn't. Knowing his female as he did, she had a plan. Hopefully, the plan involved bringing Bram's human-half back into control.

The first fifteen minutes after entering the cave dwelling, Bram had fought tooth and nail against his inner dragon and lost. He'd never appreciated his logical other half until it was gone. He also finally understood what Tristan had gone through with Melanie. Given the other dragonman's temper, Bram realized Melanie was stronger than he'd given her credit for.

After the losing battle with his dragon, Bram had hung back to conserve his energy. Sure, he enjoyed sex with Evie. Under normal circumstances, he would love nothing more than to lock her away for two days and make her come until she couldn't think straight, but he needed to find a way to break free and save his clan.

His inner dragon roared inside his head and screamed, *Why is she taking so long? I need her. I must scent her. She is mine.*

Ours.

Mine.

Fuck. He'd never seen his beast act so stubborn and possessive before, and he had no bloody idea how to fix it. He was ninety-five-percent certain the beast wouldn't stop until Evie was pregnant.

Yet that was impossible. Maybe his beast, being so dominant, was extra possessive. He had no reason to believe Evie had lied to him about being incompatible with dragon-shifter DNA.

Before he could dwell any longer on his dilemma, the toilet door opened to reveal Evie clasping a plunger in her hands. Even his dragon blinked for a second at the sight before rushing toward her. Evie said, "Stop. I'm tired. I'm sore, and I'm hungry. I want a break from sex."

His dragon growled in Bram's voice. "No. You are mine. I must make sure the others know it."

Evie tightened her grip on the plunger. "Don't make me use this to knock you flat on your arse."

Fuck. His female was challenging his dragon in the throes of a frenzy. If she wasn't careful, his beast would do something crazy, such as tie her to the bed.

Bram was forced to watch, helpless, as his beast moved their body toward Evie and said, "You agreed earlier. Sex. Now."

His human narrowed her eyes. "Look, mister dragon, I'm all for hot, slightly kinky sex, but I'm not a dragon who's gone mental and has a never-softening cock of magic. I'm human. You try having something hard thrust into you every which way for hours and see how you feel."

Anger coursed through his dragon-half and Bram wanted to scream for her to stop. While he was pretty sure his beast wouldn't hurt her, there was always a chance his dragon could go into such a state that Bram would never take back control. It was rare for it to happen, especially to someone dominant enough to become clan leader, but there were stories. Some of which, in centuries past, were still legendary, such as when one dragon razed every village in a twenty-mile radius before he'd been shot down with a catapult.

No. Bram wouldn't let that happen. He'd have to think of something quickly.

His dragon moved their body another step closer and said, "Throw the stick down or I will take it. Then I'll toss you on the bed and scent you again."

Bram pushed against the invisible boundary inside his mind. If he couldn't take back control, would his dragon really force their female? *Stop it. She is tired and needs rest. We can scent her later. No. Now.*

Evie moved the plunger a bit behind her, readying herself to swing. "Last warning, dragon."

His beast growled and moved to take the plunger. However, at the last second, Evie sidestepped and swung the wooden handle against his hard cock.

Not even his bloody beast could take the pain, and doubled over. As soon as he did, Bram felt his prison give way a little.

Clever lass. Anger was weakening his dragon's control.

Brave, too, as she swung again and smacked him in the balls. Fuck, it hurt. Pain radiated through his entire body, to the point tears formed in his eyes, but Bram felt his prison give way even more. He had a chance, and he was going to take it.

With every iota of strength he possessed, he pushed against the invisible wall trapping him deep inside his mind. The pain coursing through his body made it difficult to concentrate, but Bram had fared worse during his clan leader trials.

Each second a little more gave way. Roaring inside his mind, he gave one final push before the wall dissolved. His human-half rushed to the front of his mind. The pain was worse, but the drive to protect his female gave him the strength to toss his bloody beast into an invisible prison. *Stay. I will take care of her.*

Ignoring his dragon's roaring and shouting, Bram said through clenched teeth, "Lass, if you ever want me to use my cock again, that's enough."

"Bram?"

"Aye, it's me. Please don't smack me in the cock again."

SEDUCING THE DRAGON

He heard the plunger fall to the ground before Evie enveloped him in her arms. Since he was still bent over, she was mostly draped over his back. The warmth of her soft curves against his hard body helped him to forget some of his pain.

Evie's voice was muffled against his back as she said, "I'm sorry I had to whack you in the bollocks, but it was the only vulnerable spot on your body I could attack and have any impact."

His cock and balls still pulsed with pain and hurt like hell, but he forced himself upright and drew Evie close against his side. "Why should you apologize? My beast was being a bloody bastard and deserved it. Next time, he'll think twice about trying to take you when you say no."

Evie snuggled into his side. "You think so? I didn't mind the sex so much, but we needed you back."

By 'we', she meant the clan. Bram's heart warmed at the reference. "I'm here now, lass. However, I need to be careful. Until my bloody dragon calms down, I can't risk shifting, especially if you're nearby."

His female hesitated a second and he didn't like it. "Bram?"

Giving her a squeeze, he replied, "Ask me anything, love."

She looked up at him, curiosity brimming in her dark blue eyes. "Your dragon was acting as if he were in the throes of a mate-claim frenzy, yet that's impossible. You'd tell me, right, if there was any way a person could instantly become compatible with a dragon-shifter's DNA and make it possible to conceive a child?"

"I would tell you if I knew, but I don't. Once we take care of the dragon hunters and Murray is back safe and sound, we can try asking that friend of yours, the one who 'knows more about dragon-shifters than just anyone alive' as you put it."

She nodded. "Good idea. To be honest, we should find a way to ensure her safety. If word ever got out about her knowledge, she would become a target."

"I wish I could allow an unmated human to live on my lands from time to time, but right now, the law forbids it. Maybe Melanie's book can help change all that." Bram turned so he could haul Evie against the front of his body. He needed her warmth to battle his inner dragon's current roaring and pushing against his invisible prison. "For now, I need to check in with Kai and Finn and then both of us need some rest. Since I can't risk shifting anytime soon, I'll have to drive back to Stonefire in the morning. I don't want to leave you here, but you're easy pickings back on Stonefire's lands. A guard or two should come here once Finn's people arrive to help relieve the strain on my Protectors."

Evie poked his chest. "You had better keep me in the loop. I have the data on the laptop to sift through and I might just have to save your arse again."

He smiled. "I look forward to it. But next time, love, could you leave my cock and balls out of it?"

His female laughed. "I think I'm going to keep a cricket bat next to our bed in the future. If you thought the plunger handle was bad, just you wait. The cricket bat will have you crying like a baby."

"Then here's to hoping you never need to use it." Bram gave Evie a brief kiss and then patted her arse. "Right, you go shower while I talk to Kai and Finn."

Evie nodded. "Okay." She stood on her tiptoes and gave him a quick, rough kiss as she squeezed his arse cheeks. "It's good to have you back, dragonman. Your dragon knows how to give hot sex, but without your humor, it's not quite the same."

Seducing the Dragon

His inner beast growled at her words. Bram ignored him and gently slapped her arse. "Just wait until I have both sides of me working together. Then you'll never want to leave my bed."

"I could make a flippant remark right now, but seeing as a shitload of danger is coming, I'm going to be honest. I'm not going anywhere, dragonman, because you're mine."

Her words caused joy to course through his body and even soothed his dragon's anger a fraction. "Good, because you're mine, Evie Marshall, and I'm keeping you." After one more kiss, he said, "Now go shower before my cock recovers and I think about taking you slowly and gently."

Evie frowned. "No more sex until Murray is back. That's an extra incentive for you to finish the job quickly and come back to me alive."

While his dragon was grumbling about the 'no sex' statement, Bram didn't mind as much. "As long as you're waiting in my bed when I return, I can live with that."

Evie grinned. "Now I have something fun to plan."

"The glint in your eyes doesn't bode well for me." He stepped back and motioned toward the bathroom. "As much as I want to hold you in my arms and talk with you for the next week, Murray and the clan need my attention. Shower, love. I'll fill you in afterward."

Nodding, Evie left. Once she shut the door, he addressed his inner beast. *Until you calm the fuck down, you're staying in that prison. I need to rescue wee Murray and save the clan. When you're ready to help me, I'll let you out.*

His beast snarled. *Protect our mate first, then save the clan.*

I will protect her. But unless you want the Scottish leader to take over, you'd bloody well better get a grip, and soon.

Just as he'd expected, since Evie wasn't in the room, his dragon stopped fighting and growled. *We are the leader of Clan Stonefire. We will save them.*

Good. Prove it to me. While I sleep with Evie, you find a way to calm down. Since we survived the clan leader trials, this should be easy.

His dragon huffed. *I want her many more times, until she carries our child.*

He blinked. *Now would be the time to tell me your damn secret. Is Evie our true mate?*

Yes. I must claim her completely, until she carries our young and our scent. You should understand.

A mixture of joy and 'holy shit' hit him. *Forget the claiming bit. Why didn't you tell me earlier she was our true mate?*

Because, you would have seen her as a duty. A child would help the clan, so you would make sure she conceived without knowing her. You needed to want her for her, to make her happy.

He'd never heard of a dragon being able to rein in the mate-claim frenzy before. *You are stronger than I thought.*

Of course. You always underestimate me. I am brilliant.

One corner of his mouth ticked up at his dragon's matter of fact tone. *Well, brilliant one, not telling me the truth put our mate in danger. Don't do it again.* Silence was his reply so Bram pushed on. *I'm still keeping you in there. You've calmed down a bit with me, but Evie's scent will scramble your brain again. Work on your restraint. We will handle the frenzy once the clan is safe.*

His beast grunted. *I don't like it, but I will try. I don't want the Scottish leader and his dragon to save our clan. We should do it.*

Agreed. Now, I must talk with Kai.

As Bram moved to where he had a phone line connection, he tried but failed to push aside what his dragon had just told them.

Evie was their true mate.

He'd wanted her even before he'd known that tidbit of information, but just the thought of her one day carrying his child filled his heart with warmth. Evie would make a fantastic mother.

Except, he hoped she wasn't pregnant yet. Before the next time they had sex, he'd have to talk with her. She should have a choice in when she had a child. She wasn't a sacrifice who'd gone in knowing it would happen.

Yet to have that talk, he needed to take care of the hunter threat. As he dialed Kai's mobile phone number, Bram stashed away his feelings about Evie. His female was clever, and if he wasn't careful, she'd catch on that he was hiding something. He didn't like keeping secrets from her, but in this case, she might become distracted with the news. He needed her help to sort through the information she downloaded. Retrieving Murray wasn't going to be easy; Evie might well find the answer needed to win against the dragon hunters.

So, as much as Bram wanted to shout from the rooftops that Evie was his true mate, he bottled up his joy and stuffed it deep inside himself. The emotion would be a distraction and he needed to focus on living long enough to see what surprises she had in store for him when he returned. Only when he returned would he be able to claim Evie as his true mate.

CHAPTER NINETEEN

Finlay Stewart watched as five of Lochguard's youngest Protectors landed in the Stonefire takeoff area.

His lands might be more isolated than Stonefire's since his clan's lands were in the wilds of the Scottish Highlands and safer from outside attacks, but he couldn't risk sending his more mature soldiers. They needed to look after the clan.

His clan didn't share the same sense of unity he had witnessed amongst Stonefire's members. No, Lochguard was far more fractured than he liked, which meant petty arguments and fights broke out on a regular basis. Only his strongest Protectors could keep them in check during his absence.

The former clan leader, Dougal Munro, had done a bloody awful job of keeping the clan together, let alone encouraging them to work together as a unit. If things continued as they had over the past six months, his hair would turn gray in no time.

Finn's dragon growled and said, *Stop it. The past can't be changed. Work on the future.*

If only it were that simple. This threat to Stonefire may well soon be ours, and that worries me.

Gain the trust of our new allies. Then they will help us.

Finn knew that already, but sometimes he still second-guessed himself at winning the right to lead Clan Lochguard. Half the time he didn't know what the bloody hell he was doing. Only through pure stubbornness had he done a halfway okay job so far. His alliance with Bram Moore-Llewellyn was his biggest win to date.

One by one, his five Protectors removed the satchels tied to their hind legs before shifting into their human forms. The sight made Finn focus back on the present. His dragon was right—if he succeeded in helping Bram, then the Stonefire leader may help him in the future. The dragon clans needed to learn to work together. One day, the British government would stop trying to protect them. Finn wanted his clan to be ready for that day.

As he walked toward his clan members, who were in the middle of removing clothes from the satchels and getting dressed, his dragon said, *Working with this clan also means we can see Arabella again. She is a puzzle I want to solve.*

If the rumors are true, then she's been through hell. I can't force her to come to our lands.

Make her laugh. That will work.

Finn wondered if that were true. Then Arabella's dark brown eyes, full of intelligence, caution, and a little sass flashed into his mind. She was somewhat damaged, but he wondered what it would be like for the clever lass to simply be herself. *We'll see. For now, we must help our new allies.*

Stopping in front of his five young Protectors, he switched into clan-leader mode and asked, "Did you notice any unusual activity on your flight here?"

The leader of the wing of dragons, Faye, finished tying her long, curly, brown hair back with a hair tie before saying, "No, we were cautious and made sure to backtrack to lose any sort of tail. Care to tell us what's so urgent we had to fly the long way around to Stonefire's lands?"

At least they had come when he called. For a short while, Finn had worried about if he were still too new a leader to be trusted at the drop of a hat. Sure, these were some of his most loyal Protectors, who agreed with his vision of the future, but that loyalty had never really been tested before. "The Carlisle dragon hunters have more savvy technology than we figured. I couldn't risk them listening in."

One of the other Lochguard dragons, Shay, spoke up. "Why would Carlisle monitor us? It's the Inverness hunters who are the pains in our arses."

Finn crossed his arms over his chest and raised an eyebrow. "Oh, aye? So you're the new clan leader then, privy to classified information? I must've missed your trials and confirmation. Otherwise, you're speaking out of turn, lad."

Shay, a lad of twenty-three and barely out of his mandatory time with the British armed forces, paused to collect himself a second before mumbling, "Sorry, sir."

Finn nodded in acknowledgment. The lad had been making progress with his temper and the present was no time to castigate him in front of the others. Finn would have a chat with him again later.

He then eyed each of his five clan members in turn. "Look, Carlisle's leader, Simon Bourne, is someone every dragon-shifter clan in the UK should worry about. He's stealing dragon-shifter bairns and we think he plans to use them to create his own blood farm."

Faye said, "But that would take nearly two decades of housing a dragon-shifter before their blood was of any use to the hunter."

Finn nodded. "Aye, but for a man with ambition, time is just one of the many things they use to their advantage." After quickly filling them in on Evie's theory, he continued, "With Carlisle so close, Stonefire is their main target. Bram Moore-Llewellyn needs our help. I'm going to turn you over to Kai, the head Protector here, and you follow his orders to the letter, understood?"

Faye frowned. "And what will you do, Finn?"

Rather than tell them the truth of how Finn wanted to make sure Bram focused despite the threat to his mate, he merely replied, "I need to touch base with Bram and go from there." His wing leader nodded and Finn turned. He said over his shoulder, "Right, then follow me. I'll give the tour later. For now, just know that if Stonefire falls, Lochguard will probably be next. For all intents and purposes, they are your clan for the next day or two. Don't fuck up and don't die."

He hated being a hardass, but the clan was used to Dougal Munro's almost dictator-like style. It would take time to acclimate the clan to his slightly more laid-back methods of trusting responsible dragon-shifters to make good choices, even without him ordering them around.

As he led his team to the location previously provided by Kai to check-in, Finn's heart beat double time. The alliance and bringing in his own Protectors to help Stonefire were his first real tests as clan leader. He needed to heed his own advice and not fuck up and die.

~~~

"Evie, love, wake up"

Evie vaguely registered Bram's voice, but rather than answer, she snuggled deeper into her pillow. She was still exhausted from their sex marathon.

Then there was a whoosh and a blast of cool air. She flipped on her back and blinked her eyes open to see Bram holding her blanket in one hand and a mug in the other. Her voice was heavy with sleep when she said, "What the hell, Bram? Will I ever be allowed to wake up on my own?"

"It's better than a pitcher of ice water, isn't it, love?"

She grunted. Rather than argue, she sat up and stretched her arms. "I'm assuming there's a reason for waking me. Is it morning already?"

Bram sat down on the edge of the bed and handed her a cup of coffee. "Almost, but Nikki and Charlie are nearly at the meeting point, where I'll meet them to bring both females back here. I figured you'd want to be ready before they arrive, and maybe give me a good kiss or two to send me off."

Evie took a sip of coffee, strong with milk and no sugar, as she preferred. "So through the power of deduction, I'm guessing Charlie is another Stonefire Protector. I didn't realize there were so many female Protectors, especially given the smaller female population."

"There are only two in Stonefire, which is more than most of the British clans. Some leaders coddle their females, in the hopes they'll have more babies. You've seen the clan and know how well that would go over here."

She tucked that bit of knowledge away. "So does this mean Finn's reinforcements arrived?"

"Aye, which is why I can spare the pair of them to watch over you while I plan with Finn and Kai for Murray's rescue."

Doing a double-check, she confirmed Bram's pupils were still round. "And your dragon is okay with it? Considering his attitude yesterday, I'm surprised you're so calm at the thought of leaving me behind."

Seducing the Dragon

"My dragon and I had a chat."

She raised an eyebrow. "A chat? That's it? I somehow imagine there's more to it than that."

A corner of Bram's mouth ticked up. "Right, then, a very persuasive chat."

Evie rolled her eyes. "We'll save the discussion about how a chat with basically yourself can be 'persuasive' for later. Just answer me honestly: can you keep control of your dragon? If you're going to help rescue Murray, which I suspect you are, then you'll need to shift. The last thing Finlay or Kai needs is for you to be unable to shift back to your human form."

Bram leaned forward and kissed her nose. "You're very blunt, lass. Don't ever change."

Evie grinned. "I don't think I could if I wanted to. You're stuck with me, Bram Moore-Llewellyn. Now, don't change the subject and answer my question."

"My dragon behaved all night, even with me holding you close. With a few secrets cleared between him and me, he's doing better."

"Secrets? What secrets? How does that even work?"

The humor faded from Bram's eyes. "I promise you a lengthy discussion on how the human and dragon halves interact later. Right now, I need to meet Nikki and Charlie. You'll have about fifteen minutes to get ready." He cupped her cheek and Evie leaned into his touch. "If there's anything pressing that can't wait, ask me, lass, because I won't have time later."

In case I don't make it back alive, was left unsaid. "Just promise me you'll do everything you can to return to me in one piece."

He stroked her cheek with his thumb. "I only just found you and I'm not about to let you go."

Before she could reply, Bram kissed her. He nipped her lower lip and she opened, welcoming his tongue. Bram removed the mug from her hand and she wrapped one arm around his broad back and one around his neck. As he stroked his tongue against hers, she reveled in his taste and warmth. The thought of never holding him close again only made her clutch him tighter.

With one last stroke and then nip of her lip, he broke the kiss and laid his forehead against hers. "As hard as it'll be to function without me near, keep Kai and me in the loop about what you find in the data on the laptop."

"Yes, because my brain only turns on when you're in the same room. I don't know what I was doing for the thirty-one years before I met you."

Bram squeezed her side. "Cheeky wench."

She fought a grin and lost. "You know you love that about me."

His gaze became serious. "Aye, that and more." Bram gave one more gentle kiss before he pulled away and stood. "I need to leave, but there's a satellite phone on the kitchen counter if you need to use it, as well as a landline on the small table near the entrance. The number for my mobile is on the fridge."

She nodded. "How long before you return with Nikki and Charlie?"

"If everything goes to plan, fifteen minutes. If not, then a bit longer."

Standing up, she placed her hands on Bram's chest. "Be careful."

"I always am."

After one more quick kiss, Bram exited the cave dwelling. Evie was a resilient person; her years working with Clan Skyhunter down south proved that. Standing alone in the room, however, her eyes prickled with tears. She put up a brave front for Bram's sake, but the thought of losing him squeezed her heart.

She might only have known him a short time, but she cared for the dragonman. She hoped they would have a future together.

As a tear slid down her cheek, Evie wiped it away and took a deep breath. "Right, Evie Marshall, crying isn't going to help anyone. Bram needs information. Work on that."

She ran her fingers through her hair a few times, picked up her still warm cup of coffee, and moved to the laptop sitting on the kitchen counter. She wasn't going to waste another second. If there was something in the information she downloaded from the DDA database which could save both Murray and the clan, she would find it.

Chapter Twenty

Evie had barely sorted through the first few files on her laptop when Bram returned with two female dragon-shifters. Standing up, she smiled at Nikki and then looked at the other dragon-shifter. She was a tall woman in her late thirties with short, blonde hair, blue eyes, and a faint smile on her face. At a glance, the woman looked more like someone she'd see carting around three kids in an SUV to various after-school activities than a dedicated soldier. But Evie knew looks could both be deceiving and used to one's advantage.

Before she could say a word, Nikki turned to Bram and said, "Now that we're alone, I have news to report."

Bram frowned. "Why didn't you report during our five minute hike here? The longer I stay, the longer Murray is in the hands of the dragon hunters."

Nikki squared her shoulders. "I know, sir, but on the off chance someone was hiding in the forest, I didn't want to risk them listening in."

Bram replied, "This area is secure. Tell us what's going on."

Nikki glanced to Evie and then Bram. Once Bram nodded, no doubt to tell her it was okay for Evie to hear the information, the young dragonwoman continued. "Right before I left, I finally tracked down Olivia's location. Kai is in the process of bringing her in. I know you mentioned driving back to Stonefire, but Kai asked for you to fly back, if at all possible, so you two can question her together. Your dominance may be required to make her say something, especially concerning Neil Westhaven."

Bram was silent for a second, no doubt communicating with his inner dragon. When his pupils flashed to slits and back, Evie moved to his side. Rather than air out what had happened earlier in front of his clan members, Evie merely asked, "Are you okay?"

Ten more seconds passed before his pupils became round again. Her dragonman looked down at her. "Yes, I'm fine." He looked to Nikki. "Right, then I'll fly back." He then glanced from Nikki to Charlie and back. "You two take care of Evie and follow the protocol for reporting sensitive information." The two dragonwomen nodded. Bram then looked to her. "If you find anything at all in those data files, Nikki or Charlie will pass on the information. Even if it's the smallest bit significant, pass it on. I don't want to overlook anything."

Placing a hand on his chest, she said, "Of course. Just make sure I'm able to report to you. I'm sure your dragon wouldn't like Finn taking my call."

His eyes flashed again and she resisted a smile. She was learning how to push his inner dragon's buttons; the beast wouldn't want Finn talking to her. He would have to allow Bram to shift back to do that.

After Bram made a motion with his head, the two Protectors went to the kitchen and faced away from them. Bram lowered his head and murmured, "My beast is behaving. There's no need to prod him."

Evie batted her eyes. "Who said anything about prodding? I just stated a fact."

Bram hugged her close. "I don't have time to challenge you. I want a decent kiss goodbye. Make it good."

"I don't take kindly to orders."

"Then I'll just do this."

Bram lowered his head and kissed her. As his tongue invaded her mouth, his hands gripped her arse and pressed her soft stomach against his hard abs. Continuing to caress her tongue with his, he then moved a hand to her back and pressed her chest against his. Her hard nipples brushed against him and she moaned, not caring that two dragonwomen were able to hear her. No, then she would worry about them scenting her arousal, too.

Instead, she clutched Bram's shoulders and explored the inside of his mouth with her tongue. She would never get enough of his taste, his heat, or his scent.

As her pussy pulsed between her legs, she wished they had time to have sex one more time. Not to say goodbye, because he would come back to her, but rather, for luck.

All too soon, Bram broke the kiss, his breath hot against her lips as he whispered, "Now I'm determined to return so I can finish what I started." He moved to her ear. His whisper was quiet; to the point, she strained her ears to hear his words. "Everyone in the room knows how you're aching for my cock."

She swatted his chest. "Bram, stop it."

He chuckled before he eased back to see her eyes. "I'm going to miss you, Evie Marshall."

Evie's heart squeezed at the emotion in his words. Yet she somehow managed to keep her voice even when she replied, "Then stop dawdling and go. The sooner you save Murray, the sooner you can come back to me."

With a nod, Bram released his grip. She nearly reached out to pull him close again, but she resisted. There was too much at stake and it was no time to be selfish.

Bram cleared his throat and the two dragonwomen turned around. Nikki was fighting a smile, but Charlie's face was still as calm as before.

Her dragonman said, "Take care of Evie. You all should be safe here since I took great care in choosing this location, but don't let your guard down for a second until I return. Who knows how far Simon Bourne's reach goes, let alone where he has spies." Nikki and Charlie nodded. He looked to her. "I know you don't like orders, but stay put. When all of this is over, we'll work on some self-defense training beyond what the DDA taught you. Until then, let my people watch over you. Worrying about you is a distraction I can't afford until the clan and Murray is safe."

Evie replied, "Don't worry. I'll stay until all of this is over. Not only do I want to live, I have mountains of data from the DDA database to comb through. I haven't found anything in the fifteen minutes you were away, but I'm going to keep looking."

"Good. Then I'm off."

With one last quick kiss, Bram exited the room. Pushing aside the ache in her chest at his leaving, she turned toward Nikki and Charlie. "Right, I have a ton of information to sort through. Would anyone like to make some breakfast?"

Nikki crossed her arms over her chest. "We're your guards, not your maids."

Before she could launch into why it would benefit the clan to allow her to work, Charlie said in a quiet voice, "This job isn't always as glamorous as you'd like it to be, Nikola. Now, start looking for something to make. I'm starved."

Nikki gave a terse nod and turned toward the cabinets.

Looking toward Charlie, Evie said, "I don't think we've met officially. I'm Evie Marshall."

"I know." Charlie gestured toward the laptop. "Why don't you start working? I'll let you know when the food is ready."

Evie scrutinized the dragonwoman's face, but she couldn't detect any discernible emotion. *Not everyone will love you instantly. Focus on your work.*

"Sounds good," Evie said and moved to her computer and started reading.

~~~

Bram walked away from the cave dwelling toward the clearing surrounded by trees he would use to shift and take off. After taking a deep breath of cool morning air, he spoke to his dragon. *Do you still agree to our deal?*

His inner beast gave a sleepy yawn before replying. *Yes. I will hand control back over to you once we arrive at Stonefire's lands. Then I will be first to fuck our mate when the danger has passed.*

Bram hated that his inner beast would be in control again the next time he had Evie naked and willing, but he was clan leader. Sacrifices had to be made. *Good. Channeling some of your sexual frustration will help us rescue Murray.*

Yes. I'm strong, but I'm reaching my limit. I want our mate every second of every day.

I know how you feel. I don't ever want to let her go, and not just because she's our true mate.

My plan succeeded. You're welcome.

Bram simply shook his head at his beast's tone of surety. *She knows how to put you in your place. I'd be careful.*

206

Seducing the Dragon

She won't need to hurt us again. Next time, she will understand. She will bear our young.

How is that even possible?

Not now. I will tell you later. It will encourage you to finish the task quicker.

First Evie, and now his dragon; he was a bit worried about everyone dangling incentives for him to return in one piece. Even without the enticements, he wouldn't let down his clan.

Bram stopped in the middle of the clearing and decided he would finish the rest of the conversation later. *I'm trusting you. Don't let me down.*

We have a deal. I will not renege.

Since Bram didn't have any other choice, he allowed his dragon to rush to the front of his mind. As the inner beast took over, his legs grew into giant hind legs with talons, his arms into forelegs, and his face elongated into a snout at the same time ears and horns grew from his head. When the shift was complete, Bram's dragon folded back their wings partway, crouched down, and jumped into the air.

As their wings beat to lift them into the sky, Bram paid close attention to his inner dragon's behavior. Despite the tension humming through his mind, which he now recognized as his dragon containing the mate frenzy, the beast didn't try to force him inside a mental prison as before.

Satisfied, Bram said, *Now, fly as fast as we can without being seen. Our clan needs us.*

His wings beat in a steady rhythm as they flew over the English countryside. He was careful to pick a path with the least amount of human houses and farms. Nighttime was better for concealing a dragon in the sky, but Bram couldn't afford to wait.

No matter how many times he'd flown in his dragon form over the course of his life, Bram loved viewing England from such a great height. Everything was small, not much more than a speck. Eventually, he wanted to take Evie out during the daylight hours. She would love the view.

To do that, he needed to ensure his survival. As he made his final approach to Stonefire's secondary landing area, Bram said to his dragon, *Remember, to help me, the clan, and our mate, I need you to channel your frenzy. The dragon hunters nearly killed Tristan the last time our people rescued someone in trouble. We can't let that happen, or our mate will be alone.*

We will succeed.

As they slowed down the beating of wings to land, Bram noticed Finn and Kai off to the side, their faces grim. The instant his feet touched the ground, he nudged at his dragon to fade into the back of their mind. Five seconds ticked by before his beast complied with a grumble and said, *Remember our deal. If you don't honor it, I'll force my way out. I want Evie.*

His dragon receded and Bram took back control of his mind. He then imagined his legs shrinking into arms and legs, his face morphing back into a human skull, and his wings and tail merging into his back. Once he was human again, Bram strode toward Kai and Finn. Kai tossed him a less formal version of the traditional dragon-shifter attire. Stepping into the kilt-like garment, Bram said, "Give me the report."

Kai nodded. "Finn's people have been assigned Stonefire partners and two of our Protectors just brought in Olivia. She was sedated, but should wake up any minute. I wasn't sure who you wanted to question her."

Implied was another question: Do you trust the Scottish leader to attend the questioning?

Bram said, "I'll question her alone first." He looked to Finn. "I'd have you join me, but Olivia doesn't know you and I can't risk her keeping secrets because of it."

Finn let out an overly dramatic sigh. "Well, I'll just have to find something else to do and miss out on the fun. I need to check in with my clan, at any rate, before we go off to save your clan. Since I want a secure connection to contact Lochguard, I need to talk to Arabella MacLeod."

Bram eyed the Scot. "We have other techs who could help you."

Finn shook his head. "No, she knows what she's doing and I don't have time to interview someone new. I can't risk a fuck-up in this, Bram. We have no idea of what Simon Bourne is capable of doing with regards to surveillance."

The dragonman did have a point. Bram wanted to ask Finn's true motives with Ara, but it would have to wait. He looked to Kai. "Find someone to show Finn where Tristan lives. Ara should still be there." Kai grunted in acknowledgment. Bram looked to Finn and pierced him with a stare. "Be careful with her, Stewart. You hurt her and I'll toss your arse out in a heartbeat."

The Scottish leader gave a mock salute. "Yes, sir."

With a sigh, Bram waved the two off and headed in the direction of the building where prisoners were held whenever he had them. He didn't have time to think about how annoying Finn was. Clearing his mind with a few deep breaths, he prepped for his interrogation. Olivia might be the key to saving Murray, and he would find a way to make her talk.

CHAPTER TWENTY-ONE

Arabella brushed the soft, warm cheek of her little niece, Annabel, with her finger and smiled. While she'd been afraid to even hold the twins when they were first born, she'd become quite the protective auntie. Between her brother, Tristan, Melanie and herself, nothing would happen to the sweet babies. They would make sure of it.

And it wasn't just because the little girl was partly named after her, either. Annabel and her brother, Jack, had been vital to her healing process. Whenever she held one of them, her dragon would come out to make soothing sounds inside Ara's head. Because she came to visit her niece and nephew often, Ara was growing more accustomed to her inner dragon's presence inside her head, to the point the beast's appearance didn't incite a panic like it had done for years.

She still might not be able to hold conversations with her inner dragon quite yet, but progress was progress. At least, that was what her brother's mate, Melanie, always said.

A knock on the door caused little Annabel to scrunch her face and turn her head in the baby way which signaled they were about to wake up. With a little rocking, her niece fell back into a peaceful slumber.

SEDUCING THE DRAGON

Arabella heard footsteps coming from the direction of the door and she looked up to see who dared to disturb her niece's sleep. She did a double-take. It was Finlay Stewart.

Pushing aside her surprise, Arabella frowned at the Scottish leader. Without thinking, she asked, "Why are you here?"

All eyes in the room turned toward her, but she never stopped rocking little Annabel in her arms. The Scot was a dragonman, not a god. If there was one thing she'd learned from Bram, it was that even clan leaders needed to be questioned from time to time.

Still, to ease the worry of her friends in the room, Ara added, "I'm sorry, but if he's offended by one question, then he has issues. A clan leader deals with far worse, am I right?"

One corner of Finn's mouth ticked up. "Aye, you're right, lass. As long as you don't call me a daft, unlikeable sod, you can say whatever you like. I prefer honesty myself."

Arabella said, "I don't know you well enough to say whether you are a daft, unlikeable sod or not. I'll let you know the verdict when I come to it."

The Scottish leader burst out laughing and she couldn't resist a small smile.

Tristan cleared his throat and Ara darted a look at her older brother. There were questions in his eyes. Given the stubbornness of the MacLeod bloodline, he wouldn't give up until he had answers.

Finn's voice filled the room and she let out a mental sigh of relief. She could postpone her brother's interrogation until later.

Finn said, "Thanks for that, lass. Given the circumstances, I needed a good laugh." Finn's brown eyes stared straight into her, not even once moving to the scar on her face or the healed burn on her neck. Ara resisted fidgeting under his intense gaze. She nodded and he continued, "I'm here because I need to talk with my clan. I hate to break up the baby time, Arabella, but you know your stuff, and I need your help. Can you set up a secure video connection from here?"

She nodded. "Yes. I always keep a back-up computer at my brother's house."

"Good. Then let's get to it. I need to go back and maybe help Bram with something."

Hugging Annabel close, she replied, "A please would be nice."

"Lass, will you please help me? Pretty please? My clan would thank you."

Arabella blinked. She hadn't expected him to cave so easily. "Okay."

Avoiding eye contact with Finn, she stood up and walked over to her brother. She really didn't like the mixture of concern and determination in her brother's eyes.

Once Tristan took the baby from her arms, her dragon scurried back into the far reaches of her mind. For some reason, the action stung a little.

Carry on, Ara. There are far worse things happening right now. She moved toward the door to the little room used as an office. Just as she reached the door, her brother growled and said, "Don't follow her, Stewart."

She stopped and looked over her shoulder just as Finn replied, "Arabella is a grown dragonwoman who speaks her mind. She didn't say anything about waiting out here."

Even with the baby in his hands, her brother took a step toward Finlay. "I don't care if you're Lochguard's leader or not. This is my home. Try ordering me around and see what happens."

Seducing the Dragon

Oh, bloody hell. Ara moved between Tristan and Finn. Looking at her brother, she said, "Tristan, it's okay. With the door open, I'm virtually in the same room. I'll be fine."

Her brother's brows furrowed. *Crap.* She knew that look. When they were alone, he was going to question the hell out of her.

From the corner of her eye, she caught Finn smirking. She faced him. "Just because I didn't outright say to stay out here doesn't mean you can just enter any room you wish in someone else's house. I'm sure you have things you don't wish for strangers to see."

Finn's smirk widened. "Lass, there are things I *verra* much want you to see."

The Scot exaggerating his accent was the last straw. Ara's restraint shattered. "Stop with the innuendo. It's not sexy. It's irritating. Just for that, you stay out here. Once I have things set up, I'll call you."

Before he could reply, she walked back toward the door to the small office and entered the room. Taking out the laptop, she plugged it in and turned it on. While she waited for it to boot up, she couldn't decide whether to sigh or to laugh. The expression she'd glimpsed on Finlay's face, one of open astonishment, made her day.

Working as quickly as she could once the laptop was ready, Arabella heard nothing but silence coming from the other room. When everything was set up, she walked out to see Finn and her brother staring at each other. It was then she noticed Melanie studying her with the careful look her sister-in-law always used when trying to spot clues to solve her latest puzzle.

Bloody hell. It would be a double-team interrogation later. She hated being under such constant scrutiny. All she wanted was for her brother and his mate to allow her to recover in her own way. Yes, she'd needed the kick in the arse to leave her cottage and face the clan, but that had been over nine months ago. As Finn had said, she was a grown dragonwoman.

Rather than think about agreeing with Finlay Stewart on anything, she cleared her throat. Everyone's eyes moved to her. Arabella motioned toward the office. "It's ready."

Finn walked up to her. "Are you going to show me how to work it?"

She raised an eyebrow. "Don't be daft. You know your way around a computer. Do it yourself."

The corner of her brother's mouth ticked up, but she ignored it. Many of the clan members might be intimidated by her brother, but Ara wasn't afraid to tell him what she thought of him. Sometimes he was a right cocky bastard. She'd deal with him later.

Finn let out a long, drawn out sigh. "Right, then I'll do it myself."

As he walked toward the office, she held out her arms to her brother. "I want Annabel back."

Tristan said, "I could use her as leverage to make you answer a few questions."

His mate, Melanie, piped in. "Tristan MacLeod, stop it. I won't let you use our children as leverage. Give Ara our daughter. We can talk with your sister once things calm down."

Tristan glanced to Melanie and sighed at the stubborn glint in Mel's eyes. Arabella knew she'd won and took Annabel from Tristan's arms.

Once she settled back into the chair with her niece, she hummed a tune. Soon, her dragon joined inside her mind. While Ara should be worried about everything happening to the clan, she felt more content than she had in a long time. After all, she'd put a clan leader in his place, won a mini-battle with her brother, and was cuddling her niece again.

She refused to admit Finlay Stewart was the reason most of it had happened at all. Neither she nor her dragon were ready to face that fact.

Instead, Arabella continued humming to her niece. Putting Finn in his place had boosted her confidence. Maybe once everything was settled in the clan again, she could try pushing her boundaries even further. Until she completely overcame what the dragon hunters had done to her and her mother, she would never be anything more than 'poor Arabella' in the eyes of the clan.

She wanted to finally be allowed to be herself.

~~~

As Evie polished off the last of her English breakfast, she paused with her forkful of egg halfway to her mouth and reread the summary of the current investigation file on her computer:

Based on the number of witnesses sharing the same testimony, it is highly probable the Carlisle hunters have several escape tunnels. None of the Carlisle city plans, going back to the 16th century, show anything bigger than sewer pipes. Yet the hunters appear from behind vegetation and abandoned sheds in the area on a regular basis. More interviews and research will be conducted in three months to determine if any tunnels exist.

Bloody hell, if the hunters had constructed escape tunnels, that was something Bram and his clan needed to know.

Laying down her fork, she skipped ahead to the second Carlisle investigation conducted three months later and read the summary:

As predicted, a series of underground tunnels were detected. Using the witness testimony from three months previous, the use of radar technology confirmed two known exit points. The DDA believes the Carlisle hunters are unaware of our discovery, but the department will sit back and wait for confirmation of this supposition. This knowledge may be used for future operations.

Further down, she found the coordinates of the two tunnel exit points.

Evie scanned the rest of her files for anything else on the Carlisle tunnels, but didn't find another reference. It was almost as if the DDA had abandoned any further research, which was odd. The DDA hated the dragon hunters nearly as much as misbehaving dragon-shifters, except the DDA's reasons had more to do with inconvenience than a sense of moral duty.

Then she remembered the promotion of Jonathan Christie to Assistant Director of the DDA. His promotion had been right after the second report on the tunnels had been filed. New leadership always brought change, but her intuition sense it was something more than a mere administrative oversight. There was a slim possibility Christie had ordered them to stop looking, although she had no reason why.

Unless Christie had some kind of deal with the dragon hunters. The thought that the DDA knew about Bourne's plans to kidnap dragon-shifter children made her sick to her stomach. It was definitely something she needed to check out once she had the chance.

She clenched one of her fists. Despite the lack of enthusiasm concerning dragon-shifters for most of the higher-ups in the department, she refused to believe they would allow innocent children to be kidnapped and imprisoned.

SEDUCING THE DRAGON

Focus on the present and what you can do now. Right. Pushing aside her disappointment at the DDA, she focused on the positive. Finally, she had something Bram might be able to use.

She swung around in her chair. Charlie and Nikki were lounging on the couch, finishing up their own meals. They noticed her movement, however, and stopped eating. Nikki asked, "What? Did you find something?"

Standing up, Evie tried to keep her voice calm. "I might know the location of two secret entrances for the Carlisle hunters' den. I need to contact Bram or Kai before they fly off to rescue Murray. Otherwise, they could end up finding an empty set of rooms and not know why."

Charlie gently laid her plate on a free spot on the couch. "How reliable is your information?"

Evie straightened her shoulders. "Using a collection of reports taken from the locals, the DDA confirmed the locations with radar, so I'd say fairly reliable. The only concern is the information is a year old."

Charlie raised an eyebrow. "How do we know the hunters are unaware of the DDA's discovery and switched escape methods? A year is a long time. Any number of changes could've been made."

While not being questioned would make things easier, Evie respected Charlie's drive for certainty. "Well, to be honest, we don't know if they've changed escape plans. But even if the hunters know about the DDA's discovery of those two exit points, there are bound to be other tunnels. If they are still using them, having a dragon or two circling in the sky to look out for other exit points would be a good idea. I need to tell Bram."

Charlie gave her a once-over. "You'll do well at Stonefire." Before Evie could do more than blink, Charlie said to Nikki, "Patch her through to the secure number."

Nikki moved to the landline phone near the kitchen. Returning to her laptop, Evie scrolled to the coordinates and walked over to Nikki. Just as the dragonwoman held out the phone for her to take it, a boom reverberated through the air.

Nikki tossed aside the phone and pushed her behind the kitchen island counter. The dragonwoman whispered, "Stay here," and moved out of Evie's line of sight.

A loud crash sounded inside the cave dwelling. As dust swirled in the air above her, she decided the intruders must've blown in the door.

As the sounds of shuffled feet and flesh pounding flesh filled the air, Evie tried to think of what she could do to help. She'd spent the last seven years with the DDA, but the role never required training beyond basic self-defense. Even then, most of it was aimed toward dragon-shifters. She had no idea if the people inside the dwelling were human or not.

She had no training, no weapon, and was trapped inside a cave. Things weren't looking good.

Then she heard a female grunt of pain and Evie decided hiding wasn't going to help anyone. It was time to see if they were here for her.

Stashing the laptop inside the cabinet of the island counter, Evie took a deep breath and peeked over the counter top. Charlie was taking on two people dressed in black with bandannas over the lower half of their faces in some kind of hand-to-hand combat she couldn't identify. Glancing over at Nikki, the other dragonwoman was struggling to defend the blows from another person dressed in the same attire because of her injured arm and shoulder.

The clothing and height of the three invaders told her they weren't dragon-shifters. If she were to place a bet, they were dragon hunters.

Which meant they were probably here for her. Nikki and Charlie would just be a bonus.

As Nikki stumbled from a blow to her injured shoulder, Evie made a decision and stood up. Clapping her hands together, she yelled, "Hey, hunters, looking for me?"

Her heart thundered in her chest as all eyes locked on to her face. Not wasting a moment, she continued, "My name is Evie Marshall. If you're here for me, leave the two women alone and I'll cooperate."

Nikki said, "No, Evie, don't do it."

The person in black opposite Evie punched Nikki's injured shoulder. Hard. The dragonwoman huddled over and moaned with pain.

Evie clenched her fists to prevent herself from rushing to Nikki's side. Instead, Evie raised her eyebrow. "Well? Are you here for me? Otherwise, I have a secret weapon back here and I'm not afraid to use it."

The person in front of Nikki walked around the hunched over dragonwoman and faced her. "Love, I'd bet a million pounds you don't have a weapon back there. You're bluffing."

Her heart thumped harder, but Evie had years of practice concealing her emotions. She kept her face nonchalant, just barely. "You can either test me or answer my question. I would think if you're here for me and I offer to go with you without a struggle, it would save you some time."

One of the two people still keeping an eye on Charlie said, "She's right. Who knows when the dragonman will be back."

She detected a hint of worry in the person's voice. They must be afraid of Bram. She could use that to her advantage.

The person closest to her, whom she designated as "the leader", replied, "Protocol Y."

In the blink of an eye, both the leader and the two people near Charlie pulled a tag on their black vests and tossed small, smoking metal objects at both Nikki and Charlie. As soon as the light purple smoke reached the faces of the two dragonwomen, they collapsed and didn't move.

Evie caught herself before she cried out. Showing attachment to the pair might do them more harm than good. She would treat them as nothing more than bodyguards.

The leader looked her in the eyes. "Now that your dragon friends are out of the way, let's talk."

Remember, Evie, don't look to Nikki or Charlie, or you might breakdown. After a deep inhalation, she said, "As long as you didn't kill the two guards, my offer to cooperate still stands."

The leader kicked Nikki in the side and Evie steeled herself not to react. The leader said, "As long as our scientists didn't make a mistake with the dosage, they'll live."

Evie guessed he was telling the truth. After all, Nikki and Charlie's blood was too profitable to waste on killing them, which meant no matter what Evie did or said, they would take her friends alive.

Since her capture was all but inevitable unless Bram suddenly showed up, her priority was to leave a clue for Stonefire to use when they searched the cave dwelling later. But what could she do?

Then she remembered the phone. From the corner of her eye, she saw the landline receiver laying on the desk. If she were lucky, someone was still listening in. She could communicate that way.

She focused on the leader and said, "Right, then tell me what I need to do to keep the two guards alive."

The leader motioned with his fingers and his two team members flanked him on either side. He put out a hand and the person on his left placed a small vial into his palm. The leader held up the vial. "Drink this and we won't shoot your friends."

Evie raised an eyebrow. "You want me to drink a strange, blue liquid, no questions asked? How do I know you're telling the truth and will keep your promise?"

The leader held out the vial. "You don't, but this is the only time I'm offering it. Next, we'll take you by force and kill them."

They wouldn't. She prevented herself from calling the man on his shit and put out her hand. "Hand it over." Once the leader placed it in her palm, she curled her fingers around the vial. "Right, then just tell me this: are you with the Carlisle hunter gang?"

The leader growled. "We're not a gang, love." He took out a gun, unlocked the safety, and aimed it at Nikki's head. "Now drink the bloody vial."

Evie uncorked the vial. While the man's words hadn't been a full confession, they sounded like an admission to her. She only hoped the information reached Bram before it was too late. If she used the 'correct dosage' remark to make a guess, she decided Charlie and Nikki had probably been dosed with the periwinkle and mandrake root, which meant they couldn't shift for a few days. They would be kept alive until they could be drained of blood, but who knew what the hunters would do to Nikki and Charlie in the interim.

There was only one option to take. Evie put the vial to her lips and drank the bitter liquid. She only hoped she could find a way to save her friends. Or, if nothing else, a few days was enough for Bram and the others to find her. Evie refused to think of the alternative.

Her vision swam before the world went black.

CHAPTER TWENTY-TWO

Bram sat down across from Olivia, whose hands and feet were chained to the metal desk in front of her. Her restraints were made of hardened steel. If she were to shift, the steel would break her human wrists before eventually snapping. Despite her daft move of working with Neil Westhaven, the lass was clever enough to stay in her human form. With the entire Protector team on the watch, she would never escape with broken arms and legs.

He studied her a second. Her heartbeat was only slightly faster than normal and she wasn't fidgeting. Given the female had been quite temperamental as a young adult, he had no doubt the change was because of Neil.

Bram reached out to his dragon. *Help me question her. I need our dominance combined to make both halves submissive.*

It will be difficult. Olivia's dragon is strong for a female. I will try.

You're supposed to be oh-so-strong, cocky one. Just help me.

His dragon rumbled a not-quite-happy yes. Bram fixed his stare on Olivia and said, "Tell me about Neil."

Olivia merely replied, "No."

Bram channeled his inner dragon and forced every bit of dominance into his voice he could muster. "I'll ask one more time, lass, before I alert the clan about your activities. Your parents wouldn't take kindly to everyone knowing their daughter is a traitor." Olivia's posture gave way a bit. At least, she still cared for her parents. He continued, "You were found near Carlisle when you were supposed to be in Wales. Tell me why."

"I want guaranteed protection first."

The idea of protecting a traitor didn't sit well with him, but Bram forced aside his disgust in order to do his job. "I need something to go on first, Olivia. And I won't ask again."

As they stared at one another, Bram allowed his dragon to come and go into his mind. His eyes flashed between slits and round pupils. Olivia's bravado faded as her shoulders slumped further. She was about to give in.

He raised an eyebrow and the female said, "I was supposed to meet Neil, but the Protectors found me before he arrived."

"Why were you meeting him?"

Olivia shook her head. "I gave you something. I want guaranteed protection. The dragon hunters will hunt me down once they hear I was alone with you."

"You'll just turn your back on Neil, without so much as a backwards glance?"

"Neil was offering me power I could never obtain here, and that's no longer an option since I'm sitting alone with you. Simon Bourne will see it as a betrayal and a threat to be eliminated. My life is more important than protecting Neil's."

Olivia's words pretty much confirmed the suspicion about a traitor in the clan. Bram didn't like Bourne taking such an interest in Stonefire.

Eyeing the dragonwoman across from him, he needed to proceed carefully. He wasn't about to pamper a traitor, yet he wasn't about to lie to her, either. He said, "Even if I grant protection, you'll still be kept under house arrest."

"Again, I will be alive."

And she'll bloody try to find a way to escape. Still, every minute he spent garnering meaningless reassurances from Olivia was another minute the dragon hunters could be harming wee Murray.

Bram folded his arms over his chest. "Fine, you will be guarded but just know if you shift and try to escape, you'll be taken down and handed over to the DDA. Come to think of it, step a fraction out of line and I'll hand you over to the DDA. I don't give second chances to traitors."

Olivia nodded. He had a feeling she'd break that promise before long, but he merely said, "Then tell me about Neil's connection with Simon Bourne."

She hesitated a second before she answered quietly, "Neil has formed a tentative alliance with Simon Bourne and the Carlisle hunters. He feeds them information in exchange for money and protection from the local human authorities. It's how he's remained off the radar since you banished him last year."

He nodded. A dragon-shifter without a clan was usually taken into custody by the DDA until a clan would accept him or her into their fold. "What was your role in all of this?"

"In exchange for information about what was happening here, I received payments. My goal was to relocate to Romania, where dragon clans have more power over the local authorities."

His dragon piped in. *She wishes for the old days, but the old days were filled with death. Controlling humans only makes them want to kill us more. Working together is better.*

Bram agreed, but didn't have time to argue dragon-shifter history with his inner beast.

He raised an eyebrow. "What sort of information did Neil, and by extension, Bourne, ask for?"

She shrugged one shoulder. "What you'd expect— weaknesses on our borders and patrol; notification of clan gatherings; any sort of discord that could be used to weaken the clan's unity."

"Stonefire has the strongest bond amongst all British dragon-shifter clans."

"That was before the human DDA inspector showed up. On the drive back here from Carlisle, one of the Protectors mentioned you claiming the human as your mate. If Neil or the Carlisle hunters find out about that piece of information, it can be used against you. Not everyone in the clan will approve their leader passing up the dragon-shifter females for a human."

The bloody young Protectors and their mouths. He would mention the slip-up with Kai. After a chat with him, they'd think twice about gossiping in the future.

Bram moved his hand to the table and tapped his fingers. "Here's what else you're going to do in exchange for protection." Olivia made a sound of protest, but he ignored it and continued, "I never said I wouldn't ask for more demands. You're going to dictate everything you know about Neil and Bourne, as well as what knowledge you've passed on. One of the Protectors will stay until you're finished, with another in the room ready to call the DDA if you refuse to help. If Kai and I are satisfied with the results, I'll extend protection. If not, then I will hand you over to the DDA. I suggest you cooperate."

Before Olivia could make any sort of reply, Kai burst into the room. The worry on his head Protector's face stopped any reprimands. Instead, Bram stood up and asked, "What happened?"

Kai motioned with his head toward the door. "Not in here."

Seducing the Dragon

A sinking feeling gathered in his stomach. Kai was usually calm and collected under pressure. The worry on his clan member's face meant something awful had happened.

The instant Bram shut the door behind him, Kai said, "Evie and the others have been taken."

Bram's dragon pushed to the forefront of his mind. *I told you we should have protected her. We must find her.*

I need information first. After shoving his beast aside, Bram said, "Tell me what happened, and quickly. My dragon is not happy at the moment."

"Well, Nikki reached out via the secure line, supposedly because Evie had found something in the data. But before the human could come on the line, there was a mini-explosion, some fighting, and talking. Since the phone line was still connected, one of my Protectors was able to decipher the faint conversation."

Bram put more pressure against his dragon's invisible prison to keep him restrained and bit out, "And?"

"Evie was a clever human, and she tricked the attackers into admitting they were Carlisle hunters."

His clever lass. "Olivia didn't give me anything about the location of Bourne's headquarters, and I doubt she'll be able to. Has Zain found out anything new from the dragon hunter we captured?"

Kai nodded. "Yes, he managed to extract some locations in exchange for protection for the hunter. Everything is already in motion. Since Evie is your mate, I need to know if you want to come with us when we leave."

Bram's dragon roared. *Of course we will go. I will channel my anger to rescue her. The hunters won't stand a chance.*

Unless they bring out the laser guns.

I will be careful.

Bram focused back on Kai. "Let me call Tristan and a few others first so the clan isn't leaderless when we finally leave. I'll meet you in my office in twenty minutes to hash out the details. Also, find someone you trust to take Olivia's statements. If she refuses to cooperate, lock her away and call the DDA once all this mess is sorted."

Kai nodded and left Bram alone in the hallway. As much as he wanted to roar along with his inner beast, he forced himself to remain calm. Anger would hurt Evie. He needed his brain to save her.

Even if he died trying, he would save his mate. Simon Bourne and his dragon hunters were going down.

~~~

Evie looked around her windowless room for the millionth time and let out a sigh. The room, quite simply, was a prison cell with just a bed, sink, and toilet. Oh, and a faulty, occasionally flickering fluorescent light overhead, which made her think of bad horror movies. Hopefully, she'd avoid a similar fate to the victims in those movies.

No one had taken her in or out of the tiny room since she'd regained consciousness. Despite watching the guards and their movements whenever they brought meals, she had yet to find a way to take down the armed guards, let alone devise a plan of escape.

She also had no idea of what had happened to Nikki and Charlie. While Evie didn't know how long she'd been unconscious after drinking the bitter liquid from the vial back at Bram's hideout, it wouldn't be much longer before the effects of the mandrake root and periwinkle wore off the two Protectors.

Seducing the Dragon

Once Nikki and Charlie could shift, the hunters would drain them dry. If Bram or his Protectors didn't find them in time, the two dragon-shifters would die.

No. Evie wasn't about to let the dragon hunter bastards win. At some point, they would question her. When that time came, she would try to find a way out of her prison. It was highly unlikely she could free the two dragonwomen alone, but if she could escape, she could bring help.

The dim fluorescent light overhead flickered right before someone unlocked the outside bolt of her door. Wherever they were keeping her contained, it's wasn't a new or very solid building. That would be a major oversight if Bram found her before she managed to escape.

The door opened and she blinked against the bright light in the hall. She could just make out a silhouette of a man. He said, "Stand up. We're moving you."

His strong West Country accent marked him as distinct from the other guards who had brought her food. Simon Bourne must be recruiting nationwide.

Being complacent would hopefully lower everyone's guard, so Evie stood and blinked a few more times until she could make out the large nose, high brow, and balding blond hair of the guard dressed in black. If she managed to escape, she could look through the database of known dragon hunters. Reporting it would probably do bloody nothing, but it was ingrained in her to memorize details.

Once she was close enough, the guard took her arm and led her down a dirty hallway filled with cobwebs and debris. The building hadn't been used commercially for years and was probably condemned.

After going down one dimly lit hallway and then another, the guard halted them in front of a reinforced door. Unlike back in her cell, the door was new and made of some type of metal.

Before she could think too long about what that signified, the guard rapped on the door. It opened and her ears were bombarded by a weak dragon's roar.

Her heart squeezed. *Oh no. Please don't let it be Nikki or Charlie.*

The guard pulled her into the room and Evie was careful to school her face into a neutral expression. Just in time, too, as they entered a massive cavern of a room. People dressed in either the same all-black outfit as her guard or in white lab coats bustled to and fro. Machines she couldn't identify, medical equipment, and a bevy of weapons were spread across the room or attached to the walls. Then her eyes reached the far corner and she stopped breathing.

An adult green dragon, female if she were to guess by the size, was locked inside a giant prison cage, a muzzle on her snout and with some kind of band trapping her wings. In addition to the shackles on all four limbs and tail, various hose-like tubes were connected to the main arteries in the neck, forelegs and hindquarters. The dragon struggled to roar above a normal talking voice range. Each one was progressively weaker than the previous.

The sight simultaneously made her want to be sick as well as want to punch every person harming the magnificent creature in the face. What kind of person could put a dragon-shifter through such torture, not even drugging the dragon unconscious to spare her the pain of being drained dry?

She clenched her jaw. Dragon hunters, that's who. Nothing she'd read in reports in the past could have prepared her for the sight before her. A quick glance told her the smiling and preening hunters in all-black who were watching the struggling beast were enjoying the sight.

Sick bastards. If something wasn't done soon, the green dragon would die.

Evie tried to recall Nikki's dragon color, but couldn't remember it. She had no idea of Charlie's dragon color, either.

While she wanted to be optimistic, Evie was a realist. Catching a dragon was bloody difficult; the green dragon had to be one of Stonefire's Protectors.

Each second she stood gawking was lost time to find out what she could about her current situation. While she may not be able to save the green dragon in the cage, there was still a chance she could save the other Stonefire Protector as well as baby Murray.

Tugging on her arm to catch her guard's attention, she asked, "Why did you bring me here?"

The guard tightened his grip and she resisted a flinch. "Shut it. You'll find out soon enough."

After the guard gave one last look at the weakening dragon, he pulled Evie to the corner farthest away from the large beast.

The corner was sectioned off with a light blue curtain. The guard pushed aside the curtain to reveal a glass room. Inside was a sleeping baby with dark hair, in a see-through plastic or glass crib.

Her throat closed up. It was little Murray.

Breathe, Evie. You need your brain or you don't stand a chance. With one last exhalation, she focused on the details. The room was currently empty of anyone else but the baby. Much to her relief, Murray wasn't attached to a machine, nor did he have tubes running from his body. She knew his blood was useless at curing illnesses until he reached maturity, yet she had half-expected the hunters to be testing the little one. They still might yet do so, but for now, Murray was alive and even looked peaceful.

As she continued to scan the room for weaknesses, the guard said, "The boss wanted you to see what we do here. The dragon baby is safe for now." The guard squeezed her arm tightly, and Evie looked at his face. He continued, "Next, I'm taking you to an interview. Remember the brat and the dragon in the corner. If you want the baby and the other dragon to live, nod that you'll cooperate now."

She wasn't about to give up and tell the hunters everything they wanted to hear, especially since they'd betray her at the first opportunity. But, for the time being, Evie bobbed her head to buy herself some time.

The guard turned her away from Murray. "Right, then let's go."

As they walked back toward the same door they'd entered, Evie caught a glimpse of the green dragon in the corner. She was barely making any noise at all now, nor was she struggling.

Evie fought back tears. The beautiful dragon, who had most likely been sent to protect her, was dying.

Right then and there, she made a promise to the green dragon. *I'll find a way to expose these activities to the world. Your death won't be for nothing.*

The dragon caught her eye and she swore it nodded at her, almost as if she could hear Evie's thoughts. However, before she could do anything else, Evie was back in the dark rundown hallway again.

As they walked in the opposite direction to her cell, Evie's heart pounded in her chest. She'd been angry before, but the sight of the green dragon had made her furious. No living thing should be put through such torture. If the DDA didn't know about these activities, she would make sure they did once she was free.

And if her supposition about the DDA assistant director, Jonathan Christie, was correct and he was allowing the dragon hunters to carry on with little to no oversight, then she'd reach out to the media. Something needed to be done.

They stopped in front of an old, slightly rickety door and Evie pushed aside her anger. She needed a cool head for the 'interview'. If she let her temper out, Evie wouldn't be able to help anyone, let alone herself.

Chapter Twenty-Three

After two bloody days of planning, researching information on Evie's laptop, which they'd found tucked away in his hideout, and scouting the area around Carlisle, Bram and Kai were ready to make their move. As much as Bram's dragon wanted to fly in and deal with the threat as it came, Bram wasn't about to risk Evie, Murray, or his two captured Protectors. He owed it to his people to bring everyone back alive, not just his mate.

Yet keeping his inner beast in check became harder with each passing hour. The incessant roaring inside his head was not only irritating, but also signaled how close Bram was to losing control. No amount of scolding, let alone reasoning, had been able to silence his inner beast.

As such, Bram would be infiltrating the hideout while still in his human form.

Looking up to the night sky, he could just make out the shadows of his clan members flying in the air. To the average person, they might hear the beat of wings and dismiss it as the wind. Bram, however, knew there were two wing formations of dragons circling as quietly as possible in the sky above.

He hoped they were quiet enough to avoid notice by the hunters.

Bram signaled to his team of five dragon-shifters in human form to wait. Once two dragons swooped down and gently landed on the four-story abandoned building in the distance, he nodded at his team and moved.

Surveillance and tapping their local contacts had confirmed the Carlisle hunters were still using one of the two tunnels reported in the DDA's reports. That was how Bram and his team would try to enter the hideout.

Bram crept through the bushes hiding the entrance until he found the branches concealing the door. Picking up a stick, he pushed aside the branches and held his breath, but he didn't see any sort of alarm or keypad. Simon Bourne and his hunters were clever enough to have silent alarms, but Kai and Bram had earlier decided to risk it. After all, Bram's break-in was a decoy meant to divide resources.

Raising a hand to signal for everyone to be ready to fight, Bram rammed his shoulder against the wooden door. On the second try, the old wooden frame splintered. The door gave way and he barreled inside the dark tunnel.

The blackness was no match for his keen dragon-shifter eyesight. With each step, his dragon pushed harder against the wall inside his mind. Bram's patience with his dragon was nearing its limit. He took what few precious seconds he could spare to say, *You can help me soon. I need my human half for the plan to work.*

Let me out. I will make you stronger.

When the time comes, I'll do that. For now, stop with the bloody roaring. You're acting like a two-year-old who didn't get the sweets he wanted at the shop.

His dragon huffed. *I'll give you ten minutes of peace. If you don't use me by then, I'll find a way out of this prison.*

Bram could just make out a door at the end of the tunnel. He quickly instructed his beast, *Wait for my signal.*

Slamming up the partition in his mind again, Bram stopped in front of the new door and put his ear against the cool, metal surface. He could hear more than a few pairs of footsteps on the other side as well as the shuffling of equipment and muffled shouts. Chances were the hunters knew the tunnel had been breached.

Good. If they were occupied with Bram and his team, they wouldn't notice the other dragons' approach.

He conjured up Evie's dark blue eyes and red hair. Using her face to focus, Bram shoved against the door, but the metal didn't give. Unable to shift, he'd brought along a gun. Taking it out, he flicked off the safety and shot the lock three times. With another shove against the door, it gave way and he burst into a giant room of chaos.

People were running about, picking up supplies. On the far side of the room, a large group of human men and women dressed in black formed a protective circle around a smaller group of humans in white lab coats. Before he could try to guess what they were moving, the white coats escaped the room via the exit on the far side.

It was then his eyes fell on the green, unmoving dragon in the corner. The restraints and tubes told him what had been done to Charlie, and his inner dragon howled with grief.

The female Protector was dead.

Bram growled. The grief and sadness would have to wait. More than just about anyone, Charlie would understand the need to focus on saving the living before grieving for the dead. Channeling some of his inner dragon's anger, Bram gave the signal and rushed toward the twenty or so black-clad humans still inside the large room.

SEDUCING THE DRAGON

It was time to give Kai the distraction he needed to save the others. Bram refused to believe Evie, Nikki, or Murray were also dead. No, if he had any say, no more of his clan members would die in this building at the hands of the hunters.

~~~

Evie had been abandoned to the dilapidated conference room for about twenty minutes. There was a guard outside her door, so escape wasn't an option.

After a quick check of the room and not finding any real faults, she sat down. Rather than processing everything she had seen in the last half-hour, the silence had brought back memories of the dying green dragon. A dragon who was most likely dead.

First, human sacrifices had died because of her. After today, a dragon's death would also be on her head.

For someone who had joined the DDA in hopes of protecting life, Evie saw more death than she liked. Even though she'd saved more lives than not, it was still difficult to digest.

Only remembering what she told Bram, about how she survived the two human sacrifices, helped with her guilt about the dragon. She would analyze what had caused the dragon's death later and find a way to prevent it from happening again. Evie refused to believe this old building full of dragon hunters and scientists would be her final resting place. Somehow, some way, she'd escape and find help.

The door opened behind her. The sound sharpened her focus, although it took everything she had not to ask what had taken so bloody long.

She turned to see a male dragon-shifter in human form swagger into the room. The dragonman's hair was longer and he sported a short beard, but there was no mistaking the eyes, the tattoo, or the slightly crooked nose of Neil Westhaven.

Instead of screaming "murderous traitor," Evie merely raised an eyebrow and asked, "What do you want?"

The dragonman flipped around one of the chairs and sat with the back facing his front. "I'm guessing by your nonchalance you're either quite calm in stressful situations or you've seen my face before."

"Both, but I'm more curious about you. They're killing a dragon in this facility for their blood, yet you don't seem to care."

He shrugged. "Stonefire interfered in my private life. When they chose to protect the human sacrifice over one of their own, I stopped caring about them. I left and made sure the human female got what she deserved. The only good thing to come of it all is the child has secured my position here."

His tone was almost bored, the bastard. *Punching him in the face won't accomplish anything. You need information, Evie Marie, or you'll never make it out of here.*

Right, then. With a deep breath, she forced her voice to remain neutral when she said, "So they're starting a blood farm here, aren't they?"

Neil didn't so much as blink an eye at her question. "Clever human. I'm not sure how you found out about that piece of information, but it proves you might be more useful than the other DDA inspectors."

Evie clenched her hand into a fist under the table; otherwise, she would punch the dragonman in the nose. "If you've been working with Simon Bourne this whole time then you know it's only a matter of time before he discards you, too."

Neil waved a hand in the air. "You know nothing of my deal with Bourne." The dragonman leaned forward. "Now,

enough chit chat. It's time for you to answer some questions."
Evie opened her mouth to reply but Neil cut her off. "Don't try
to bargain or use your wits to outsmart me. You do anything daft
and we'll drain the other Protector. Her life is in your hands."

She gritted her teeth. "What do you want?"

"You're going to help me take down Bram Moore-
Llewellyn."

Un-bloody-likely. "And what makes you think I can do that?"

"Don't play coy and waste my time. The only reason Bram
would carry you to a secret hideout himself is that you mean
something to him." Neil's nose scrunched up. "I reckon he wants
to take you as his mate, not that I understand why he would
choose a human female willingly."

Yes, her urge to punch him was growing harder to resist.

Luckily, her time down south with Clan Skyhunter had
prepared her for dealing with dragons of the arsehole variety.
"Listen, we can waste time while you make your snide, passive-
aggressive remarks, or we can get to the point. Take your choice."

Neil's jaw clenched and she resisted a smile. The
dragonman said, "Only because I'm not allowed to kill you will I
let that slide, human. Now, tell me the truth: Does Bram intend to
take you as his mate?"

Since Neil knew about Bram taking her to the cave hideout,
Bourne's spies were probably everywhere. Lying would be
pointless. The truth might just give her the time she needed. "Yes.
But before you make a snide comment about how I stink or Bram
must be desperate, tell me why you think Bram will trust me if I
miraculously walk out of here and back to Stonefire?"

"Male dragon-shifters are careless when they think with
their cocks."

"Are you speaking from experience?"

Neil growled. "I'm the one who will ask the questions from here on out. Bram will trust you. That's enough. So if you want the other captured dragon to live, you'll cooperate. Understand?"

Evie didn't want to make a blanket promise, but she was running out of ways to stall. The dragonman's eyes had flashed to slits a few times. If she wasn't careful, she would provoke the inner beast. Unlike Bram, she didn't think Neil would restrain himself. There was a lot he could do without killing her.

She was about to wing it when a light started flashing in the corner, near the ceiling.

Neil stood. "Fuck, there's been a breach." He looked at Evie. "No doubt, it's your dragonman. Stand up. You're coming with me."

While waiting earlier, Evie had inspected the boarded-up windows, hoping to find an escape route. While they were sealed up tight, maybe, just maybe, if there were dragons flying around outside they could scent Neil. They would be looking for any dragon-shifter inside the building. If she could make some noise to signal her location, it might speed along her and Neil's discovery.

It wasn't like she had the strength of a dragon-shifter to punch out the wood covering the windows. The chairs, however, were old and of the four-legged metal variety rather than the newer roller chairs every office in Britain sported these days. She could lift one and make as much noise as possible.

Decision made, Evie stood. As Neil reached for her, she dashed to the end of the conference table, picked up the plastic back of the chair, and hurled it at the nearest window with every iota of strength she possessed. The board held, but a large smack reverberated through the air. *Please, oh, please, let that attract their attention.*

Seducing the Dragon

In the next instant, Neil had her arms behind her back. He tugged and she drew in a breath at the pain radiating from her wrists and shoulders. Neil said, "You're trapped, human. Pull a stunt like that again, and I'll knock you unconscious."

Her heart thundered in her chest. Not because of the fear of the dragonman behind her, but rather she waited to see if her last ditch effort would save her.

Yet as Neil maneuvered her out the door of the conference room, her hope faded. *Damn it.* She'd failed. The remaining Protector was most certainly going to die because of her actions. Not to mention Murray's future would be as a prisoner in a cell.

Bram, where are you? Just because Evie was used to taking care of herself didn't mean she didn't need help. She was definitely in over her head. The instant she gave up her faith in Bram, it would be game over.

Neil dragged her to the end of the hallway when a loud crash sounded behind them. Glancing over her shoulder, she saw a large, gold dragon staring straight at them. The conference room behind him was gone. The dragon was holding on to the edge of the remaining floor with his talons.

Neil pushed her forward, forcing her head to turn back around. Then she heard the faint crackling sound she'd heard before, when Bram had shifted. A male voice shouted, "Running won't help you now, laddie."

It was Finlay Stewart.

He whistled and another dragon crashed in front of them. If many more dragons made the same entrance, the building would collapse.

The red dragon snarled and Evie hoped it was intended for Neil and not her.

Neil extended and pressed a half-talon against her throat and said, "Fly away, mates, or I kill the human."

Before the red dragon in front of them could do anything, Evie heard a thud, and Neil dropped to the ground. She blinked, turned, and saw a piece of twisted metal poking out of Neil's back. Looking up, a very naked Finlay Stewart strode toward her. He said, "Not the smartest bloke in the world, giving me his back." He put out a hand. "Come, lass. I'm going to shift back and take you out of here."

Evie's momentary shock concerning the dead dragon-shifter at her feet wore off. "What about Murray and the others?"

Finn took her hand and pulled her toward the gaping hole in the side of the building. When she dug in her heels, he stopped and turned toward her. His eyes flashed to dragon slits and back as he said, "I don't have time for your stubbornness right now. Just know that Bram is providing a distraction to give the rest of us time to find you and the others. I don't have telepathic abilities, so I don't know if the others were rescued or not. But I do know the longer we dawdle, the greater the chance your male will be hurt."

Bram was in the same building as her. The thought warmed Evie's heart.

Looking at the Scottish leader, she wondered about trusting him. But if Arabella, who had been through hell and back, didn't mind his company, Evie would go with her gut feeling that Finn was only trying to help her.

Besides, once they were free and clear of the dragon hunters' den, Evie had inside information that might help Stonefire's rescue efforts.

Decision made, she put one foot in front of the other until she tugged Finn's arm and he matched her pace.

Reaching the edge of the gaping hole, he released her hand and rolled his shoulders before giving her a piercing stare. "You try to run away while I'm shifting, and I won't be so gentle next time. Understand?"

His tone was full of dominance and brooked no argument. She was starting to see why Finn was a clan leader.

Evie nodded and watched as Finn ran and jumped into the hole. Before she could even reach the edge of what was left of the floor, a gold dragon's talon swooped inside and wrapped gently around her. Finn beat his wings and took them into the sky.

It took her a second to catch her breath as the city of Carlisle and then the English countryside sped beneath her. She might not be afraid of heights, but Finlay Stewart was going to receive an earful once they landed and she ensured everyone was safe.

She was also going to ask him how he shifted mid-air. In all her years working with dragons, she had never heard of anyone being able to do that.

As each mile passed below them, Evie hoped she had made the right decision to go with Finn. She had always been a reasonable person and made the most rational choices. In this instant, however, she was doubting herself. Would the other dragons find Murray and the remaining Protector? Would Bram make it out alive? Judging from her experiences with his inner dragon, he probably wasn't helping matters. If the inner beast was too distracting, Bram could die.

And if anyone else died because of her, she wasn't sure how she could face the clan again.

Chapter Twenty-Four

Bram ducked another fist and swept the hunter bastard's leg with his foot. Once the man was on his back, Bram crouched down, smacked the human male's head against the ground, and turned toward the next dragon hunter.

While some of the hunters had escaped, Bram and his team were working their way through the rest. None of these low-level hunters had anything resembling the periwinkle and mandrake root concoction used on Quinn several days ago. That told him the use of the mixture wasn't widespread.

If nothing else, he'd succeeded in that part of his mission.

As he moved to the side to dodge another blow, he punched the human male in the kidney. It was time to finish them. His effectiveness at being a distraction had worn off. If his people hadn't rescued Evie and the others already, they probably never would.

He signaled his team to shift and take care of the remaining humans. One by one, the five people in his team shifted into a multitude of dragon colors. A few seconds of knocking hunters against the wall with their forelegs and tails, and it was done.

Looking at the five dragons towering over him, Bram instructed, "Sniff out the exits and ensure everyone in the room is unconscious. I'm going to take care of Charlie."

Seducing the Dragon

Trusting his people to do their jobs, he rushed toward the unmoving bulk in the corner. Since the dragon was no longer a threat, the cage door was open. Bram went inside and put a hand on his fallen clan member's head. He whispered, "I'm sorry we failed you, Charlie. I will look after your mate and child and protect them to the best of my ability."

The green dragon didn't move or respond, and Bram's inner dragon released a mournful croon.

Patting Charlie's head one more time, he reached into one of the pockets on the vest he wore and pulled out a syringe. He lifted Charlie's right eyelid and plunged the syringe through the eye to the brain. Once he inserted all of the contents, he pulled out the needle and stepped back.

Even dead and drained of blood, Charlie was only freshly dead. When put directly into a dragon-shifter's brain, the chemicals in the mixture Dr. Sid gave him should force one last shift back.

He held his breath, hoping it wasn't too late. As much as he didn't want to leave her, there was no way they could carry her body in its dragon form back with them.

Another second ticked by and Charlie's body flashed. She lay on her stomach in human form, pale and motionless.

His throat choked up at the once strong and loyal dragonwoman. Charlie had been one of the first females ever to become a Protector in Clan Stonefire. She had been one of the handful he trusted enough to guard his mate.

Even now, he didn't blame Charlie for Evie's capture. Bram's own pride and cockiness had cost him. No location would ever be secure as long as Simon Bourne was still free.

Noticing his dragon brethren moving toward the exits, Bram pushed aside his memories and anger. Charlie may be dead, but hundreds of others still depended on him.

Clearing the emotion in his throat, he scooped up his fallen clan member into his arms and headed back toward their escape point. Four members of his team were back in human form, with one remaining in his dragon form to stand guard. They all glanced down at Charlie's body.

Losing one of the clan was never easy, but losing a female was even worse given how few of them there were. He couldn't allow his men to be distracted.

Looking at each of his men in turn, Bram said, "Charlie's mate deserves the chance to give her a proper goodbye, but he won't be able to do it if we don't return. Save your grief until we reach home." His men straightened their shoulders and gave slight nods. "Right, then two of you go in front of me and two behind me." Bram moved his gaze to the purple dragon standing above him. "Once we're clear, you know what to do."

The dragon bobbed his head. Bram adjusted his grip on Charlie's body and said, "Right, then let's go."

Two of his men entered the tunnel and Bram followed, careful to keep Charlie's body close. He wasn't about to damage her any further by accidentally banging her head against a sharp rock.

As soon as they reached the tunnel's exit point, he was greeted by the sight of two dragons with large baskets, waiting to carry any wounded back to the clan.

Even though his dragon's impatience had eased at the sight of their fallen clan member and Bram could probably shift to fly home, it felt wrong to leave the dragonwoman alone for her last flight in the sky.

Seducing the Dragon

His dragon said, *Stay with her. It is best for when we land.*

Rather than think about facing Charlie's mate, Bram crawled into one of the waiting baskets and hugged the dragonwoman's body in his arms.

Soon they were all in the air. Bram barely paid attention to the purple dragon bursting free of the building below him, nor the ensuing collapse of the building. The death of one of his own was always hard, especially when she had been on an assignment given by him. There was also the chance more blood was on his hands if Evie, Nikki, or even wee Murray were also dead.

The thought of never seeing Evie again made his stomach drop. She'd wheedled her way into his heart in a short time. Not only would his clan be worse off without her, he would be, too. Life would be lonely without his human.

His inner dragon said, *Our mate must be alive. I would know otherwise.*

Dragons aren't telepathic. You have no way of knowing if she's alive or not.

She is alive. I won't think otherwise.

His beast was right. Charlie's death was hard enough; constantly thinking of Evie being dead as well would distract him from protecting his clan. As with most of his adult life, his needs would have to come second.

Still, Evie had bloody well be alive. If the hunters had killed her too, he would unleash his dragon on any hunters he could find until Simon Bourne was dead. Bram was done playing nice and by the rules; the next time the hunters messed with his clan, they would regret it. No one else was going to die on his watch if he could help it.

~~~

Evie had no idea how long she and Finn had been flying before she recognized some of the surrounding peaks and valleys. They were approaching Stonefire's land.

She was nearly home.

Evie blinked back tears. The adrenaline had mostly worn off during the long flight. After two days of little sleep or food, she was on the verge of crashing.

Yet if she gave in and crashed, she would have to wait even longer to find out who was still alive. Finn mentioned Bram serving as a distraction. Had her dragonman survived? Sure, she believed in him, but after what had happened with Nikki and Charlie, it would only take one canister of periwinkle and mandrake root to bring down the leader of Clan Stonefire.

It wasn't just Bram she was worried about. Murray could still be in the hands of the hunters; it also killed her not knowing which female Protector was still alive.

Her throat closed up and Evie closed her eyes. Tears wouldn't help anyone. If anything, it would sap what little strength she had left. No, she should focus on what needed to be done once she landed. Even if everyone was whole and hearty, there was a lot of shit still to tackle. Stonefire was her clan and she wasn't about to see them fall because of her or the stupidity of the dragon hunters. Her main concern, apart from everyone being alive, was that it was past her deadline to check in with the DDA. While she rather doubted it given the DDA's track record, they could be lying in wait at Stonefire's gates. Handling them wouldn't be easy, but she could do it.

No, she was more afraid of the media circus that could also be waiting. Given everything that had just happened with the dragon hunters, she didn't want the media to make any connection between the incident in Carlisle and Clan Stonefire. Any act of violence, even in most cases of self-defense, ended in a suspension of the sacrifice program, sometimes indefinitely. While Bram would be strong for the clan if that happened, she knew it would devastate him.

Bram. Her dragonman had bloody well better be alive. Life without him would be lonely. She'd miss his humor, his cleverness, and, she wasn't afraid to say, his cock. Stonefire's leader was the whole package and had ruined her for all other men. Since she had no plans of living as a nun, her will alone would ensure his safety. She knew that was impossible, but her willing him alive with every cell of her body couldn't hurt, especially since she was falling in love with him.

Already she dreamed of adopting Murray and starting a family with Bram. If they could ever spend some time together without another threat to the clan or her life, she would fall hard and fast for her dragonman.

Finn made his final descent. Opening her eyes, she clung to the hope that Bram would be there to greet her. *Bram, please be alive. I don't know if I can help pick up the pieces of your clan and mobilize them without you.*

The Scottish leader slowed his wings and much like Bram had surprised her with his agile movements, Finn was the same way as he rotated his grip on Evie until she was no longer horizontal with her stomach facing down but vertical.

She had just enough time to notice a large tent off to the side of the secondary landing area before the windy backlash forced her eyes shut.

Her feet touched the ground. Before she could open her eyes, Finn released his grip. As the sound of him flying away filled her ears, she wobbled and opened her eyes.

Despite the spinning sensation in her head, Evie scanned the area. When she looked toward the tent, a familiar face raced toward her.

It was Nikki.

She could barely string together the fact Charlie must be dead before the young dragonwoman embraced her in a one-armed hug and said, "Evie! You're alive." Nikki hugged her more tightly. "I'm so sorry we failed to protect you. Bram's words about the place being secure had put me off my guard." The woman leaned back and her brown eyes searched Evie's. "But even so, the fault is mine. I'm done being naive and stupid. If you give me another chance, I will protect you with my life next time."

Tears prickled Evie's eyes. "Don't be daft. You have nothing to prove to me. I'm just glad you're alive." She squeezed the dragonwoman's good shoulder. "Charlie didn't make it, did she?"

Nikki's face shuttered. "No, they killed her."

Sensing the young dragonwoman's guilt, Evie gave her friend a little shake and said, "Blaming yourself won't accomplish anything. Channel your anger and sadness toward defeating the dragon hunters. Understand?"

Nikki searched her eyes. Her voice was quiet when she said, "You sound like Bram."

"Well, I like to think he sounds like me." Nikki gave a small smile and Evie was glad. She continued, "What about Murray? And speaking of Bram, where is he?"

Nikki motioned with her head toward the tent. "Bram hasn't returned yet, but Murray's over there. Kai's wing of dragons rescued him from the fleeing scientists. He's fine, but Dr. Sid is checking him over one last time inside the medical tent just to be sure."

Rather than think on why Bram hadn't returned yet, the desire to see Murray to verify he was okay rushed through her body. The little boy was alone, both of his biological parents dead. He needed a family, and Evie wanted to be his new family.

Giving her friend one last squeeze, Evie ran across the field and into the open-air tent. Scanning the interior, she saw Dr. Sid's trademark ponytail and rushed over to her side. Murray was lying in a makeshift cradle and drooling in his sleep. The sight of him alive eased the tightness around her heart a fraction.

Her voice cracked. "Murray." She looked to Dr. Sid. "Can I hold him? Please?"

Dr. Sid studied her a second before she replied, "I can't find anything wrong with him, apart from needing some sleep. Just be careful not to wake him up."

Nodding, Evie gently lifted Murray's little body and laid him against her shoulder. She breathed in his warm baby scent and closed her eyes to keep herself from crying. The baby might be sleeping and oblivious, but holding his warm weight in her arms brought on a fierce protectiveness she couldn't describe. Maybe the feeling was what mothers felt when holding their children.

Squeezing him tighter, she vowed to make sure Murray, and all of the other dragon-shifter children, would have a much safer future. Whatever Melanie Hall-MacLeod needed to help launch her book and make it successful, she would do it. There was no bloody way she'd allow them to be used as blood slaves.

Evie had no idea how long she stood there with her eyes closed, holding Murray's warm little body, but the sudden shouting behind her snapped Evie out of her bubble of baby bliss. Opening her eyes, she looked toward the commotion and saw a wing of dragons approaching. One of them even carried a basket.

She wanted to hold Murray and never let go, but Evie forced herself to lay the little boy down. He would be safe enough with all the medical staff and other dragon clan members watching over him inside the tent. With one last brush of his soft, chubby cheek, Evie moved toward the crowd in front of the medical tent.

Scanning the dragons in the sky, she saw one blue beast, but the size and shape was off. It wasn't her dragonman.

Her heart hammered in her chest. Where was he? If Kai and Finn had both returned, then the dragons in the sky should be the final wave. Bram should be with them. Unless he was hurt and being carried in the basket.

Or, worse, he could be dead.

No. With a deep inhale, she pushed aside her fears and mustered up her DDA inspector persona. She needed to be strong not only for herself, but also for the others. If she showed worry, the rest of the clan would no doubt echo it.

Raising her chin and straightening her shoulders, Evie barked, "Clear the area. If someone's hurt, we don't want Dr. Sid wasting time to push you lot out of the way."

The various clan members glanced at her. For a split second, she hesitated, but then remembered no one in the crowd would hurt her. Unlike with Clan Skyhunter, Evie had special protections. The clan members would never hurt their leader's mate.

Right, Evie. Be the hardass inspector. You can do it. On the next exhalation, she raised an eyebrow and made a shooing motion with her hands. When the dragon-shifters created a pathway, she let out her breath.

Dr. Sid squeezed her arm as she rushed past. As soon as the black dragon laid the basket on the ground, Bram stood up with a naked woman in his arms.

"Bram," Evie whispered. Her dragonman met her eyes and the world stilled around her.

Even at a distance, his pale blue eyes were filled with sadness. Glancing toward the woman in his arms, she saw it was Charlie.

Aware of the clan's eyes on her, Evie made her way quickly but efficiently toward the basket. By the time she reached it, a male dragon-shifter had also approached the basket. Bram's gaze moved to the dragonman. She heard him say, "I'm sorry, Hudson. It was too late. The hunters were cruel, but your mate died fighting to the end. The entire clan will remember her sacrifice and forever honor her service. She will not be forgotten."

The dragonman took Charlie's limp body from Bram and hugged her close. His eyes were wet and voice scratchy when he said, "Thank you for bringing her back to us. Now we can give her a proper goodbye."

Evie's throat closed at the sight of the dragonman holding his dead mate. Evie would also look after Charlie's family. After all, the dragonwoman had been captured protecting her.

Bram nodded and the dragonman walked away with Charlie in his arms.

Then Bram looked at her and she stopped breathing. She was torn between scolding him for taking so long to return and pulling him close to kiss him until they both lost their breaths.

Before she could so much as blink, let alone make a decision, Bram leaned over, picked her up, and placed her in the basket with him. He pulled her flush against his hard body and whispered, "Evie, love. You're alive."

And then he kissed her.

Chapter Twenty-Five

Bram had given in to his dragon's need, hauled Evie's soft body up against his, and not caring who saw, he kissed her.

As he seamed her lips with his tongue, she opened and he devoured her mouth with hard, strong strokes. He'd seen the anger in her eyes and he was determined to make her forgive him. An argument would fire his blood and as much as he wanted to take his mate hard and fast, he didn't have the time.

No, he'd merely have to placate her with his tongue.

As he continued to explore her mouth and squeeze her soft curves against his body, her arms finally wrapped around his chest and hugged him tightly, never surrendering her mouth to him.

The lass had forgiven him.

His dragon roared. *The kiss is not enough. I need to feel her skin. The frenzy is becoming harder to control.*

Sensing his dragon's tension, he roamed Evie's body with his hands. He cupped her face with one hand and placed his other on her arse. He squeezed her large arse cheek, wishing he could mold and shape her soft skin without any barriers. But as his dragon roared again to take their mate to safety and claim her, Bram caressed Evie's face with his thumb. The skin-to-skin contact eased his dragon's tension a fraction.

His inner beast said, *Please. I need her. Deal with the clan so we can fuck her.*

Breaking his kiss with Evie was one of the hardest things he'd ever done, but it was better than taking her in front of everyone.

Staring into Evie's dark blue eyes, he could make out relief, happiness, and even affection. Every cell in his body wanted it to be love, but it was too soon.

Caressing her jaw again, he whispered, "I'm sorry, love. I have plans involving us both naked and alone, but right now, I need to check on my clan."

Evie ran a hand up his chest and gave it a pat. "You mean our clan."

He smiled. "Yes, our clan."

"Good. I only have one condition before you go."

He frowned. "Now isn't the time for conditions, love. I need to see who's hurt and then check in with Kai and Finn. The hunters could be planning an attack right now."

The stubborn glint was in her eye and he resisted a groan. She said, "Just listen a minute, dragonman. It's important."

"Make it quick, love."

She bristled but shook her head. "I don't have time to argue. My condition involves Murray."

He blinked. "Murray?"

Evie nodded. "Yes. I just need you to tell Dr. Sid it's okay for me to take him home and then you can do whatever needs to be done." She leaned against his body and whispered, "We'll both be waiting for you when you're finished. I might even forgive you for taking so long to come back to me and let you fuck me once or twice."

Bram's heart skipped a beat. His dragon tried to take over at the mention of fucking, but he pushed the beast aside to focus on the other half of her words. "You want to look after wee Murray?"

Evie smiled. "More than that, I want to adopt him. He can be the start of our new family."

Ignoring his beast's attempts to break out of his mental prison, Bram searched Evie's eyes. "Are you sure?"

Evie frowned. "You should know by now that if I suggest something, I mean it."

Stroking her waist, he murmured, "Sorry, love, but the last two days have been hell. I can hardly believe it'll end happily for anyone, let alone me."

His mate softened. "I'm here, Bram, and I want to make sure nothing happens to Murray ever again. I think together we can give Murray the love he deserves as well as make sure he's safe." She frowned again. "Just make sure you stay alive to help me. Being a single mother with a dragon-shifter baby is not something I want to experience. Murray needs his dad."

Hearing her call him Murray's dad warmed his heart. "I don't want the lad to be fatherless, now, do I? That's only slightly worse than upsetting my mate."

Evie smiled and he knew he'd won. She gave him a quick kiss. "Good. Now that's settled, let's see Dr. Sid so you can finish up with the clan and come home to me."

He nodded. "Also, I'll have Melanie and Tristan sent over to you. You've been imprisoned for two days and while you're strong, you may yet go into shock."

"I'm not a delicate flower, Bram Moore-Llewellyn. But I can use the help as I need to shower and have not the faintest bloody idea of how to care for a baby."

He squeezed his mate. "You'll do fine, love." He kissed her one more time and pulled away. The loss of her heat stabbed his heart. "Now, I need to find Finn. I hear he's the one who rescued you."

"Yes, he did. But he also killed Neil Westhaven."

Bram blinked. "What?"

Evie brushed his chest with her hand. "You didn't know?"

"No."

"Don't be too hard on him. Neil was threatening to kill me at the time."

His dragon growled. *It is good the traitor is dead.*

Yes, but he should have faced trial. Killing one of our own plays into the image all dragon-shifters are monsters.

If the traitor was threatening our mate, then our mate's life is more important than trying to impress the humans.

His dragon had a point, but he didn't have time to argue. He'd already spent more time with Evie than he should have. While the hunters' base near Carlisle was destroyed, it didn't mean they wouldn't attack again.

Bram crawled out of the basket, helped Evie out as well, and then faced the members of his clan standing in front of him. "I want everyone to return to their cottages and remain alert. Until I release the order, off-site visits won't be allowed."

A male voice shouted, "How long, Bram? I can't run my business if I can't deliver goods to the humans."

Bram looked at his clan mate and said, "Don't worry, Alex. I won't keep the restriction in place any longer than necessary. But I think staying alive is more important than delivering your wood carvings, aye?"

The same male replied, "Aye."

Bram nodded and then did a sweep of the crowd in front of him. "Go. I'll let you all know when things have returned to normal."

Seducing the Dragon

As the crowd dispersed, Bram took hold of Evie's hand and tugged her inside the tent. While he'd taken care of Murray a hundred times in the last five months, he was anxious to see the lad. From here on out, Murray wouldn't be a charge but his and Evie's son.

Sid and her core nursing staff were finishing up the minor wounds on Bram's team. Sid noticed him, gave an order to one of her staff, and stood in front of him. After giving him a once-over, she said, "You'll have a bruise on your jaw, but you'll live. Do you have any other injuries I should be worried about?

Evie moved slightly in front of him and gave an assessing glance. "Stubborn dragonman, if you're hurt, say so."

He put up his free hand. "I'm fine. Before the two of you insist on checking every inch of me to verify my words, Sid, I want you to let Evie take Murray home. Provided, of course, he's well."

Sid moved her gaze to Evie and back. "Yes, he's healthy if not a little tired and dehydrated. But does your mate know how to take care of a dragon-shifter child?"

Evie's grip on his hand loosened and he squeezed her fingers in reassurance. "She'll be fine. I'm sending Mel and Tristan to help until I finish with clan matters."

Sid turned and Bram followed, tugging Evie along until they stood over wee Murray. The babe was asleep, but his cheeks were full of color and the lad seemed content. His dragon chimed in, his previous tension somewhat diminished. *Our son will be well.*

That was fast. I expected it to take longer to claim him.

Our mate wants him, so I want him. The baby will make her happy.

Bram watched as Sid lifted Murray and placed him in Evie's arms. The sight of his mate holding the babe caused a rush of warmth to spread throughout his body. He said to his dragon, *The baby will make us all happy.*

He brushed Murray's soft cheek. "Be a good lad, Murray, and mind your mum until I return." Glancing over at Evie, her eyes were wet. He rubbed her back and said, "You'll do all right, love. Don't worry."

Evie met his eyes. "I'm not worried about that. It's just that I never thought I'd have the chance to be a mum. Hearing you call me that makes me happy."

"Evie." He gave her a gentle kiss. "This is just the beginning for us. We'll see how you feel when he wakes you up at four a.m. The reality might be a little less rosy."

She frowned. "Don't you have clan matters to attend to?"

Bram laughed. "I can take a hint. You want to enjoy the rosiness of being a new mum without a reminder of the realities to come."

Scanning the tent, he noticed Nikki sitting in a corner. He shouted her name and motioned for her to come. As she made her way toward them, he whispered to Evie, "I really do need to take care of some clan matters. Nikki will take you home. Are you okay with that?"

Evie's stern voice returned. "Why wouldn't I? Blaming her for my capture and Charlie's death is pointless. A number of factors contributed to that happening."

The corner of his mouth ticked up. "Good. My clever lass understands." Before Evie could reply, Nikki approached. Her expression was unsure and her posture a little less confident. Bram decided to fix that. He ordered, "Take Evie and Murray to my cottage and help her settle in. Then call Melanie and Tristan to come over. I want you to watch over them all until I return."

Nikki twisted her hands. "Are you sure you want me to do it?"

"Nikola Gray, unless there is a valid reason for why I shouldn't send you, then you have your orders."

Nikki's voice was faint when she replied, "The last time I was given an assignment, Charlie died."

Pushing aside the loss of his clan member, Bram focused on healing the one still alive. "You aren't responsible for Charlie's death. If anyone is to blame, it is I. Now, do you wish to keep arguing or will you take Evie and Murray so I can ensure the clan's safety?"

Nikki glanced to Evie, but his mate smiled and bobbed her head in encouragement. Nikki looked back to him. "I'll take her."

Bram nodded. "Good lass." He turned toward Evie, kissed Murray's forehead and then hers. "I'll be home soon. Don't destroy the place in the meantime."

Amusement danced in Evie's eyes. "I'll see what I can cook up."

As he watched his family walk away, his dragon said, *Hurry up. I want our mate as promised.*

You are calmer than five minutes ago.

Tasting our mate and claiming our new son helped, but I need her. I am strong, but even I am reaching my limit.

His inner beast's words rang with truth. Bram couldn't risk the mate frenzy breaking out while the clan was still in danger. *Then let's find Finn and Kai.*

After checking in with Sid, Bram left the tent. It was time to talk to Kai and find out what Finlay Stewart had done.

~~~

Finn knocked on the door of Tristan MacLeod's cottage. He didn't have long before Bram found him and while Finn stood by his decision to kill Neil Westhaven, the act might break the new alliance with Stonefire. If that happened, he wanted to see Arabella MacLeod one last time, both for his dragon and himself. For some reason, he didn't want the lass to think ill of him.

The door opened. Instead of Tristan's glare, Arabella's dark brown eyes greeted him. She frowned and said, "What do you want?"

"It's nice to see you, too, lass. Can I come in?"

"Why? Everyone is gone. It's just me."

"Aye, that's why I'm here."

She hesitated. He'd gleaned from his last visit that the lass didn't like being alone with strange men. "We can talk out here, if you like."

"Since we've spoken twice, I'm sure all you need to say can be said whilst standing at the door."

He gestured at his body, clad only in a casual kilt. "It's a wee bit cold out here and the warmth from the door is enticing."

Her eyes darted to his chest and lingered. Finn was leaner than most dragon-shifter males, but only because he was taller. The lass's eyes didn't seem to mind and his dragon rumbled. *I want to feel her skin.*

Not now.

His beast growled, but Finn ignored him and cleared his throat. "If you're quite done with the view, let me in or toss me a jumper." Arabella's cheeks flushed and he grinned. "Unless you want a longer look at my epitome of male perfection."

Seducing the Dragon

The dragonwoman rolled her eyes and stepped back. "If coming inside will help stem your cockiness, then hurry up."

His dragon crooned. *She likes us. This is good.*

Rather than dwell on his inner beast's words, Finn stepped inside the cottage and headed into the living area. Once he plopped down on a chair, he dove right to the point. "Have you considered my invitation to come to Lochguard and set up the secure connection?"

She stayed standing on the far side of the room. While her heart rate appeared normal, he didn't like the distance.

Arabella answered, "I told you I'd think about it. My answer hasn't changed."

"In my experience, maybe means no. Come, Arabella. It would benefit us both."

She frowned and her voice was careful when she said, "Explain that last bit."

His dragon cautioned, *Don't scare her.*

I won't coddle her. She doesn't want it. "You've proved your skills to me and I won't have to double-check your work, which saves me time."

"And what is the benefit to me?"

"You'll have the chance to interact with people who will treat you with care because you're a stranger, not out of pity for your past. While I've only heard the rumors, I expect everyone on Stonefire knows the truth."

Arabella took a step toward him. "I don't want your charity."

His dragon piped in. *Don't fuck up.*

Finn stood up. "It's not charity, Arabella MacLeod. I need your skills and you desperately need a break from the clan. Even your brother coddles you."

She took another step toward him. "Leave my brother out of this."

"It's true, aye? Your brother is as careful as the rest. I don't know about you, but living day in and day out with everyone walking on eggshells must be exhausting. Yes, you've gone through something terrible. But isn't it time for you to face the world and live your life?"

They were only a few feet apart from one another. Finn never flinched from her gaze. Aye, she was angry, but there was longing there too.

Arabella's voice was quiet and full of steel when she said, "I think you should leave."

His inner beast roared, but Finn ignored him. "I'll leave, but think on it, lass. Lochguard may not be perfect, but it could be a fresh start for you."

Provided, of course, he hadn't fucked up the alliance with Stonefire.

Before the dragonwoman could reply, there was a knock on the door followed by Bram shouting, "Finlay Stewart, I know you're in there. We need to talk."

Arabella retreated to the far side of the room. It took everything Finn had not to walk over and corner her against the wall to provoke her fire again. Both man and beast liked her fire, maybe a little too much.

There was more pounding on the door and Finn sighed. "It looks like you're getting your wish, lass."

He waited a beat, but Arabella remained silent. Rather than push too far, he gave a flourishing bow and went to the door. Opening it, Bram glared up at him and said, "Where's Arabella? Is she okay?"

Finn motioned behind him. "She's back there. Lass, care to shout out so he doesn't kill me?"

Arabella peeked her head around the corner. "I'm fine, Bram. Finn was just leaving."

Bram looked between him and Arabella, but if the Stonefire leader expected an explanation, he wasn't going to get one.

Finn raised an eyebrow. "You're letting the heat out. If we're walking and talking, then let's go."

Bram gave him one more assessing stare before he turned around and started walking. Finn took one last look at Arabella and dared to say, "Think on it, lass. I mean it."

Then he was out the door. As he lengthened his stride to catch up with Bram, Finn hoped that wasn't the last he saw of Arabella MacLeod. The lass deserved to have laughter and light in her life and Finn wanted to be the one to give it to her.

When he caught up with Bram, Finn decided not to delay the inevitable. "Care to tell me if the alliance still stands or not?"

Bram stopped and turned toward him. "As much as my dragon doesn't like it, I can handle you being the one to rescue Evie. She's alive and I thank you."

Finn raised an eyebrow. "But?"

"But killing Neil Westhaven was never part of the plan. You were supposed to help capture him and bring him back alive."

Finn's dragon huffed. *Why would he want the traitor alive? It's better that he's dead.*

He likes to play by the rules.

Hmph. Sometimes the rules are meant to be broken.

Finn agreed, but from what he'd learned of Bram Moore-Llewellyn over the last week, it would take a different way of thinking to preserve the alliance. "He had your mate in his arms, a talon at her throat, and was one slice away from killing her. The idiot had his back to me and I took advantage. Wouldn't you have done the same?"

Bram stared at him a second before he answered. "Maybe. My concern is you acting out of turn and ignoring what we agreed upon for the alliance. You being unpredictable could hurt my clan."

Finn's dragon snarled and he pushed back his beast. "The foundation of the alliance is helping each other out and protecting one another when needed. I plan on doing that. My ways may differ from yours, but after what happened today, I reckon you and I need to stick together. The rescue was too easy."

Bram's tension eased a bit. "I feel the same. Simon Bourne isn't an idiot. I can almost guarantee he allowed us to rescue Evie, Nikki, and wee Murray. I just don't know why."

"Right now, neither do I. But think about it—if we're both gathering intelligence and keeping an eye on the dragon hunters, then our clans both have a greater chance of surviving whatever Simon Bourne may throw at us."

The Stonefire leader assessed him, but Finn didn't waiver. While the alliance would make his life easier, he could find another way to protect his clan if it came to that. Giving up wasn't in Finlay Stewart's vocabulary.

Another second passed and then Bram nodded. "Right, we'll keep the alliance for now, but on one condition."

"What?"

"Leave Arabella MacLeod alone."

Finn's dragon growled. *No. I don't like that.*

Rather than answer his dragon, Finn merely replied, "If she seeks me out, I won't turn her away."

Bram searched his eyes. "While not quite the answer I was looking for, it's better than nothing. You hurt her, and I will cut off your bollocks.

His inner beast said, *We would never hurt her.*

I know, but he's blind to what Arabella needs. Let's humor him for now.

His dragon conceded. Finn put out a hand. "So the alliance remains?"

Bram took his hand and shook. "Aye, but you've yet to earn my full trust."

"Good, because you have yet to earn mine."

CHAPTER TWENTY-SIX

Evie halfway closed the door to the spare room off the main living area. Melanie had brought a bassinet for Murray to sleep in and Evie had just managed to get Murray back to sleep after feeding him. She was glad the little boy wasn't fussy. Her exhaustion was setting in and it had taken every bit of strength she had left to coo Murray to sleep without crashing herself.

She stood outside the door for a few more seconds to make sure he was truly asleep before heading into the living area. Melanie and Tristan sat together on the sofa. Each of them held a sleeping baby in their arms as they leaned against one another. The thought of her and Bram doing the same thing, albeit with some argument or another filling the room, made her smile.

Melanie grinned. "You have the new mother glow. I imagine not having to recover from birthing two stubborn dragon-shifter babies and nearly dying makes it all a bit more fun."

Tristan growled. "I thought we agreed you couldn't use that against me anymore."

Mel looked at her mate. "Two days of labor and me dying for a few seconds means I can use it whenever I want."

Tristan grunted and Evie pounced. She didn't have the strength to listen to them argue. "Thanks for coming over. I never would've known to mix a little soy milk into the formula to help calm the restless dragon inside Murray."

Mel waved a hand in dismissal. "No worries. I had no idea, either. Dragonwomen have something similar in their breast milk that we lowly humans don't. You'll be surprised at how much even half-dragon babies can eat. Their inner dragons might not be able to talk to their human halves until they're about six or seven years old, but their energy carries over into the babies' actions." Melanie looked up at her mate. "Sometimes, it's handy to be mated to a dragon-shifter teacher. If you have any questions, I'm sure Tristan will help."

Tristan grunted which Evie took to mean "if I have to". She still didn't understand how the mostly nonverbal dragonman had won Melanie's heart. At some point in the future, Evie would ask for details.

Evie settled down in the armchair across the room from the pair and released a sigh as she snuggled into the cushions. A shower and some food had done wonders to revitalize her, but exhaustion was too tame a word for the tiredness coursing through her body. On top of that, she was anxious for Bram's touch.

While this was a prime opportunity to ask questions about dragon babies, Evie's brain didn't want to cooperate. With each passing minute, her attention span and intelligence were slipping. *Bram had bloody well better come home soon so I can get some sleep. I can't do anything to help Stonefire with a brain that feels like a bowl of pudding.*

Melanie, on the other hand, hadn't been through hell over the last few days and had no problem saying, "I have an idea I wanted to run by you."

Evie folded her hands over her belly and resisted a sigh. "What is it?"

Mel shifted the baby in her arm. "I imagine Bram will be mating you soon, am I right?" Evie nodded and Mel continued, "How would you feel about inviting some of the human press to the event?"

Evie rubbed her forehand with her hand. "Care to tell me the bigger reason behind it? Because I have a feeling there is one."

Mel nodded. "You know how I'm nearly done with my book about Clan Stonefire? Well, I want to test the waters before dumping a large amount of information on the human population."

Even in her tired state, Evie knew it was a clever move. With herculean effort, she forced her brain to work and said, "That way, if chaos breaks out or incites violence against the dragon-shifters, you know to hold off on releasing the book."

Mel smiled. "Exactly. So will you do it?"

Sitting up, Evie replied, "You want me to share one of the dearest memories of my life with a bunch of journalists and hope they don't slander Bram and me the next day?"

Melanie shook her head. "We'd only use the most trusted news outlets and they'd be required to sign a legally binding document between you and them."

"And since I'm human, the law will hold."

"Yes. On top of that, no recording devices or mobile phones will be allowed. It'll be an old-school style reporting job, with pen, paper, and film-only cameras."

Evie raised an eyebrow. "Have you discussed it with Bram yet?"

Melanie winked at her. "No, but I figure if you agree, you have more persuasive ways of convincing him."

Tristan chimed in, "Melanie, I don't need to think of my clan leader's sex life."

Melanie lightly slapped her mate. "Don't be such a prude."

Tristan merely shook his head and Evie took control of the conversation again. "Let me discuss it with Bram first."

"Awesome. Between you and me, he should say yes."

Evie didn't like the thought of Melanie convincing Bram of anything.

However, before Evie could warn off the other woman, the front door opened and Bram's voice carried down the hallway, "Evie? Are you awake?"

Her exhaustion melted at his voice and she rushed into the hall to wrap her arms around him. Snuggling into his chest, she murmured, "You're home."

He squeezed her tightly against his body. "I missed you, too, love. How's Murray?"

"He's asleep. Mel and Tristan gave me a crash course in how to care for dragon babies."

"So does that mean you don't need my help at all?"

Evie looked up and frowned. "Don't you dare tease about that. If you think I'm going to take care of Murray ninety-nine percent of the time without you, then you're in for a big surprise."

Her dragonman chuckled. "If you remember the first day we met, I was doing a fine job taking care of him all by myself."

She laid her head back on Bram's chest. "I'm too tired to match wits. How about we thank Mel and Tristan, send them on their way, and take a nap?" Bram's chest tensed under her cheek. Looking up, she saw his pupils flashing between slit and circles. "What's wrong with your dragon?"

His pupils remained round as he replied, "Remember the secret my dragon had been keeping from me? Well, you're my true mate, Evie Marshall, and I'm not sure how much longer my inner beast can control the frenzy."

She blinked. "True mate? How is that even possible?"

Bram's eyes flashed more frequently. "Tristan, I know you can hear us. Explain it to Melanie and leave." He looked down at her, his pupils flashing even more quickly. "Please, Evie. If I can claim you once, I might be able to stave off my beast long enough to explain it all."

His voice was gravelly, almost as if the man and dragon halves were talking at the same time. Bram sounded like he was in pain.

Whatever exhaustion she had before melted away as adrenaline pumped through her veins. Her mate needed her and Evie wanted to take care of him.

She framed his face with her hands, the feel of his warm skin giving her some energy. "Then take me to your room and fuck me, Bram."

He growled and raised his voice. "Tristan, show yourself out." Then Bram took hold of her elbow, and guided her to a room not far from where Murray was sleeping. No doubt, her dragonman could scent their son and didn't want to be too far away in case something happened. The thoughtfulness warmed her heart.

As soon as they entered the spare bedroom, she forgot about Murray as Bram tore off her pajama top and bottoms until she was naked. He then pushed her onto her back on the bed, shucked his clothes, and covered her body with his. The feeling of his warm, chiseled body and hard cock pressing against her stomach made her pussy pulse. She was already wet and ready for him.

Bram's slitted pupils stared at her as his hand caressed between her legs. One brush of his finger against her clit made her cry out. He growled and thrust two fingers inside her. "My mate. I need to fuck you until you carry my young."

If it weren't for Bram thrusting his fingers long and slow inside her, she might question that statement. Then he brushed against her clit with his thumb, and she decided not to argue. She opened her legs wide. If there was a child, so be it. She would love him or her. "Then take me. I'm waiting for you."

With a growl, Bram removed his fingers and thrust his cock into her. While it had only been a few days, his size made her moan and dig her nails into his back. The act triggered something primal and her dragonman squeezed her breast as he moved his hips.

As he increased his pace, he leaned down and took her nipple into his mouth. He bit her hard and Evie cried out at the mix of pleasure and pain. Then he swirled his tongue over the tender bite before sucking her deeply. Moving a hand to his hair, she pressed him against her breast, urging him to do it again. When he bit her a second time, lights danced in front of her eyes before an orgasm exploded inside her.

When Bram released her nipple with a pop, she cried out in protest. The sound then prompted her dragonman to pull out of her completely.

Blinking in confusion, Evie demanded, "Why did you stop?"

Glancing at her dragonman, she watched his flashing pupils again. In a gravelly voice, Bram said, "I need to taste you first. Then I'll allow you to come again."

She frowned "Allow me to come? Bram..."

His warm, rough hands rubbing over her breasts, her stomach, and then her plump thighs stopped her in mid-sentence.

As he continued to caress her skin, she almost forgave him for pulling out.

She parted her legs when he pushed and Bram stared at her pussy. He whispered, "Mine," before leaning down and licking her slit with his warm, wide tongue.

Evie clutched the sheets as he continued to flick and lick her sensitive flesh, careful never to touch her clit. With each passing second, her frustration grew until he finally swirled her clit with long, hard strokes. She drew in a breath and clenched the sheets tighter. When he nibbled, she moaned and whispered, "Oh, god, yes."

He growled and the vibrations went straight to her clit. Another few swirls and nibbles and another orgasm took her as she cried out Bram's name.

She'd barely stopped spasming when Bram moved away from her pussy, flipped her over, and raised her arse in the air. He thrust into her from behind and she moaned at the fullness. "You're going to kill me with sex, aren't you?"

"Not kill. Make you carry my young."

His words shot straight between her legs. Yes, when the clan wasn't in danger, she rather liked his dragon's primitive nature.

He slapped her arse and moved. Between two orgasms and a dragonman's giant cock moving inside her, she forgot about everything but the man behind her and the way he made her body come alive.

CHAPTER TWENTY-SEVEN

Three Weeks Later

Evie snuggled into Bram's chest and sighed. Half-awake, she nestled up against her dragonman feeling warm and content, especially since her morning sickness had yet to rear its ugly head.

Placing her hand on her stomach, Evie smiled. The DNA compatibility test she'd had as a teenager only seemed to hold true for any dragonman who wasn't her true mate. As Bram's dragon had said, true mates would always be compatible. It had only taken five days of mind-blowing frenzied sex interspersed with eating and taking care of Murray before Bram had scented her pregnancy. She would keep the joy on his face in her memory until the day she died.

Murray squirmed in his bassinet to the side of their bed and Evie waited to see if her little man would wake. Once Bram's frenzy had stopped, they had decided to keep the little one in their room for a few weeks. Dragon-shifters often relied on scent for comfort, Bram had told her, and Murray being near his new parents and branding their scent into his memories would help with the transition.

While Bram was filling in the gaps of her dragon-shifter knowledge, she was also educating Bram and the Stonefire Protectors on the ways of the DDA and on British law. Most of her free time, however, was spent taking care of their newly adopted son and Bram.

Not that she'd have it any other way. Murray was Bram's and her son. Anyone who tried to take him again would feel the combination of their wrath. The dragon hunters had been quiet, but the clan was prepared for another attack. Especially given what was to happen today.

Bram nuzzled her cheek and whispered, "I can hear you thinking." He placed a hand over hers on her abdomen. "Is the wee dragon baby making you sick again?"

"No." She gave him a gentle kiss. "But I'd be lying if I wasn't a little worried about today."

He nibbled her earlobe and some of the tension eased out of her body as he said, "You're already my mate, Evie Marshall Moore-Llewellyn. Today is just a ceremony contrived by you and Melanie to give the humans a taste of our clan in preparation for Mel's book release in a few months."

"I know, and I understand how much our clan needs this exposure, but what if the journalists don't keep to their signed contracts and paint the clan as monsters who force human women to marry them with threats to their lives?"

Bram ran a hand to her hip and squeezed. "Be yourself and every human in the room would think twice before suggesting I force you to do anything, love."

She smiled. "It's good you finally realized that I'm in charge here."

Her dragonman rolled until he was on top of her, trapping Evie with his body. He whispered against her ear, "Is that so, my little human?"

His hard cock pressing against her stomach made her pussy throb, but she wasn't about to let him win completely. "Sex is different than every other aspect of our lives." She moved against his cock and Bram hissed. Smiling at her power over him, she said, "Although if I told you to take me right now, would you listen?"

Bram gently bit her neck as his hand roamed down her body and under her nightshirt. "I was planning on fucking you anyway before I let you out of this bed, so it's a moot point."

Then his fingers rubbed the swollen flesh between her legs, and Evie had to bite her lip to keep from moaning and waking the baby. She whispered, "I could get out of this bed if I wanted to. You know I keep a bat nearby."

Her dragonman smiled against her cheek. "That's for my dragon, and he's not in control right now."

Bram teased her slit and wetness rushed between her legs. *Damn it.* She couldn't let him win.

Clenching down, she managed, "If you ever act the part of an arsehole, I'll smack you in the balls, too."

Her mate's eyes flashed to slits and then he said, "Enough talking."

He thrust a finger inside her pussy and Evie bit her lip harder. When he found her g-spot and rubbed, Evie lightly scored her mate's back with her nails. "Then stop teasing and fuck me, Bram."

"Is that an order?"

Frowning, she opened her mouth to reprimand him again when Bram thrust his cock inside her and Evie clutched his shoulders.

As he moved, she widened her legs before pulling his face down to hers and kissing him. His tongue was as possessive as his cock, exploring and stroking the inside of her mouth. Then the cheeky bastard thrust harder into her pussy, daring her to make a sound, but Evie wasn't about to concede defeat. Let him do his best; she wouldn't be the one waking the baby.

Instead, she moved a hand to his arse and dug in her nails. Bram gave a faint growl and his eyes flashed to slits and back. His dragon always liked it when she was a little rough. She dug her nails a little harder, but he was on to her game and merely pistoned so hard the bed moved.

She was about to scrape his back with her nails in warning when Bram pinched her nipple and she swallowed her moan. If he kept his attention on her nipples, she was in trouble.

Then her dragonman twisted ever so slightly and Evie cried out in pleasure, the sound muffled inside their joined mouths.

Bram stroked her tongue as he pistoned his hips faster. The pressure was building. Evie was done playing games. Moving her hips in time to his rhythm, she needed to feel him come inside her, and not just because it would cause another orgasm. No, even after three weeks, she needed to feel he was alive and still with her.

She loved him with all her heart, even if she hadn't yet told him. She would never tire of him. Her only fear was if Bram, her other half, would be taken from her before she was ready.

Evie clutched his shoulders tighter and brought his chest closer to hers. Bram was her mate and she was never letting go.

Then her dragonman rubbed her clit. Each stroke sent pleasure coursing through her body. Her tender thoughts were temporarily forgotten.

Bram scraped her clit lightly with his nail, and his action pushed her over the edge. She moaned into his mouth as lights flashed inside her eyelids. Her pussy clenched and released Bram's cock as he continued to move.

He then stilled and took their kiss deeper to drown out his own cry.

Since he was her true mate, each spurt of semen ignited one orgasm after another, pleasure to the point of pain coursing through her body. It was a good pain, though, but when she finally came down, she was no more than a boneless heap in Bram's arms.

As she lay on Bram's chest, listening to his heartbeat and Murray's soft snores, Evie realized how much both of the males in her life had come to mean to her in such a short time. She hugged Bram close and the thought of never sleeping in her dragonman's arms brought tears to her eyes.

Blinking them back, she nuzzled into Bram's chest. *Silly pregnancy hormones.* Still, the emotions were true. Bram was her partner in both love and in life. As his warm, rough hands caressed her back, Evie decided she needed to tell him how she felt. Sure, she had no idea if he felt the same or not. After all, they'd only been together about a month. By most standards, that was too fast, but Evie and Bram had never been an ordinary couple.

Still, she wasn't one to back down. Taking a deep breath, Evie propped herself up on her elbows and met her mate's gaze. *Damn the man.* The bastard's eyes were smug.

She still loved him anyway.

Bram patted her arse. "You came close to winning this round, love."

"You didn't make me wake the baby, so it's a tie."

He grinned and squeezed her arse cheek. "Will everything be a competition with you?"

Poking his chest, she said, "Well, someone has to keep your ego in check. No one else will bloody do it, except for maybe Finn."

Her dragonman growled. "I don't like you mentioning his name in my bed."

She rolled her eyes. "So I guess this means the alpha caveman is here to stay?"

"It's alpha dragonman, and yes." He hugged her tightly. "And as much as I'd like to go another round and win, Melanie will be here soon to collect you. I wouldn't want to face her ire, so I'd get up if I were you."

Her heart thumped in her chest. *This was it.* She could leave the bed and tell him she loved him later. It would be safer to make sure Bram felt the same way as her. But a small part of her urged her to keep going. It would only take one dragon hunter raid to steal the love of her life away from her. The thought of him never knowing her true feelings gave her the courage she needed.

Running her hand through the patch of dark hair on his chest, Evie said, "I love you, Bram Moore-Llewellyn."

The one second Bram remained silent seemed like an eternity. Then he grinned and cupped her cheek. "I was wondering how long it'd take for you to tell me with words what I've known for weeks with your expressions." He stroked her cheek with his thumb. "You're everything I never knew I needed. I love you, Evie Marie."

"So you've loved me all this time and never said anything?"

He squeezed her waist. "Bloody woman, I'm trying to pour my heart out here. Can you work with me a little?"

She grinned. "Maybe. If you make it up to me later."

Growling, he raised his face to hers. "Aye, I think I can manage that."

The tenderness in his eyes warmed her heart and Evie decided to stop teasing her dragonman. As he caressed her cheek with his thumb, she whispered the truth, "I don't think I was truly living until I met you, dragonman. So you'd better stay alive or else."

Bram moved his thumb to her lower lip. "Or else what?"

"Or else, this."

She tickled his armpit and Bram's laughter echoed inside the bedroom. There was something about the large, muscled clan leader being ticklish that made her laugh right alongside him.

Two seconds later, Murray's crying stopped the tickling. While the mother side of her was upset Bram woke the baby, the Bram's mate side of her preened at finally winning against him.

Still, Murray's cries went to her heart. She tried to go to the baby, but Bram prevented her a moment and gave her a quick, hot kiss first before releasing her as he said, "Round two will be mine."

Evie smiled at his challenge. "I look forward to you losing again."

Bram laughed as she moved from the bed. She picked up Murray and bounced her baby boy to try to calm him down. Her eyes met Bram's. The love shining in his eyes for both her and Murray brought tears to her eyes again. And for once, she didn't care that her pregnancy made her emotional. This moment was one she'd keep with her always.

~~~

Bram adjusted the sporran-like pouch over his crotch and resisted straightening his formal dragon-shifter attire for the hundredth time. He still didn't know how Evie had convinced him to go through with inviting outsiders to be a part of what should be their special day.

Still, as he scanned the crowd in front of him, the four journalists sitting in the front room were furiously scribbling in their notebooks. He only hoped he'd made the best decision for his clan. While the dragon hunters had retreated for the time being, Stonefire and Lochguard were still searching for the reason why the Carlisle rescue attempt had been so easy. No doubt, Simon Bourne would strike again and Bram had a feeling that next time, more than one person would die.

His eyes fell on Finlay Stewart sitting in the back row. Bram would rather have spent his mating day without the Scottish bastard's grins and winks, but Evie had convinced him to invite the Lochguard leader.

At least Finn was sitting on the opposite side of the room from Arabella. He'd kept his word concerning the dragonwoman, although the glances Ara kept giving the Scottish leader worried Bram a little.

Moving his gaze, Bram checked that Kai was stationed at the rear door, keeping an eye out for any uninvited guests. The journalists had used their contacts in Westminster to gain permission to be on a dragon-shifter's land. It was only a matter of time before others, or Evie herself, figured out a loophole to allow others to visit. His head Protector was determined to make sure any unwanted visitors didn't try to harm the clan.

Then his mate entered from the back dressed in a traditional dragon-shifter dress of cream and he forgot about everything but his beautiful female. The sight of her glowing face and the way the dress hugged her curves warmed his heart, as well as a few other places. When she winked at him, he suddenly forgot why he'd ever try to resist her charms.

A traditional human wedding march played as Evie made her way up the aisle alone. Even if her parents didn't live abroad, they wouldn't have been allowed on Stonefire's lands. Evie had decided to walk alone, as she'd done her entire life until meeting Bram.

His inner dragon said, *She will never be alone again. She is ours. Ours now, eh? I'm glad you decided to share.*

His beast bristled. *The frenzy made me unstable. You know that. Aye, but it's fun to tease.*

No more teasing. Our mate is here.

Bram put out a hand and Evie placed hers in his. Squeezing her fingers, he led her up the three stairs to the raised dais. While he had a second, he whispered, "You're beautiful."

In a rare occurrence, Evie blushed. That made his dragon smug. *She is ours.*

Ignoring his beast, Bram focused on his mate. He could hear her heart hammering in her chest. To give her strength, he squeezed her fingers again, leaned over, and murmured, "Be strong for me, love. We all need you."

She nodded and they took their final places in the middle of the dais. Unlike in a human wedding, there wasn't anyone officiating the ceremony. Dragon-shifter matings were between two people and no one else.

Never taking his eyes from Evie's, he picked up the smaller silver mating band in the box next to them, the one engraved with "Bram's" in the old dragon-shifter language, and the room fell silent. That was his cue to begin.

Bram projected his voice. "Evie Marie Marshall, today I take you as my mate. You are clever and brave with an inner strength rivaling any dragon-shifter. I offer you my mate claim today in front of the clan. Will you accept it?"

Evie stood tall and offered her upper left arm. "Of course I accept."

Good lass. Grinning at his brave mate, he slipped the silver cuff around her arm. The sight of his name on her arm satisfied a primal need deep inside him. Later, he would claim much more than her arm.

Evie reached behind them to take the large silver cuff engraved with "Evie's" in the old language. Holding it up, her voice was loud and steady as she said, "Bram Moore-Llewellyn, I love you and not just because you're clan leader, although that is a bonus." A chuckle went through the room. Leave it to his lass to lighten the mood. She continued, "I love you because you are a strong, caring, and stubborn dragonman who never gives up. I accepted your mate claim. Now, will you accept mine?"

He turned his arm without the tattoo toward her. "Of course, bloody woman, now hurry up. I want everyone to see your name on my arm."

Evie grinned as she placed the cuff on his bicep. His dragon crooned. *I approve of our mate's name on our arm. We should never take it off.*

We'll discuss that later.

Bram took Evie's hands in his, brought them to his lips, and kissed each one in turn. Then he tugged her close and stopped a hairbreadth away from her lips. His whisper was meant only for her as he said, "Shall we put on a good show and convince them how in love we are?"

"Oh, Bram, there's no need for a show. One taste of me and you lose your mind."

He squeezed her tightly. "I rather thought it was the other way around."

"Just kiss me. I love you and want this to be over so we can celebrate both with the clan and with each other."

Bram whispered, "I love you," before taking her lips in a possessive kiss. Uncaring about who was watching, Bram made sure everyone in the room knew Evie was his.

Or, at least, he claimed her as thoroughly as possible while they both still had their clothes on. That possession would come later.

Epilogue

Two Days Later

Evie was typing out a chapter on her current work in progress, *Understanding the UK Department of Dragon Affairs*, when Bram came into the room carrying Murray in one arm and a stack of newspapers in the other.

Her heart rate kicked up. The articles about their mating ceremony had finally arrived.

She rubbed her hands against her trousers before turning from the computer. "Did you read them? What did they say? Are riots breaking out in the streets?"

The corner of Bram's mouth ticked up. "Riots in the street, love? It's just some bloody newspaper articles about our mating."

"Now is not the time to tease me, Bram. I'm pregnant and my hormones are not amused."

He shook his head as he bounced their son in his arm. "You need to come up with a better excuse. That one is becoming a tad old."

With a sound of frustration, Evie stood up and took the papers from Bram's hands. "I'll find out myself, then."

As she scanned the first newspaper, her stomach churned, warning her that if she didn't sit down, she'd be losing her breakfast.

SEDUCING THE DRAGON

When Bram's look turned into one of concern, she knew she must be pale. Her mate's teasing tone was gone. "Are you all right, love? Should I get the trash bin?"

Shaking her head, she moved toward the sofa. "I just need to sit down."

Plopping down on the sofa, she closed her eyes and breathed in and out until the queasiness subsided. Once she no longer felt like throwing up, she opened her eyes to find Bram standing in front of her. He asked, "Are you better, love?"

She waved a hand. "I'm fine. Just let me read the papers."

She barely noticed Bram sitting down next to her as she read the first few paragraphs:

Saturday saw a monumental event in modern British history. For the first time, journalists were welcomed onto a dragon-shifter's land to witness a mating ceremony, which is the equivalent of a marriage between humans. The event took place near the Lake District, on the lands belonging to Clan Stonefire.

Even before the ceremony began, everyone was excited about another dragon-shifter clan leader sitting in attendance. His identity remains a secret. While a few journalists were invited, it was clear the dragon-shifters were wary of the humans on their land.

The ceremony, held between Stonefire's clan leader, Bram Moore-Llewellyn, and former-DDA employee, Evie Marshall, only lasted five minutes before the celebrations began. Everything from the exchanging of arm cuffs to the dancing after the ceremony was fascinating to watch. The traditions between humans and dragon-shifters are similar, yet different.

Evie scanned the rest, which detailed everyone's appearance and behavior. By the end of the article, even she wanted another peek into how the dragon-shifters lived.

Reading the Telegraph, the Guardian, and then the Times, Evie felt the same way after each. The articles were entertaining yet informative and lacked any of the malice of the anti-dragon-shifter crowd.

When she was done, she looked over at Bram, who was bouncing Murray on his knee. She would never tire of the big dragonman playing with the tiny baby.

She smiled and said, "Everything seems fine. The journalists upheld their agreements. All of the articles were fairly objective."

Bram glanced at her. "Aye, I told you not to worry and before you ask again, no, there aren't any riots in the streets. So far, the news has been received well."

"And you couldn't have told me this sooner?"

He grinned. "You're the one who likes to find things out for yourself."

Ignoring his teasing, she pushed on. "Anyway, the reception of the articles bodes well for Melanie. Her release might go ahead as scheduled."

Murray put out his arms and reached for her. Evie took her son from Bram and cuddled him on her lap.

Bram said, "The reception also bodes well for you, love. The DDA should stop harassing you after this. You've turned into the darling of the press."

Evie leaned against her dragonman's shoulder. "I guess now all we need to do is watch out for the dragon hunters."

"Aye, but Finn and I have things in hand. If Simon Bourne makes a move anywhere between Birmingham and the Orkney Islands, we'll know. Things might be a bit boring from now on."

Evie smiled. "Life with you will never be boring, Bram. In nine months' time, you'll not only have to look after the clan, you'll have two babies as well."

Seducing the Dragon

Bram put an arm around her shoulder. "And you, love. I'll look after you."

Leaning into his warmth, she murmured, "And I, you."

Evie glanced up and as they stared at one another, warmth and happiness spread throughout her body.

Cocking an eyebrow, she stated, "Well, I guess I succeeded in the end, then."

"Succeeded with what?"

"I managed to seduce a dragon-shifter."

Bram's gaze turned heated and he leaned in close. "Aye, and you're welcome to do it anytime you like, love."

Evie tried her best seductive smile. "Well, Murray's due for nap in ten minutes. Maybe I'll try then."

"Lass, that sounds like a plan."

Bram kissed her. As her dragonman teased her mouth with long strokes of his tongue, most definitely a preview of what was to come, happiness warmed Evie's heart. With her mate and her son, she had a bright new life ahead of her. With time and Melanie's help, their children might just grow up in a world where humans and dragon-shifters could marry whomever they liked.

Dear Reader:

Thanks for reading *Seducing the Dragon*. I hope you enjoyed Bram and Evie's story. If you're craving more of this couple, then know they do have a follow-up novella later in the series (*Loved by the Dragon*). Also, if you liked their story, please leave a review. Thank you!

The next book is a follow-up novella for Melanie and Tristan and is called *Revealing the Dragons*. It may be about half the length of their original book, but a lot happens! Turn the page for the synopsis and an excerpt.

To stay up to date on my latest releases, don't forget to sign-up for my newsletter at www.jessiedonovan.com/newsletter.

With Gratitude,
Jessie Donovan

Revealing the Dragons
(Stonefire Dragons #3)

After more than a year, Melanie Hall-MacLeod finally releases her book about dragon-shifters. Everything seems peaceful until her first public appearance.

Tristan wants nothing more than to whisk his mate and two children off to safety, but Mel refuses to hide. As the danger increases and threatens his new family, Tristan battles the need to protect his mate with the need to make her happy.

Melanie is determined to change the future for her children and all dragon-shifter in the UK. Is it even possible? Or, will they be forced into hiding for the rest of their lives? Read to find out!

CHAPTER ONE

Melanie Hall-MacLeod brushed the cheek of her five-month-old daughter, Annabel, one more time before looking up at her sister-in-law and saying, "Remember, she'll only go to sleep if she has her stuffed green dinosaur. And Jack needs his baby blankie."

Her sister-in-law, Arabella MacLeod, raised an eyebrow, which also raised the scar near her temple. "Have you temporarily forgotten the last five months? You know, when I was here at least three times a week helping out with the twins?"

Before Mel could reply, the third woman standing near the door, Evie Marshall, interjected, "Give her a break, Arabella. This is the first time she'll be away from her babies for an entire night."

Ara replied, "Yours and Bram's cottage is a five-minute walk from here. We could probably hear Tristan if he shouted."

Melanie was about to set them straight when she felt Tristan's presence at her back before he rubbed up and down her arms. His touch soothed some of her tension and she leaned back against his muscled chest. His arms went around her and she let out a sigh. The world could be ending and Tristan's touch would still ease her worries.

His deep voice rumbled, "If you two have everything you need, then maybe you should go."

Evie raised an eyebrow. "You are aware that we're watching your children for free, right?"

Tristan said, "And?"

Evie shook her head and Melanie jumped in, "Ignore him. We're extremely grateful for you two volunteering to watch Jack and Annabel. I've spent every moment either taking care of them or finishing my book. A night off, despite my mother-half worrying, will hopefully refresh me for the shit storm to come after the book releases next week."

Evie tilted her head. "I don't know if it'll be that bad, Mel. After all, the reception of the article about mine and Bram's mating ceremony went well. Not one attack, and if anything, more people are 'dragon watching' more than ever before, hoping to catch a glimpse of a flying dragon."

Mel leaned more against her mate's chest. "A mating ceremony is one thing, but a book humanizing, for lack of a better word, the dragon-shifters is another. Doing that might push for equality, which many most definitely don't want. Permanent change can be scary, especially if it involves giant dragons maybe moving into your neighborhood."

Evie adjusted the sleeping Jack in her arms. "Nothing you're doing is breaking the law. Besides, even if people become upset, you're safe here. Bram would never allow anything to happen to you." Tristan grunted and Evie rolled her eyes. "Or, I should say, Tristan won't allow anything to happen to you."

Mel sighed. "I know, but what happens if it fails? I'd one day like my children to be able to see their grandparents and uncle."

Tristan squeezed her gently and said, "Soon, my little human. We'll find a way."

"I hope so," Mel whispered. She'd been on Stonefire's land for a little over a year. While phone calls and video chats helped, she missed her parents and younger brother so much it hurt.

Evie gave her a sympathetic look before straightening her shoulders. "Right, then, Arabella. Let's leave the two lovebirds alone. I'm sure they have lots of catching up to do."

Tristan said, "Yes, so only call if it's an emergency. I plan to keep Melanie very, very busy."

She elbowed her mate. "My definition of an emergency and Tristan's vary. His involves blood and dying. Mine includes things like high fevers and uncontrollable crying. Call if you need anything."

Arabella finally spoke up again. "If we don't know how to handle something, Bram will." Ara looked to Evie. "Let's go before Melanie thinks of another reason to keep us here."

Evie nodded. As the human woman and the dragonwoman walked away, Mel shouted, "Thank you! Remember to call!"

Evie raised a hand in acknowledgment. Soon, the two women disappeared behind a cottage.

She sighed. "I hope everything goes okay."

"It will."

Tristan walked them back a step inside their cottage and shut the door. Melanie turned in his arms. "You checked your phone, right? It's fully charged?"

Tristan raised a hand to her cheek and brushed her skin with his fingers. "Yes, love. Fully charged, although Bram knows what he's doing."

She placed a hand on Tristan's chest. "It's just, with Jack and Annabel gone, it feels like a part of me left with them."

One corner of Tristan's mouth ticked up. "If you're like this now, what are you going to do when they're old enough to live on their own?"

Swatting his chest, she frowned. "That's a surefire way to ease my worry. You're the worst, Tristan MacLeod."

He chuckled. "And yet you're the one who agreed to be my mate."

His gaze turned heated and Mel's heart rate kicked up. "You have your moments."

Leaning down, Tristan brushed his cheek against hers. "Then I'll make sure this is one of them."

As one of his hands rubbed down her back and rested on her ass, heat spread through her body. "You're not even going to try to woo me first?"

He massaged her bum. The feel of his warm, strong hands molding and sculpting her flesh sent a jolt between her legs. With each squeeze, it became harder for Mel to stand upright.

Even after being mated a year, all her dragonman had to do was touch her and she turned wet and needy. Not that she would ever give in easily to him.

With a husky voice, he said, "Who needs words when I can do this?"

He nibbled her earlobe and she leaned against his chest for support. Then he kissed his way down her neck until he bit where her shoulder met her neck. As he soothed the bite with his tongue, Melanie whispered, "I love our children and can't imagine life without them, but I've missed not having to squeeze in sex in between feedings or naps."

Tristan moved so he could look into her eyes. "Me too, love. However, our twins are in the hands of capable people and I have the whole night with you to myself."

Seducing the Dragon

She batted her eyelashes. "And what in the world should we do? Maybe clean the kitchen? Or catch up on laundry?"

Her mate growled and hauled her body against his. His hard cock poked her stomach through his trousers. "Forget the bloody cleaning. My plans include devouring you properly."

Her pussy pulsed as memories of Tristan lapping between her legs filled her mind. "Then, dragonman, you'd better get started. After all, we only have twelve hours before Evie and Ara bring the twins home."

"I think learning to function on little sleep will work to our advantage tonight."

She laughed. "Just make sure to feed me once in a while or I will get cranky. Not even your hot dragon self will be safe."

He nuzzled her cheek. "Soon you won't be able to say anything but my name. I think I'll be fine."

She opened her mouth to reply but then Tristan kissed her. As his tongue stroked hers, Melanie decided words could wait.

~~~

As Tristan explored the inside of his mate's mouth, his dragon growled. *Why are you waiting? It's been too long. Fuck her now. She likes it hard.*

Shut it, or I won't give you a turn.

His inner beast hissed. *You can't deny me. I am stronger.*

Last warning.

As his dragon sulked and retreated, Tristan hugged Melanie tighter. The way her soft stomach cushioned his cock made him even harder.

He broke the kiss and ran a finger under the band of her jeans, loving the softness of her skin. "Take these off or I rip them off."

Melanie raised an eyebrow. "At the rate you rip off my clothes, I soon won't have anything to wear."

He undid the top button and slowly unzipped her jeans. "Then wear skirts with nothing underneath. I like easy access."

"I need some barriers between me and your cock. Taking care of twins is exhausting and as much as I love you, there are moments when I don't want anyone to touch me."

Tristan stilled. "You've never mentioned this before."

Melanie shrugged one shoulder. "I didn't want to risk your dragon getting out of control due to lack of sex."

His dragon huffed. *I can refrain sometimes. She only needs to ask.*

Cupping her face, he ordered, "If you ever need a break, tell me. I can't take care of you if I don't know what you need."

His mate smiled. "Oh, Tristan. You can be sweet when you try."

He grunted. "Don't go ruining my reputation now."

Melanie laughed and some of his tension eased. As much of a bastard it might make him, he very much wanted to fuck his mate senseless as soon as he could get her naked.

When she ran a hand up his chest and around his neck, she played with the hairs at the back of his head; his hope soared higher.

Mel's husky voice caressed his ears. "Let me be very clear about tonight. I want you both on top of me and in me, dragonman, so hurry up and fuck me."

Seducing the Dragon

Want to read the rest?
Revealing the Dragons is available in paperback

For exclusive content and updates, sign up for my newsletter at:

http://www.jessiedonovan.com

Author's Note

Here we are at the end of another Stonefire Dragons story and it still feels like a dream. I'd like to thank all of my readers for their support and word-of-mouth. Without you, I would still be working an office job and scrambling to find time to write. Thank you!

There are some people I'd like to thank for their help:

• Clarissa Yeo is an amazing cover artist and I'm lucky to have her. She captures my dragon-shifters without even really trying.

• Becky Johnson and her team at Hot Tree Editing. She was awesome about my short turnarounds to make my pre-order deadlines. She has also made me a better writer. Thanks, Becky!

• Iliana and Donna are my beta-readers and their input has been vital to this series. Part Four in particular was a lot less awesome before Iliana told me it was missing the "Wow Factor". Honesty is a rare thing and I am lucky to have it from both of my betas!

Thanks again for reading and I can't wait to revisit Melanie and Tristan in *Revealing the Dragons*. After *Revealing* comes Finn and Arabella's story, *Healed by the Dragon*, followed by Kai's story (Stonefire's head Protector). I hope you continue to follow the story of Clan Stonefire.

See you around! :)

ABOUT THE AUTHOR

Jessie Donovan wrote her first story at age five, and after discovering *The Dragonriders of Pern* series by Anne McCaffrey in junior high, she realized people actually wanted to read stories like those floating around inside her head. From there on out, she was determined to tap into her over-active imagination and write a book someday.

After living abroad for five years and earning degrees in Japanese, Anthropology, and Secondary Education, she buckled down and finally wrote her first full-length book. While that story will never see the light of day, it laid the world-building groundwork of what would become her debut paranormal romance, *Blaze of Secrets*. In late 2014 she officially became a *New York Times* and *USA Today* bestselling author.

Jessie loves to interact with readers, and when not reading a book or traipsing around some foreign country on a shoestring, can often be found on Facebook:

http://www.facebook.com/JessieDonovanAuthor

And don't forget to sign-up for her newsletter to receive sneak peeks and inside information. You can sign-up on her website:

http:///www.jessiedonovan.com

CPSIA information can be obtained
at www.ICGtesting.com
Printed in the USA
LVHW11s0812111018
593101LV00002B/79/P